Readers love *Warlock in*
by TJ NICHOL

"This fantasy story is truly brilliant."
—Gay Book Reviews

"Engaging characters,
interesting and
compelling world,
and outstanding story
telling. I wholeheartedly
recommend this book to
any fantasy lovers out
there."
—Joyfully Jay

"WOW! The world
building and emotion
in this book bowled me
over!"
—The Novel Approach

"*Warlock in Training* tells
a unique, complex, and
addictive story that is
hard to put down."
—Joyfully Reviewed

"A book that provokes thought as it entertains."
—Binge on Books

By TJ NICHOLS

STUDIES IN DEMONOLOGY
Warlock in Training
Rogue in the Making

Published by DSP PUBLICATIONS
www.dsppublications.com

ROGUE
IN THE
MAKING

TJ NICHOLS

DSP PUBLICATIONS

Published by

DSP Publications

5032 Capital Circle SW, Suite 2, PMB# 279, Tallahassee, FL 32305-7886 USA
www.dsppublications.com

Rogue in the Making
© 2018 TJ Nichols.

Cover Art
© 2018 Catt Ford.
Cover content is for illustrative purposes only and any person depicted on the cover is a model.

Trade Paperback ISBN: 978-1-64080-451-7
Digital ISBN: 978-1-64080-452-4
Library of Congress Control Number: 2017919629
Trade Paperback published May 2018
v. 1.0

Printed in the United States of America

This paper meets the requirements of
ANSI/NISO Z39.48-1992 (Permanence of Paper).

ROGUE
IN THE
MAKING

TJ NICHOLS

PREVIOUSLY IN
WARLOCK IN TRAINING

ANGUS DONOHUE never wanted to be a warlock like his father, but with no other options, he went to Warlock College. People with magic either went to college and became warlocks, or they remained untrained wizards—and the college made sure wizards were considered dangerous.

Every warlock-in-training must summon a demon who would become their conduit of magic from Demonside. The demon Angus summoned was a mage, a powerful demon who had plans for the human he was bound to. Saka took Angus to Demonside, where magic is visible and the rivers flow deep underground. But those rivers were sinking as the magic of Demonside was being stolen by the warlocks. There Angus learned more about magic in a short time than he had in his entire first year at college, including the three ways to rebalance magic: blood, sex, and soul. He also discovered he quite liked learning about magic with Saka—and having sex with him.

But the magic must be rebalanced, and soon. Demonside was drying up, and the ice sheets were growing on the human side of the void because the warlocks had stopped paying for their magic.

Unable to open the void from Demonside—it can only be opened from Humanside—Angus had to wait to be retrieved by the college. He expected his father to leave him because he was such a disappointment. But he was rescued and questioned. The warlocks tried to erase what Angus had learned in Demonside, but they don't yet know they've failed.

While he continued at Warlock College, Angus joined the underground, a group of wizards and disaffected warlocks who planned to take down the college. He met Terrance, a rugby player, warlock, and underground spy, and found a friend who didn't want him just for his magic. Angus loved Demonside, but he wanted more than magic in his life.

As tensions between the college and the underground escalated, Angus had to make choices. He could see through the lies the college told—the propaganda about magic and the truth about why the human world was getting colder.

When his father demanded that Angus hand Saka over, Angus refused. They fought, and Angus was stabbed. His father opened the void between the worlds, intending to strand his son there to die, but Angus dragged his father through too.

The demons questioned and killed his father and healed Angus.

In defying his father and the college, Angus had become a rogue warlock and a wanted criminal. Unable to live in Demonside, as it would drain the life and magic out of him, he is now reliant on the underground, both to retrieve him from Demonside and to protect him from the college.

But the underground will have its own demands.

CHAPTER 1

WHILE THE wound had been healed with magic, the new skin was tight, and the memory was raw. Angus Donohue kept his hand over the scar on his abdomen as though he expected his skin to tear open. He knew it wouldn't, and it didn't stop the pain, but he couldn't drop his hand and walk easily either.

The red sand was warm against the soles of his feet, and the bells around his ankle jangled as he left the shade of Lifeblood Mountain. For the first few days of his recovery, he'd stayed close to the tents of Saka's tribe. When he wanted to go out, Saka was with him. Each day a little more magic was worked to make sure all of his intestines were properly repaired. His body was healing fine.

But when he was going to sleep, he felt the blade of the knife thrusting into his stomach, twisting and tearing. He was so used to Saka's sharp knives and the way they cut skin with no whisper of resistance. The knife his father had used wasn't designed for magic or ritual. It was a knife for killing.

Angus walked and sang softly to himself, even though dizziness darkened the edges of his vision. He would get there and back on his own. He was tired of being trapped in the tent and having people—demons—thinking him a fragile human. He lifted his gaze. The orange sun was low but crawling its way up the cloudless violet sky. He had plenty of time to return to Saka's tent before the intense heat of midday. If he fell over, he was sure someone would be watching him anyway.

Someone was always watching him. He wasn't a human trainee sent across the void by the underground. He was Angus, the human apprentice mage—which was something else entirely.

3

Though no one had actually explained the difference, he seemed to be an honorary demon.

His father would've been horrified.

Angus's lips twisted into a bitter smile. His father died knowing that all his stolen magic was being returned to Demonside with every drop of blood and smothered scream. Maybe he didn't bother to hold back his cries. Maybe he yelled and threatened until his voice was hoarse. Yes, that was more like his father.

Angus stopped three yards from a small cairn that marked his father's grave. It was well away from the river, the mountain, and the area where the tribes camped. Their tents were colorful blocks in the distance. His chest tightened. Was he too far away?

He scanned the sand for telltale ripples and increased the volume of his singing—a human pop song that blended seamlessly into a demon ballad. It didn't matter what he sang, only that he made noise to keep the riverwyrms away. The bells around his ankle were another simple deterrent. After one near brush, he had no desire to have a closer look at how many spade-like teeth the creature had for tearing off limbs and dragging its victims beneath the sand to the underground rivers.

He shuddered, not sure which was a worse way to die—bleeding to death, suffocating in sand, or drowning? He'd come so close to finding out.

The demon-style loose pants and shirt fluttered around him in the warm breeze, and the sky stubbornly remained cloudless. His father's death had lifted a river, but it had sunk just as quickly. Everyone was waiting for rain, hoping that clouds would gather after the next ritual. He dug his toes into the sand and tried to suck up the heat, but the cold in his bones remained.

If there was no rain, Demonside would die. It was already on the edge. For Demonside to live, the magic trapped across the void had to be returned. Human blood would be spilled that night in the hope of rebalancing some of what had been taken.

He closed the last three yards and knocked the top stone off his father's cairn. "Because of you."

4

He shoved another and another off. They rolled down the sides and landed softly in the sand.

"Because of warlocks like you." He picked up a rock and threw it. The fresh pink skin of his scar tugged. He pressed his hand harder to his stomach, but the pain wasn't in his gut. His gut was healed but tender. His heart was torn open, and no magic could heal that wound.

"You don't deserve a marker." He used the ball off his foot to kick off another rock. "You stabbed me. You tried to kill me."

His father had almost succeeded.

"I hope your death hurt. I hope you regretted everything you'd ever done in your life." His mother had lost her husband, and her son was a wanted criminal for siding with the underground and refusing to turn Saka over to be killed by the college. His father had told the college that Angus was a rogue warlock. He'd never be able to live in Vinland without looking over his shoulder. His mother would be heartbroken.

Tears welled, and he didn't brush them away. "What was so important that you had to kill me? Or was it just that you hated me?"

A breeze tugged at his clothes, and the bells added their tune. There was no other reply. All Angus had needed to do to please his father was graduate from the Warlock College and become a warlock of standing, just like him. He shuddered. The idea of being anything like his father was abhorrent.

He'd tried to avoid going to college. Then he tried to get kicked out. He couldn't even do that right, because that was the day he met Saka, and Saka had brought him to Demonside.

In one day he'd seen the destruction the warlocks were causing with their quest for power—the way they manipulated the media to blame the demons for the cooling of their world and the increasing rampages.

There was only one flaw with their spin—no one could open a tear in the void from Demonside, not even a human. The void could only be opened from Humanside. A warlock had let the demons through, let them cause fear, and then killed them for their magic.

Too much magic taken and not enough rebalanced. His father's blood had barely wet the bottom of the dry riverbed.

Angus picked up the rocks he'd knocked off and rebuilt the cairn. The anger was there, but he'd get no answers from a week-old corpse.

Fast footsteps on the sand made him look up.

It wasn't a demon, but a human.

He lifted his hand and squinted. If it was one of the humans being kept for rebalancing, there was nowhere for them to go. Running would only bring their deaths sooner. He didn't like the squirming sensation caused by the idea of humans being treated like cattle. But without them, Demonside would die before there was any chance of saving it. If Demonside died, Humanside would freeze over. Ice ages didn't sound like a whole lot of fun, and already the winters were longer and colder, and crops were failing.

He dropped the rock in his hand. Two worlds were dying so a few could control all the magic. The demons should have thrown his father's body to the scavengers....

The running human came toward him—not a sacrifice but a trainee.

"I wanted to talk to you before you went back to the camp." Jim huffed out the words and put his hands on his knees.

"Town... it's a town, not a camp." A town that could be packed up and moved to wherever the water was, which left few options these days. Saka had told him how all the land around Lifeblood had once been green and littered with trees. Now it was hard to see even the twisted dead trunks. Many of the tribes were going to stay close to Lifeblood instead of breaking away like they usually would. Fear was in the air and whispered on the breeze.

If Jim wanted to talk to him out here, then it was something he didn't want to say around demons.

"You didn't have to run to catch me alone. I'm not speedy at the moment." Angus patted his stomach. It could've been him buried in the sand with no one to mourn his passing. That wasn't entirely true.

6

Saka would be saddened. He picked up the rock and placed it back on the cairn. He was a better man than his father.

Jim pushed his hair back as he stood. "Yeah. How is that?"

"Fine." He wasn't in the mood for chatting with his ex. It hadn't been long enough for the little flip to stop when he saw Jim smile, but Jim had moved on. He was dating another underground trainee, Lizzie.

Jim picked up the other rock Angus had thrown. He tossed it from hand to hand as he walked back. "How is it really going here? With Saka?"

Ah, so that was what Jim really wanted to know. Angus held out his hand for the rock, and Jim gave it to him. "Good."

The word fell from his tongue without thought. Saka had been with him, healing him, helping him. Some days they were closer than mage and apprentice. Some days it felt like they were lovers playing with magic the way he and Jim once had, although the amount of magic that he and Saka played with was very different from his early fumblings with Jim.

"Back to rebalancing?" Jim's eyebrow twitched upward.

Angus swallowed, but his throat was dry. He untied the waterskin from his waist and took a sip. It was warm, but enough. He offered it to Jim, who hadn't brought water—a foolish thing to do in a desert.

There'd been no talk of rebalancing with blood or sex. The third kind of rebalancing required soul. His father had paid in blood and soul for his magic. Angus doubted the ritual would've made a dent in the amount his father owed.

"No, I haven't been doing much but healing." And learning about how it was done. That was what he was interested in. He'd wanted to be a doctor, not a warlock.

Jim didn't have a demon. He had no bond with Demonside, and he couldn't draw magic via a demon. He was, in Angus's father's words, "a know-nothing wizard and not worth wasting your time with."

"The college will know he's dead." Jim handed back the water skin.

Angus had no doubt it had been reported. Everyone knew the demon who spied for the college under duress. What Ruri told her warlock was carefully discussed with the other mages—enough to keep the college happy but not enough to give them any ideas. His father's death wasn't a secret that could be kept.

Dead. It was so final, so unreal, even though he was standing at the cairn. He waited for sorrow or even remorse to kick in. When his father stabbed him, Angus made the snap decision to drag his father to Demonside with him. He knew his father would die there, and it hadn't stopped him. He might as well have held the blade that took his father's life.

But he didn't regret bringing his father there. Beneath the anger was the lightness of relief. His father would never hurt anyone, human or demon, again.

"I know. The Warlock College will blame me for not having the decency to die alone." He was making a habit of not doing what they wanted. What lies would the college tell his mother this time?

Jim drew in a breath. "You aren't to blame. He made his own choices. We all did."

"What do you mean? You regret coming here?" The wizards who volunteered to come to Demonside to learn magic were in a unique situation. They learned from the mages as though they were apprentices, and they learned how to pay for their magic to keep the balance, but they had no bond with their demon. The bonus was that magic was visible in Demonside. It made learning so much easier.

Jim shook his head. "It's weird, but it's good to know how to use natural magic, how to be strong without a demon…."

Angus was learning that too. He didn't want to be reliant on Saka for power. The underground was made up of rogue warlocks and wizards who resented the stranglehold the college had on magic. It was an uneasy alliance, made only because they had a common enemy.

Jim shoved his hands into the pockets of his pants. He wasn't wearing demon-style clothing. None of the trainees did. "He's dead, so you should know the truth."

Angus went still. "About what?"

For a moment nothing moved. Even the breeze and the endless sand were still. It was too quiet, too unnerving. Angus stamped his feet a few times to hear the bells.

Jim scowled. "He paid me to break up with you. I couldn't say anything because he threatened me. The college versus a wizard—it was never going to end well."

"So you took the money and ran." Angus bit out the words. *Give him a chance to explain.*

Jim looked at his feet. "I didn't have a choice."

The rage bubbled up and threatened to suck him under. *There's always a choice. You took the easy one.*

Angus pressed his fingernails into the tender skin on his belly. The pain grounded him. If he pressed harder, he might draw blood, and then he'd be able to open the sand beneath Jim's feet and let him vanish the way he had months before. He relaxed his fingers and pulled together a fragile calm. He didn't care why Jim had taken the bribe, but that didn't make it all right. "Sometimes it seems like we have no choice because the alternative is too terrifying."

He sounded like Saka. Maybe he was spending too much time around mages.

Jim looked up, and hope lit his eyes. "So you understand?"

Angus blinked and assessed his former lover. The man who had first introduced him to sex magic—they had tried and failed at it. The man who had introduced him to the teachings of the underground and made him question the college. He nodded because he didn't want to put what he really felt into words.

Betrayed by someone he thought he loved and who he thought loved him.

He wouldn't let it happen again.

He liked Saka for his magic and for the sex, but a human couldn't love a demon, and demons couldn't love humans. No matter how much he wanted more from Saka, he was never going to get it. He shouldn't want it either. Humans were destroying Saka's world. Their alliance was so delicate that Angus wasn't sure how it would survive.

Jim smiled.

That time there was no stirring or fondness to the memory of what they'd had.

His father and the college weren't done trying to ruin his life. Some days it would be easier to be demon.

CHAPTER 2

THERE WERE animals from Humanside and humans in a larger number than Saka had ever seen. The animal herd was tended by demon volunteers. The cows would be food, and their blood would also be used in rituals to rebalance some of the magic. The animals were a gift from the underground, as was the hay. There was little around Lifeblood that the cows would be able to eat.

Saka's feet scuffed the sand as he walked through the towns at the base of the mountain. He'd been hoping to find Angus, but the warlock had vanished. Saka would not let himself worry. He had to believe that Angus would be fine, even if he was pushing himself too much after such a severe injury. This was his home, or at least part-time home.

This close to Lifeblood, there should be plants and trees all year round. Even though they had raised the rivers in the area, it had brought only ribbons of green along the banks. The lushness of his youth was long gone. He dug his fingers into the sand until he could feel the moisture below. Two hands deep—that was a good sign. The sky was still brutally free of clouds. That would change. They would release enough magic that night to bring rain.

Hopefully.

Every demon held their breath on the results. He turned his gaze from the animals to the more miserable camp of humans—a few ill volunteers who had chosen to die there and some criminals who hadn't been given a choice. The others, he didn't want to know. The underground had acquired them and delivered them.

They were all adults, which eased his conscience a little. A few had already attempted escape. Two had died in the desert, but their deaths returned only a touch of magic. It was a waste of their souls. The other three made their way back and were sick from the heat, the way Angus had once been. Reddened skin and racing heart. Saka had healed Angus, and he could heal these humans, but no mage would. No one would admit to being able to heal when the humans were there to die and make their deaths count. Their suffering would be ended on the blade of a knife.

His mouth was bitter with the knowledge that he had voted in favor of the temporary solution. His one vote wouldn't have made a difference, even if he had refused, but every other mage would have looked at him and wondered why he wanted Demonside to die.

If human warlocks hadn't killed so many demons for their magic, he wouldn't be surrounded by red sand and contemplating killing. He'd be in the shade of fingerfruit trees, teaching magic to an eager apprentice. There were few trees, and fewer crops. Fewer herds.

They'd all be dead from starvation before the drying of Demonside was complete. It was little comfort that Humanside was freezing, and their crops were also failing.

He turned away from the humans. Most of them wouldn't be killed. Soul magic, while powerful, was a one-off event. Most of those humans would be kept alive and bled, prolonging their use and the magic that could be returned. Most of them would hold some magic, but nothing like a warlock.

It would be good to have another warlock to bleed. He'd seen the release of magic from the death of Angus's father. And warlocks were the ones who should pay. How many demons felt that way about Angus and the humans they were training? Not all the mages were in favor of deepening their ties with the human world, but Saka didn't see that they had a choice.

Humans had to stop the humans. All the demons could do was offer support.

He would kill that night, because if he didn't, there was a very good chance he would lose his position as head mage of his tribe. He would not let go of that and surrender to the will of those who wanted to kill every human they could get their hands on. That was not the way to save Demonside… or Humanside.

Saka gave up looking for Angus and walked up Lifeblood Mountain to get ready for the ritual. The knives strapped to his arm were sharp and ready. Inside he was dull.

On the path up, he met other mages. There was little talk as there was nothing left to say. They were surviving, not living.

CHAPTER 3

IT WASN'T Saka returning from the mountain that woke Angus. It was excited chatter. He drew up some magic and created an orb of light in his hand. In Demonside it was something he could do almost without thinking. Magical energy was everywhere. It was part of the fabric of the world.

He got out of bed, pulled on pants, and padded across to the flap of the tent. He pushed it open to see what the commotion was. Other demons were also waking.

"Look, above Lifeblood." A woman touched his arm and pointed up.

The sky that had been a deep purple bruise when he went to bed, tired and aching from the simple walk to his father's cairn and a little magic practice by the river, was no longer clear. The bright yellow stars were hidden.

He rubbed his eyes and squinted, but there was no mistaking what he saw. Clouds were forming, spreading out. The top of the mountain rippled and shimmered with energy from the ritual the mages were carrying out. In the same heartbeat, Angus wanted to be up there with them and also to throw up. He wanted to be part of the magic, even though he knew what they were doing to rebalance and it turned his stomach.

Even though demons were celebrating the clouds and what it would mean—many of them putting out pots and bowls to catch as much of the rain as they could—there was a certain reverence about it. They weren't celebrating the death. They were celebrating the rain. In their red desert, rain meant life.

That was the reprieve they had bargained for, that he helped create—a few lives taken so they could spend the coming year finding a way to bring down the Warlock College and release the magic the college had somehow stored. If the underground failed, if he failed, then it would be war between demons and humans, and no life would be sacred.

It could still fail. The clouds could tear apart as fast as they formed.

So he joined the vigil with the other demons and watched the sky. The clouds swelled and spread. The mountain crackled and glowed with the darkest blue. Occasionally there was a flash of gold or red or sickly green as the magic was released and returned to Demonside.

The air around him cooled, and a hush fell. The desert went silent. The usual noises of the town stopped, even the singing and drumming. The livestock were quiet, as though they too knew the importance of the moment.

Angus drew his nails over the cuts he'd made that day—his way of rebalancing the magic that had been used to heal him. Blood, souls, and sex. Saka hadn't touched him since he almost died. There was a distance between them that Angus couldn't place entirely at the feet of his injury or on Saka being consumed by his duties up the mountain. Jealousy was so ugly, but it was there. He'd given up his chance to be because he knew he wasn't ready, but he could've stayed and been part of something much bigger than himself.

His blood dripped into the sand and shimmered faintly. Longing wasn't enough to release much magic. Lust and fear worked best. Would he have the courage to kill another human in ritual? He knew the answer. He hadn't even worked up to being able to cut Saka. It was one thing to put a blade to his own skin, but another to do it to someone else.

Please let there be rain. For all our sakes—human and demon on both sides of the void.

He repeated the words in a constant litany as his blood dripped onto the sand. He tilted his face to the sky and was almost able to taste the rain. There was a sweetness in the cool air. He licked his lips and anticipated the first drop.

His heart beat hard. The tension thickened with every breath.

He felt the split in the air a moment before something splashed onto his cheek. He touched the drop of rain with his fingertips, not sure he could believe it. He'd never seen rain in Demonside.

Around him people gasped as they felt the drops. Abruptly those few scattered drops became a downpour. The rain hammered his skin as though trying to pummel him into the ground. Laughter bubbled up. Someone broke into a song of thanks, and others joined in.

He was drawn into an impromptu dance, stamping in the wet sand. It splattered on his feet and legs. His skin became slick, and his hair was plastered to his head. He drank from the sky and let the relief and joy sweep through him. It was only when he went back to bed that he remembered the rain had been bought with blood.

GRAY DAWN light woke Angus. He lay still and took in the smell of the rain and the sound of the drops hitting the roof of Saka's tent. It was still raining. That had to be a good sign.

He turned over, expecting Saka to be in bed with him, but Saka hadn't come back.

The joy of last night's celebration vanished. He didn't know how to bridge the gap that had formed between them, and he wanted Saka's touch. He missed rebalancing because it had become more to him than just ritual.

He shouldn't want anything more than to learn.

Maybe it was time he went back across the void. He couldn't stay in Demonside forever. Eventually it would suck the life out of him. Demons couldn't live on the human side of the void either.

But he had no home to go to, and he was a wanted criminal, thanks to his father calling him out as a rogue warlock. And he could add accomplice to murder to his crimes because of his role in bringing his father to Demonside.

He wasn't ready to go back, and he needed to get on with his training. There wasn't time for him to waste lying around. He traced his fingers over the smooth red scar on his stomach. He had to stop reminding himself how close death had been, how much of his blood had been spilled on the sand. Saka claimed that he had expected the worst. For a man who thought his lover, his apprentice, his something, was dying, he was notably absent.

At some point Saka would have to take his teaching duties seriously, or it would reflect badly on him, but Angus didn't want to be a duty or a burden. Somehow the fun had gone out of magic, and he wanted it back.

He got up and pulled on clean pants. The ones he'd worn the night before were spattered in sand and soaked. He'd draped them over a stool, not sure what else to do with them. Drying freshly washed clothes had never been an issue before. But with the rain, everything was wet. He glanced at the roof and wondered how much rain the tent could handle before it sprang a leak.

When he stepped out and took in the state of the sky, he realized the rain wasn't going anywhere. There wasn't a patch of purple blue to be seen. Even the fat orange sun was hiding. Instead, for as far as he could see, there were green-tinted clouds.

People walked around and got on with their day, even though they were soaked. Children ran and laughed between the tents as though amazed by the falling water. Some of them had never seen real rain. He recalled Saka saying that the rain had been nothing more than a light shower in previous years.

Despite the rain, the day was heating up. The air thickened with humidity. He'd forgotten what a summer rainstorm could be like. Vinland hadn't had a real summer for years. He used a little magic to create a shield to act as an umbrella of sorts and went to find some food. The underground had donated rations, so he might be able to get some bread or porridge instead of the traditional demon fare of dried fruit wrapped in something bread-like.

A demon reached out and touched his dry shirt. "You do not like the rain?"

That drew the attention of others. Then he was surrounded by pinched worried faces, as though he were ill again.

"I do... I just...." He didn't have a good explanation for not wanting to be wet, so he dropped the shield. Rain hit his head and trickled down his face. Within seconds he was drenched. Water ran down his back and slipped into his pants and down his butt crack.

The demon smiled. At least someone was happy that he was having an impromptu, fully clothed shower.

"Do you not prefer to be dry?" he countered.

The demon, whose pink tufts of hair were limp instead of upright, looked at him as though he'd said something borderline offensive. Most of the time he got things right, but not that day.

"But we are dry the rest of the time. Why wouldn't you want to be wet? Celebrate the rain and the life it brings." She took his hand and spun him around like the night before. She stamped on the sand and splashed him as though it were the done thing to make people muddy. Then she laughed and walked away.

The rain wasn't cold, and it wouldn't last long. Maybe he should enjoy it. It would be another year before the rain came again, assuming it did. He turned to keep going to the market but stopped at the sight of his demon.

How long had Saka been standing there?

Demons walked between them, on their way to do whatever they needed to do. Neither Saka nor Angus moved, but one of them had to. Saka lowered his gaze to his hands.

In that moment Angus knew why Saka hadn't returned to his tent the night before. After what he'd done to bring the rain, he couldn't face his human apprentice. Angus drew in a breath, not sure what to do, only that he had to do something before the gap got much wider.

Angus crossed the path between tents. Saka should be accepting their thanks with a smile and a nod, in his usual manner. He needed to celebrate the rain. Looking miserable would only make the tribe question whether he was up to the job of head mage. Angus had no doubt that Usi, the second mage, would pounce on the hair-thin fracture in Saka's composure and force it open. They were rivals, even though they worked together.

Saka's reddish skin usually gleamed like metal in the sun, and he glittered as the rain clung to him. Where the rain rolled off Angus in rivulets, it seemed to catch on Saka's rougher skin. His black horns were sleek, and his eyes dark as he watched Angus approach. The way he rocked back on his heels made it appear as though he were about to turn and go.

"You made it rain." Angus would not mention or ask for details about what had happened up the mountain. Even if he did, Saka wouldn't say. He couldn't, because Angus wasn't a mage, therefore not entitled to know what happened on Lifeblood Mountain where the mages met. It would be years before he had enough training to attempt the initiation requirements—longer if Saka didn't get back to teaching him.

"Yes." Saka nodded. "It hasn't rained like this in a long time."

"So I keep hearing." He didn't know what to say to ease the weight in Saka's heart. "It's good for the people, for Demonside."

"I know." Saka glanced away. "But it sits ill."

It sat no better with Angus, even though the sacrificed people had been sick and dying or criminals serving life sentences. If the college caught him, he'd never be sent back to Demonside. He'd be left to die in prison. "Now we have the time we need. You've shown that, with the underground, Demonside can survive."

Saka pressed his lips together. "We shouldn't have to beg for survival. How long until your Warlock College starts to draw the magic back across?"

Soon. They both knew that. The Warlock College wanted to gain control of all magic and was somehow storing it instead of allowing it to naturally flow between worlds. They had created the imbalance.

"For one day, let's just celebrate the rain. It could be gone tomorrow." Not that he was enjoying it slipping down the back of his shirt or the way the cloth clung to his body.

Saka shook his head. "This will last another two nights… maybe three."

"How can you tell?" Angus looked up at the clouds as though there were a clue written on them. Was it the shape or the color? Rain splashed on his face, and he blinked the drops away.

19

Saka touched his arm. "Perhaps it's time to teach you something new, if you feel strong enough?"

"I am." He was also bored of lying around healing, although yesterday's walk to his father's cairn had left him exhausted.

Saka considered him for a drawn-out moment. Then he inclined his head and angled his horns toward Angus's face. "You still trust me, then."

"Nothing you do could change that." They were trying to save two worlds. What had happened on Lifeblood was better than the alternative, which was all-out war between demons and humans. Some mages wanted that. If it happened, whenever a tear in the void was opened, demons would rush through and grab as many people as they could for rebalancing. They wouldn't care who they were or what they'd done. And while Angus was glad he didn't have to make the call on who should be sacrificed, at least the people who gave their souls had been carefully selected or had volunteered.

"Let's pack some food and follow the river for a bit."

"Where are we going?"

"Somewhere quiet, so you can feel Arlyxia awaken from her summer slumber."

CHAPTER 4

SAKA SHOULD smile at the rain. It was what he'd hoped for. He'd proven to all the doubters that they could stave off the dying and go after those responsible without starting a war they couldn't win. The humans could simply stop opening the void and wait it out, hold on to their stolen magic until the demons died.

Last night his hands had been sticky with blood. His ears had rung with the death cries of too many. He needed time to find peace within himself. He'd never seen so much death, and he'd been one of the mages who caused it. It went against what he believed, even though he knew that, in a roundabout way, it was exactly what he believed.

Everything must be in balance for the worlds to thrive. He'd helped return that balance as quickly as possible.

That morning he'd stood in the doorway of his tent and watched Angus sleep. The scar on his stomach was visible, even in the dawn light. How could he lie next to Angus after what he'd done? Yet he would have to find a way. He couldn't, and didn't want to, hand Angus off to another mage for training.

They took a little of the food the underground had donated—a gesture of goodwill until the rains came and crops could be grown. While Angus liked the familiar food, Saka couldn't say the same. Porridge made from oats was gluey. The potatoes were tasteless. The cows had proven to be the most useful, because they gave their souls and blood to rebalance. And they were good to eat. They couldn't smoke any meat in the rain, but they would all enjoy the fresh roasts.

With some cold meat and some flatbread in a bag, they followed the river away from where everyone was camped.

Angus kept his hand over his stomach as he walked. He didn't realize how close to death he'd come. Magic could do many things in the hands of a skilled user, but bringing back the dead wasn't one of them. Some wounds were too great to be healed. Angus was lucky to have been helped so fast. There were some mages who'd have been happy to watch him bleed out. The mages who helped Angus could easily have claimed that Angus was too far gone and done nothing. Saka had thanked them, but he suspected there was a debt that would eventually need paying.

The river flowed swiftly. Water had surged to the surface, drawn up by the magic and fed with the rain. He hoped the magic was strong enough that it would take a long time for the rivers to sink, but that all depended on how fast the warlocks drew on the magic of Demonside.

Beneath his feet, grasses pushed up. Trees grew as he watched. In the desert the plants were used to making the most of the rain when it came. Herds of animals grazed and also made the most of the sudden wet. Some demons would too. Hopefully next year there would be some babies. There had been so few over the dry years.

They should have done a ritual sooner.

"You're quiet today." Angus glanced at him and then returned his gaze to the rapidly changing landscape. Dormant plants unfurled. Their leaves spread out like uncurling fists. That was the Demonside he remembered from his youth—bands of green along rivers that only dried for a short time. His mentor remembered a time when Lifeblood Mountain was lush and the rivers never sank.

For the moment, the desert looked very livable, but that was an illusion. An awakened desert was just as dangerous as a sleeping one—maybe more so.

"There is a lot to think about." He couldn't lie and say last night didn't weigh on his mind. He suspected thoughts of death were filling a lot of minds. "I can't teach you everything before you need to go back. So what do you need to learn?"

Saka glanced at his hands. There was no red blood caking his nails. He'd scrubbed well. But it would be a while before he could face teaching Angus any more blood magic.

Angus's eyebrows drew down. "You're asking me?"

"I know that you want to learn healing, but you aren't ready for that." And it wouldn't be useful for fighting warlocks. "What do you need to defeat the college? You know them better than I do."

Angus was silent. Until then, lessons had always been decided by Saka. They had gone through basics like sex and blood magic, and the drawing up of magic from what was around. But using that magic and directing it with purpose was much harder to do and do well. Mages spent years learning. Angus—and Demonside—didn't have years.

"I need to be able to defend myself." He touched his stomach again.

"I can get another to teach you to fight." He would check to make sure Angus was truly healed before he let that happen. If something tore open, it would be longer before Angus could go back. And as much as he didn't want Angus to leave, the longer he stayed, the more risk there was that Demonside would leach the life out of him.

"I meant with magic too. I was able to deflect the rain, so I stayed dry this morning. There must be a way to use magic to stop magic...."

Saka considered him for a moment. "We don't attack each other with magic. That would break the oaths we swear as mages."

"Warlocks aren't mages. They use the power they have."

"Your father used a knife."

Angus stopped walking. "If he'd used magic, I'd be dead. He was counting on his demon ensuring I died here. That way he could honestly say I'd been taken again."

"And then argue his demon was dangerous and should die, thus giving him more magic."

Angus nodded. "Something like that."

"I can't teach you what I don't know." They had stopped near a part of the river that widened into a lake. The lake was fed from underground and should be there all year round. It had been dry when they arrived at Lifeblood.

Rain pattered on the leaves above their heads. Away from the tents, the noise of life had faded.

"If it weren't raining, it would be nice to swim." Angus smiled as he looked at the lake.

"Either way you would be wet, so what does it matter?" It was nice to feel the rain instead of the sun on his skin. Angus didn't seem to enjoy it as much as everyone else.

"I guess it doesn't. Shall we swim? Do you know how to swim?" He walked toward the lake.

Saka grabbed his hand. He didn't swim. No one did. "If you go in there, you will be taken by a riverwyrm."

"What? Don't they live underground?"

"They live in the rivers, above and below ground. They surface to swim and hunt in the lakes, especially the deep ones like this." Saka had wondered if they'd died out, but Angus had seen one up close, so they were very much alive. "Perhaps the first thing you should do is see if you can find one."

"Why?"

"Why not? Looking for things is important."

"And when it swims over for a taste?" Angus didn't look very convinced.

"There are ways of discouraging animals from attacking."

Angus stamped his foot, and the bells around his ankle rang. "I know."

Saka considered Angus for a moment. While mages didn't attack each other, they did know how to dissuade a hungry pack of scarlips or turn away a riverwyrm if the noise wasn't working. "Maybe there are some basic defenses I can teach you."

Their hands were still linked, and Angus brushed his thumb over Saka's skin. "Maybe that could wait?"

The air between them crackled with expectation. He knew what Angus wanted, and it had nothing to do with magic. Between Angus's injury and the release of soul magic on Lifeblood, rebalancing with Angus had been pushed from his mind.

"Celebrate the rain with me. We both know where it came from, but I don't want to dwell on it, or I might start to doubt what I'm doing." Angus stepped closer.

He hadn't realized Angus had his own doubts. He'd thought Angus comfortable with death. Humans killed many demons for their magic. "If we do nothing, we die."

"I know." He looked away, the rain streaking his cheeks. "I don't want to think about it. I want to be happy, even if it is for only a short while."

Saka reached out and cupped Angus's chin, so he was forced to look at him. "You shouldn't put your happiness in another."

Angus tugged his rain-slicked hand free. "Do you not know how to fall in love?"

"I can't. I have to put the tribe first."

"So what is this?" Angus indicated between them. "I thought there was something."

"There is." But Saka didn't know what it was either. How could he want a human, a warlock who was bound to him? But he did.

Angus set his jaw. "Magic."

There would always be magic between them. There was a whole void and two dying worlds between them.

"Can you not cast off the responsibility for even a few minutes? There's no one here to see you drop your guard. No one is trying to take your position or prove you wrong." Frustration made Angus's words sharp.

"You may not be healed." Saka had hoped that, by giving them both space, he could find more stable footing. He had failed.

Angus swore. "I'm fine. We both know I'll be going back soon. I'd rather leave with a sweet taste in my mouth than bitterness. This life was paid for in blood." He pointed to the trees. "Instead of dwelling on the death, can we not be happy?"

25

"Everything and everyone has a price. Most of the time, we don't think about it because we are happy with the trade." He wanted Angus, and while they had blurred the line before, he didn't know if it was a good idea. He should know better. He was supposed to be the teacher.

"Yeah. I should've read the fine print on this trade."

"You wanted to help. You want to save your world from an ice age and from the college. What do you think they will do with all the magic they have gathered and stored?"

"What they always do, seek more power. There will be war between the magic-using countries. My father hinted at that." He drew in a breath. "The cost is I only get you on your terms, when you have a lesson in mind. Not when I need you or want you."

Put like that it sounded brutal. Saka closed his eyes for a moment and tipped his face to the rain. He should feel a measure of joy or pride. He should be able to revel in his success. The rain would ensure that Demonside and all the demons would survive another year. Hopefully by then there would be progress on the other side of the void.

Would Angus still be his apprentice when the danger was gone, or would Angus go back to living on Humanside, keen to forget the life he had with Saka?

And he did have a life in Arlyxia. When Angus was dying, people left gifts to lure him back.

"I'm reconciling what I must do. It is not easy to hold the knife and kill another."

"No." Angus nodded. "Do you know what they call people like me back home? Those who consort with demons? Those who fuck demons?"

"Smart warlocks who know magic is about balance?" Everything was. They were standing in the first heavy rain Demonside had experienced in too many years. The death was done. Life was ensured.

Angus's lips quirked up at the corner. "I wish."

Saka closed the distance between them. "You are right. I need to celebrate the rain. There will be worse to come before we are safe."

"That's what worries me."

26

"It worries all of us who care." He swept his thumb over Angus's cheek and then kissed him. He almost expected Angus to push him away, but he returned the kiss, and his mouth opened, hungry for more.

They hadn't lain together since before Angus almost unwillingly gave his soul to Demonside. Angus skimmed his hand up Saka's side. He'd missed Angus's touch. Away from the tents, he didn't have to be Saka, the head mage. He could just be. They were two people celebrating the rain and the life it brought.

The sand beneath his feet was gritty, and puddles formed in his footprints. There would be no lying down. Now he had given in to the idea of taking pleasure in the moment, his body woke. Heat spread through his blood and demanded to be fed.

In three steps he had Angus backed against a tree. The bark was smooth and cool, and when Saka reached out with magic, he could feel the tree growing both taller and deeper, its roots seeking out the underground rivers. Maybe more trees would survive if they were able to get deep enough in the growing time they had. There would be more food. That night there would be a feast with new fruits and the gifted cows—the official celebration he dreaded.

Now he found a reason to anticipate it.

He pressed his hips to Angus's and ground against him. His warlock was hard and not keen to wait. His hand was already on the fastening of Saka's pants. Angus's shirt was plastered to his pale skin and left no line of his body to the imagination. But Saka knew every curve of muscle, every freckle, and every scar.

Saka opened Angus's pants and wrapped his hand around his cock. Angus groaned as Saka caressed the hot, hard length. He could give Angus the release he wanted in a few short strokes, but that wouldn't satisfy Saka, and at the back of his mind, he knew that the more lust there was, the more magic would be released when Angus finally came. Was he doing it for Demonside or for himself? He hesitated.

"No games this time," Angus said through gritted teeth. "You can torture me tonight."

"Is it that bad?" He brushed the sensitive head with his thumb, around the ridge, then over the slit.

"One day I will make you beg to come," Angus said between kisses sweetened with rain.

The threat was something Saka looked forward to. "Then I will know I have trained you well."

Angus slid his hand between their bodies to rub against Saka's length. His touch was firm and his kisses harder. "Train me another time."

"Tonight." It was a promise he made to himself as much as Angus. He could take the moment, but only if he made up for it later.

Angus smiled. He looked happier than he had in days, and his eyes were bright. But before Angus could take another kiss and seal his victory, Saka turned him to face the tree.

Saka traced his fingers down Angus's back and cupped his buttocks. The fabric of his clothes clung to his slick skin as Saka peeled down the pants to expose the firm flesh of Angus's ass. He kissed between Angus's shoulder blades. He shouldn't think only of his pleasure, but he wanted nothing more than to sink into Angus and forget last night.

The burden of being a mage in such dire times grew heavier with each passing day, but he couldn't say those words out loud. People would think him weak. He'd lose his position. But there was no one to see him here.

He lapped the sweet rain from Angus's skin and kissed his neck. Angus rocked his hips back to press against him, and Saka pressed a finger to the tight ring of muscle. He hadn't brought anything with him. He hadn't planned or even thought about it. He didn't want to hurt Angus, and he wasn't sure that Angus was telling the truth about being fully healed.

"I'm unprepared," he murmured, but he didn't stop the teasing stroke of his fingers. There were other things they could do. He hadn't felt Angus's mouth on him in far too long, but he didn't want to see his desire reflected in Angus's eyes. He should wait until that night, when it would mean something. His pulse quickened and his blood sharply carved its way through his body. He could control lust... but this was something else.

He nuzzled Angus's neck, and the taste of his skin mixed with the rain. The feel of the warlock's body was what he'd missed. He needed Angus.

Angus pushed back. "Do it already. I want to feel you."

Saka sank one finger in, and Angus groaned. He could give Angus the release he wanted without doing much more, take him in hand and stroke that pleasurable spot deep within him. He could drag it out until the magic rose.

None of that was what he wanted. He wanted to sink in, give in to the pleasure that was being offered without reason. Angus had nearly died. They should be able to celebrate his life. He should be allowed a moment of joy.

He hesitated for a moment longer and then gave in to the need that had simmered for so long, untended and unwatched. He kissed his way down Angus's spine and pushed aside the shirt so he could feel the smooth skin beneath. He flicked his tongue over the dimple on the back of Angus's hips and then at the top of the crease.

Angus drew in a breath. The magic was building between them, but out here there was no way to collect it… no need to collect it. There were no circles. Just them. But his training was in his thoughts, no matter how hard he tried to sweep it aside.

He spread Angus's asscheeks and watched the rain trace over Angus's flesh and form a rivulet that ended as it dripped from his balls. Saka buried his face between Angus's thighs to taste the water. Angus flinched and spread his legs a little farther, but Saka didn't linger.

All he wanted was Angus ready to take him. He danced his tongue over the rosy pucker. Circled and teased. Angus's breathing quickened, and the magic eddied around them, uncontained. He could gather it and make it count. It would be so easy to fall back into his training. Even if Angus were a demon, they could use the lust to draw up magic. It was only because he was human that they could use it to rebalance.

Saka trailed his fingers up the inside of Angus's thigh, brushed his balls and the underside of his shaft.

"I thought you were going to save the torment for tonight." Angus's words were breathy.

Saka stood and pulled his cock free of his pants—something made more difficult by the wet cloth—then pressed into Angus. The tight heat surrounded him and took his breath. He didn't move for several heartbeats before he thrust deeper. "Better?"

"Yes." Angus flexed his fingers against the tree. If he had claws, they'd be digging into the bark.

He withdrew slowly before thrusting in. Angus hissed out a breath but pushed back, encouraging Saka to go deeper and harder each time. Just once, he wouldn't care about rebalancing. All he wanted was pleasure. Then he'd go back to being a mage. He'd pick up the burden he'd volunteered to carry and keep going.

Saka put a hand on Angus's hip and another on the tree, covering Angus's hand, and drove in hard. His raw need hadn't been released since he'd taken his mage vows on Lifeblood. It flowed through him and bubbled like the underground rivers as they finally resurfaced. For too long, sex had been entwined with magic. And while he enjoyed it, he had a level of responsibility.

Angus moved his free hand to stroke himself, but Saka caught it and returned it to the tree. Angus responded by tilting his hips to find the right spot with each thrust. Saka used his tail to hold Angus's balls and tease his cock. Instead of drawing out each stroke or being cautious not to let himself reach climax too soon, he took what he needed.

He hadn't realized how hungry he was for something so simple until Angus offered a feast. Saka gave in completely and focused only on his own need. His thrusts became more urgent. For a heartbeat, he didn't think he'd be able to come so simply. Then it rushed through him, took his breath, and left his bones molten and his muscles quivering. He rested his head against Angus's shoulder. It was only then that he released Angus's hand so he could grasp his length and give him the release he wanted. In a few quick strokes, it was done. Angus groaned, and his hot come splashed on the tree.

Guilt immediately punched Saka in the heart.

30

It was a wasted chance to rebalance. Even though rain pattered on his skin and there was no need for it, he couldn't shake off his responsibility to the tribe that easily. He drew away and vowed to make up for it that night, but he hated himself for the weakness that had overtaken him. Angus leaned against the tree, and his back lifted with each breath.

Was he all right?

Saka reached out a hand to offer a reassuring touch, but then drew it back. He wasn't sure what to do. No one had ever made him act so recklessly, and he wasn't sure he liked it in the aftermath.

Then the moment was gone, and Angus dragged up his pants. Wet sand clung to them, but he didn't seem bothered. His lips turned up in a smile, as though Saka's fall was exactly what he wanted.

Saka opened his mouth.

Angus shook his head and pushed wet hair off his face. "I don't want to hear it." He walked to the lake, washed his hands, and took a drink. "I'm more than a way to rebalance. I'm on your side." He glanced over his shoulder at Saka. "I may not be your equal, but I can be your partner if you let me."

Saka swallowed. He wasn't talking about being a magical partner or an apprentice. He was talking about a deeper connection. Mages didn't have family or lovers. They had to put the tribe first. Always. Angus knew that, yet he still wanted more.

Angus wasn't demon. How could he understand?

Saka didn't say anything. He knelt at the lake's edge and washed. As he dipped his hands in again, he felt it. There was a deeper ripple, a colder current in the water. He glanced over at the light-footed tenga drinking on the other side of the lake. "Can you feel it?"

"What?" Angus put his hand in the water. He frowned as though he could force the connection. "The water's moving?"

The tenga lifted their heads and looked around, ears laid flat against their heads as they chirped at each other. Some moved away from the water's edge. They sensed it too.

"Get back," Saka ordered.

Angus and Saka scrambled away from the edge. A couple of heartbeats later, the lake erupted. Something dark sped across the surface, and the tenga ran and scattered—except one that was too slow to get away from the edge. It was dragged under. After another couple of breaths, the water was still.

Both he and Angus were on their asses, a couple of body lengths from the edge. Even though Saka knew what it was and that it preferred deer, his heartbeat was as erratic as it had been with lust not that long before.

"Riverwyrm?" Angus asked. His eyes were wide and fixed on the water.

"Yes. That is why we don't swim in the lakes." Around them the world was too quiet. They were far from the tribes and the noise of life.

Angus nodded. "Maybe we should get back."

While he wouldn't admit it, that was exactly what Saka had been thinking. It would be best if the morning were forgotten entirely—much like the tenga, which had forgotten the riverwyrm and had already returned to drink and graze.

CHAPTER 5

ANGUS'S BODY ached, but it always did after one of Saka's rituals—part fatigue and partly too much delayed pleasure. The side of Saka that he glimpsed when they were alone by the lake had been replaced again with the mage who would do anything for his world. His skin tightened at the memory, and heat washed through his veins. He wasn't sure which he preferred, the heat and the rush that left him tender or the prolonged pleasure and the release of magic.

He'd spent two weeks in Demonside recovering from his father's failed attempt to kill him, and it was almost nice to step across the void and back home. Except that it was freezing cold and the Warlock College had declared him a rogue warlock. If they found him, he'd be locked up somewhere filled with magic dampeners.

The floor was cold beneath his bare feet. He was used to the sand that was warm despite the rain. He missed the heat already, though not the humidity. That had started to make him feel like he was never dry, even when he was in the tent.

The other trainees had returned with him, and they seemed to be in a similar state of freezing. They rubbed their arms and stared out the window at the falling snow. Winter had well and truly set in, though it was only autumn.

Angus shivered.

A couple of underground warlocks watched. They wore masks because they were still affiliated with the college and didn't want their identities revealed—in case they ended up like him, wanted for being rogues. The wizards didn't cover their faces because they had nothing to hide.

"The debriefing will start in half an hour. Put on some appropriate clothes," a masked man said.

Some of the trainees had adopted demon-style clothes while they were across the void. It made sense to dress as a demon, given how hot it was there. Angus glanced at Jim, who was holding Lizzie's hand. Had he told her that the only reason he and Angus had split up was because Angus's father had bribed him? Probably not. He hadn't spoken to Jim since that day at the cairn, and he had nothing to say.

The trainees dispersed to their rooms in the building the underground used as their base. Would anyone have bothered to get him clothes? He opened the door and was surprised to see not just clothes, but his clothes. He picked up a shirt and held it to his face. It smelled of the cheap-scented laundry powder he'd bought—summer scents or something. It didn't smell like summer at all, or was he thinking of the spice on the air in Demonside?

Three pairs of his shoes were neatly lined up, and so were some of the books that had been on his desk at college. Someone had gathered his things before the college could either confiscate or trash the whole lot.

Terrance.

As though magic summoned him, Terrance appeared in the corridor. Angus grinned at the former rugby-playing warlock. He was the best part of returning to Vinland, but Angus was never sure of what they had. His heart didn't care. With Terrance there was nothing but pure attraction and affection and the potential to be more. What he had with Saka was complicated and heady and best consumed in small doses at the risk of being consumed himself. But he kept going back, though he knew there was no future beyond mage and apprentice. He couldn't let himself fall for Saka, no matter how easy it would be to do—some days he thought he was halfway there.

Even though he liked Terrance, he wasn't going to be a fool again. He didn't want to admit it, but Jim's betrayal chafed. Would warlocks convince everyone he was close to that they should turn on him?

34

"I heard the trainees had returned." Terrance's gaze slid down Angus's body and then snapped back to his face. He smiled as though nothing had changed, as though Angus hadn't been away.

But so much *had* changed. "Yeah."

"And you're okay?"

Angus nodded. He didn't want to talk about what had happened. "You?"

"Still trying to figure out what I'm going to do with my life, now I can't finish college."

"Not even a nonmagical college?"

Terrance shook his head. "The Warlock College made sure no one would touch me. Professional Rugby Association is interested, though. I have a meeting next week."

"You'd be playing for the PRA?"

"Yeah, which is all I wanted in the first place. Should never have taken the scholarship offer."

"If you hadn't, I wouldn't have met you." As he said it, he wondered if Terrance felt the same. Angus's presence in his life hadn't exactly been what one would call a positive influence. But Terrance had been part of the underground long before Angus started college. And Terrance had known the college was dishonest when he took the scholarship.

"True." Terrance took a few steps closer. "I got your things."

"Thank you." Angus meant that. It was comforting to have his things. He had so little on that side of the void. He held Terrance's dark gaze for a moment. There was no blame or hurt there, only heat. Angus's lips twitched. "Do I want to know how?"

"No. Better that you don't."

That probably meant Terrance had broken into the college to get them. "You didn't have to do anything dangerous. You could've bought me some new things. I'm sure the underground has funds for that."

"What's the fun in that? It was nice to show the college up one last time. Their rooftop security isn't that great. Nor is flying by dragon." Terrance rolled his shoulders.

"Pinches under the arm." Angus had been carried by winged demons, known as dragons, and their claws tended to dig into the soft tissue.

Terrance nodded.

"I'm going to throw on something warmer." His toes were numb. He wasn't sure he'd ever be warm again. "Did you want to come in?" His cheeks heated, and it wasn't sunburn. Whenever he was around Terrance, he fumbled as though he had no idea what he was doing.

They hadn't been on a date yet, but they'd fallen into bed once. It had been so nice to have something nonmagical in his life. The idea that he had someone waiting for him was very appealing. But it was because of him that Terrance's demon had been killed and Terrance had been questioned by the college and wore the bruises to prove it.

There was a moment of hesitation, and Angus's heart sank. Then Terrance stepped forward.

"Sure." Terrance closed the door behind him and sat on the only chair in the room.

For a couple of heartbeats, Angus didn't know what to say. "So, what's changed while I've been away?"

Angus pulled off the damp shirt and looked for a place to hang it. The room was even smaller than his room at college, but at least he had somewhere to stay while he was in Vinland—somewhere safe to stay. He put his shirt on a coat hanger, which he then hung on the wardrobe door. Hopefully it would dry.

"Not much. The college is still blaming demons and the underground for the weather. The early winter meant some crops weren't harvested. They're talking rations—real rations, not just asking everyone to reduce waste and so on. I read that if summer is shorter or colder this year, there may be no successful crops in Vinland at all. Food will have to be imported."

If Vinland had nothing to spare, it wouldn't be just humans going hungry. There'd be nothing to send across to Demonside. "What about the other magic-using countries?"

"The underground says there's talk of sanctioning Vinland. It's not just Vinland suffering. And the places that have banned magic are apparently banding together to point out the evils of magic use. You won't hear that on any official news source, though."

Angus stripped off his pants, and Terrance looked away. Living in Demonside had made Angus too comfortable with being naked. "What sources are you listening to?"

He pulled on dry clothing and socks. The fabric rubbed against his skin, but he ran his hands over his pants and luxuriated in the feel of dry clothing. It didn't cling or suck at his skin, but it was heavy and much thicker than what he was used to wearing across the void. He shrugged into his old, familiar jacket. He needed the extra layer to be warm.

"Other countries have an online network. Some people showed me how to access it."

"Is it real news?" Or were the other countries creating propaganda?

"Yeah. It's not like Vinland said out there. Sure, there are places that kill all magic users, but there are other places that use demon magic like us. But they aren't our allies either."

Angus frowned. "You'd think the Warlock College would want allies."

"You would, wouldn't you?" Terrance lifted an eyebrow.

"Does that mean the underground has allies in these other countries?"

Terrance shrugged. "I'm not that high up. I run errands. That's all. And if I get drafted by the PRA, then I won't be doing that either."

And it would be that much harder to see Terrance if he wasn't around. Angus stared at his striped socks. He wanted to keep seeing Terrance. There was still the untaken first date. It was supposed to be a movie, but that had never happened. He couldn't ask Terrance to continue fighting with the underground when he'd already lost more than he ever planned on giving up. "I hope I get to see you play."

"I'd like that." Terrance smiled. "We can't go out at the moment, but I'm sure we could catch up or something while you're here?" Uncertainty had crept into Terrance's voice.

"I hope so." Every time Angus came back, they had to rebuild the fragile thing between them.

Terrance reached out a hand. Angus took it, and Terrance drew him onto his lap so they were face-to-face. Terrance kissed him. It was soft and undemanding. He settled his hands on Angus's hips. Angus put his arms around Terrance's neck.

It was too easy to slide into Terrance's embrace. Maybe they didn't have anything but sex. Maybe that was all he was good for on both sides of the void. He should pull away until he knew what was going on, but he didn't. His skin was sensitive, but the desire Saka had so carefully coaxed and fed the night before was still warm, and it caught fire with the simple kiss.

His hunger was never quite met across the void because there was too much going on and too much to do, but it had almost been sated when he was by the lake with Saka.

He traced Terrance's lip with his tongue and let the heat rise. The kiss deepened, and Terrance pulled him closer. Hardness pressed against him. There would be no pleading for release with Terrance. That alone was tempting.

A knock on the door shattered the moment and reminded Angus he still had things to do before he could relax. Those occasions were becoming few and far between. For a heartbeat he considered walking away from the underground the way Terrance planned to do. But he couldn't. He'd never be able to look in the mirror, knowing he'd done nothing but sit by and watch two worlds die. So he drew back and looked at Terrance. Terrance had believed in the fight and that he could make a difference. But where once idealism had lit his eyes, there was only doubt.

How much did he have to give before the battle took everything? He glanced down, and Terrance kissed his forehead.

The person knocked again.

"Coming," Angus called out. Then in a softer voice he added, "How about tonight?"

"I'll arrange something, since you have meetings." Terrance smiled, and warmth bloomed in Angus. Terrance might have lost his desire to fight, but there was plenty of other desire left.

Angus gave him a last kiss and got up. "I look forward to it."

ANGUS LISTENED as some of the trainees talked about their shock at the human sacrifices. But the leaders of the underground didn't want to hear about that. They wanted to know what the trainees were being taught, and that all depended on the demon who was doing the teaching and the trainee. There was no standard syllabus, and that didn't impress the leaders. They wanted to be able to tick off a list of things the trainees had learned, like they did at Warlock College. Most of the trainees had spent their time in Demonside having their abilities and interests assessed and learning how to draw up large quantities of magic.

Eventually they were dismissed, and Angus was left alone with the leaders. He swallowed and tried to ignore the coiling sensation in his gut, even though he knew better.

They wanted to know about the mage who was bound to a warlock and what kind of information she had given him. Angus wasn't sure, but he knew the mages discussed what would be revealed, not that he would confess that. It wasn't going to be much better when he admitted that he was no longer part of the rituals on Lifeblood, but at least they'd stop asking him questions he didn't want to answer. His admission that he stepped aside because he wasn't ready to be on Lifeblood didn't go down well.

The leaders scowled and wanted to know why he'd give up the power. They didn't understand that it wasn't about power.

Had they been hoping he'd betray the mages' secrets?

He should be able trust the leaders. They were part of the fight to save both worlds… but shouldn't they be more interested in stopping the college than in what happened up on Lifeblood? Why weren't they doing something? Maybe they were, but they didn't trust him enough.

He held their stares, their eyes dark behind their masks—no names, just faceless warlocks. They seemed to outnumber the wizards. The leaders drew away to the other side of the room to confer. They could've let him leave first. There were things he wanted to do while

39

he was on this side of the void and many more that he couldn't do, in case he was recognized and arrested. Instead he sat on the cold wooden chair and waited.

Angus studied his nails. They needed to be cut and cleaned. In Demonside he hadn't worried or noticed. His hands were rough, with cracked nails and calluses and dirt ingrained around his joints. Around his forearm was a tan line where his shirt ended and his unprotected skin had gotten browner—not that he really got a tan. He just seemed to get a denser scattering of freckles. His feet were tougher from being barefoot all the time. He wriggled his toes in his joggers. They were his favorite pair, his most comfortable shoes and yet he couldn't wait to take them off so he could be barefoot or at least pad around in socks.

He glanced up as the murmurs across the room died down. They were done talking, and he was sure he wasn't going to like their decision.

"We will need to speak with Warlock Dentin about his demon," the tall man in the mask said.

Angus frowned. They were going to ruin what was happening if they spoke to him. "But the demons are feeding him false information."

"And some truth. It's too dangerous to leave him where he can do damage."

Damage to whom? The person most at risk was Dentin's demon. "What are you going to do?"

"That doesn't matter to you. You will be the lure. That's all you need to know." The man dismissed Angus's concerns with a flick of his fingers.

Bait. They wanted him to be bait and to go against what the council of mages had voted for. "The mages thought it best—"

"Are you a human or a demon?" one of the leaders snapped. His voice was harsh from behind the safety of his mask.

Angus flinched. He curled his fingers, and magic slid toward him as though he were herding dust bunnies to do his bidding. He wanted to rip their masks off. Maybe they would be more reasonable if people knew who they were. He drew a breath and swallowed but didn't let the magic go. "Human."

Although sometimes he wasn't sure. Sometimes when he was in Demonside, he felt demon. They treated him as one of them. Other times, when there was something he should know but didn't, he felt like an ignorant tourist—human and confused. When he was in Vinland, he didn't know what he was, only that he didn't fit.

He didn't fit anywhere—not Demonside, not college, not with the underground.

"Then you'll do as you're asked. We must take down the college before we're all trapped in an ice age no one can break."

That was something they had in common. It should be their only goal. "Rebalance more magic." That was the way to stop the advancing ice and the longer winters, but they knew that.

From the way they looked at him, it was clear they thought him stupid. "It's gone beyond that."

Angus doubted it. He'd seen the rain in Demonside. He'd watched trees grow in hours, stood beneath a fingerfruit tree and fed it his blood, watched it fruit and, at dusk, eaten what he helped create. Rebalancing changed everything.

That was also the reason why Demonside would eventually suck him dry and kill him if he stayed there too long. The more he gave, the less time he could spend there. That was the balance. He needed to come back to his side of the void to refill.

But he wanted to go back.

He immediately felt bad because Terrance was waiting for him, and he wanted to spend time with Terrance. He liked him, and it had nothing to do with magic, yet at the same time, his body craved magic and rebalancing. But that couldn't be a good thing. No sensible person should get caught up in the rituals and enjoy what happened.

But part of him craved the drawn-out release, and the buildup of lust until he thought his heart would implode. He had a level of trust with Saka that he'd never had with anyone else.

But it was just magic. Saka needed him, and he needed Saka. And when the worlds were safe? He couldn't think that far ahead. While he was in Vinland, he'd make the most of his time with Terrance. Terrance deserved so much more than that.

He nodded meekly as though he understood things were too dire to just rebalance. Once he would've believed without hesitation, but now he questioned everything. Saka had ruined him in that way, with prodding, discussion, and debate.

"We'll come and get you when plans have been made," the man who liked to be obeyed said.

Again Angus nodded, but he had no plans to sit around and wait. He needed to tell the mages what was going on.

Who should he obey?

The human underground or the demon mages?

CHAPTER 6

THE COLD brushed against Saka's skin as the void opened. He was being summoned. He moved away from the people he was eating with, bowl still in his hand as the tear widened. The others could see it, but they no longer pitied him for having a warlock. Angus had gained some standing and was treated the same as a demon apprentice. That had also lifted Saka's standing, as had the human trainees.

While it was no longer raining hard, a light drizzle kept everything damp. Soon the tribes would leave Lifeblood. It would be another year before they regathered. Although some wouldn't go far from the surface rivers around Lifeblood because their mages weren't strong enough to draw up water for a whole tribe.

He crossed the cold gap between worlds with his bowl in hand. If he had to, he could use the hot stew as a weapon. Human cows were tasty, both the first night and the second, when the roasted meat leftovers were boiled.

Angus sat on a chair in a small room. None of the tension that had once existed when Angus summoned Saka remained. It was then he realized that if Angus was sitting, he hadn't walked to make the circle. He held the circle out of will alone.

And Angus wasn't by himself. To the side was another man. Tall and dark-haired, he had his arms crossed over his chest and was doing his best not to look concerned. A small smile played over his lips, but it didn't reach his eyes. That was the warlock who'd had a scarlips for a demon and who liked Angus—who Angus liked. Angus might be relaxed, but tension inhabited *his* body.

He was a mage. Angus was his apprentice and could do what he wanted. They were not partners or life mates or anything close. But that didn't explain the claws that dug into Saka's heart.

If Angus was truly to be a mage, he would have to give up connections to individuals and take on the responsibility of serving the tribe and his tribe of humans. But Saka knew how good it felt to step away from that weight for even a few moments. For a heartbeat he felt the cool bark beneath his palm and the heat of Angus's body around him—the need and the release with nothing to complicate what was between them.

He drew in a breath and then took a spoonful of the stew. He would not think about that. It was an error, but it was one he would treasure.

"Sorry for interrupting your meal," Angus said. He smiled, but his voice was level.

Saka took another bite, but he no longer enjoyed the taste of the cow. It was like sand in his mouth. He chewed and swallowed. "It must be important."

Angus wouldn't summon him unless it were. That was what they'd agreed on. In Vinland Angus was supposed to put into practice what he'd learned in Demonside and be more wizard than warlock. Wizards drew power from around them. They didn't need a demon. There was less magic in Vinland, though Angus was capable of drawing some up. Was that why Terrance was there? The college had spent a long time making sure that people thought wizards were weak… and then they moved on to controlling all magical studies.

Saka had no idea how humans had let that happen.

Something changed in Angus's face—a slight hardening around the eyes. The friction was back between them because he'd said a few careless words. Of course it was important, but it annoyed him that Terrance was there and Saka couldn't be alone with Angus.

The harshness faded with Angus's next breath. "The underground plans to go after Ruri's warlock, Dentin. I thought you should know."

It was clear there were no secrets between Angus and Terrance, and that neither of them had thought it worthwhile to keep underground secrets to themselves.

Saka wasn't sure what to say. The underground was supposed to be on the same side as the demons. Though apparently that only went so far. "What will they do with him?"

"Maybe only question him." Angus shrugged. "They didn't tell me. All I know is I'm supposed to be the bait to get him to the trap location. They don't care about the misinformation. They think he's a risk."

"And you?"

"I don't know. You both make good points."

Saka almost smiled. How demon Angus was sounding when he looked at both sides but didn't make a decision. It was the lack of decision-making that had led the demons to this point. If something had been done when they first noticed the drying, neither world would be on the verge of death. But it was too late to dwell on past errors. All they could do was learn from them.

"I will let the council know." Guda would not be pleased, as she had put a lot of faith in the underground and her warlock. Without her support Saka's ideas would never have been given due consideration.

"Thank you. Is it still raining?"

"Not continuously. We will be moving soon. Miniti doesn't want to linger." She wanted people to know she had two strong mages who could draw up water. "We will absorb another, smaller tribe."

"And the trainees?"

"We are still deciding if they should remain with the tribes at Lifeblood or if they should travel in smaller groups."

"You need someone who can open the void for them," Terrance said.

"You have no demon." Saka studied the dark-haired man as jealousy nipped at the edges of his mind. He needed to remember that Angus belonged in Humanside. It would behoove him to not become too attached to his human apprentice. He took another mouthful of his dinner, and the congealing in his gut suggested that he already cared

45

too much. He'd kept a bedside vigil while Angus fought for his life. What had Terrance done?

"But I can open the void in an emergency."

"Do you want a demon?" Saka asked. Terrance hesitated. That was all the answer Saka needed. No, he didn't. But he should be glad Angus had people who cared. Saka forced gratitude and hoped it would become real as he spoke. "Thank you for your offer. It will be considered."

And disregarded.

A look passed between the two humans, and Saka knew they had already made their own plans. He would have to wait for Angus to tell him in his own time and ignore the thorn that twisted in his side.

What was wrong with him?

"If that is all?" His meal was cold and unfinished, but he'd lost his appetite. What a waste of food. He'd make himself eat it. When the rains stopped and the rivers sank there would be lean times again. He already dreaded those last months before they gathered at Lifeblood next year. Maybe it wouldn't be so bad. There had already been plenty of rain.

But that all depended on how much magic the warlocks sucked out of Demonside, and he knew they wanted it all.

"You don't want to stay?" Angus looked surprised. Had he thought they'd all sit around and talk magic? Maybe he had.

"Terrance is not a trainee. I cannot teach everyone I stumble over, and neither can you."

"He's been teaching me. I can open the void without the walking ritual."

"I noticed. You are becoming stronger." Angus was at the point when apprentices became a little too sure of themselves and accidents happened. "Be careful you do not overestimate your abilities."

It wasn't meant as a barb, but Saka saw the moment it hit and knew that was how Angus had taken it. Perhaps when Angus came back, Saka would let him see how easy it was to go too far. A lesson in control, or rather, the lack of it. Gathering power was the first simple step, but like any child who had just learned to walk, Angus thought he could run.

Saka hoped he wouldn't fall and do himself too great an injury on the human side of the void.

"If you want a demon, then I'm sure there would be a mage willing to take you on, Terrance." It was the only concession Saka could make, but it didn't cover the wound his comment had left. He stepped back through the void before he could make the situation worse.

The heat washed over him, but instead of rejoining the people he'd been sitting with—new demons to Miniti's tribe who were getting to know everyone—he walked through the tents until he reached Guda's.

As soon as he sat, his bowl was topped up with more food that he had no stomach for. They were being polite, and he couldn't refuse.

After pleasantries and conversation that he couldn't be bothered with, he and Guda retired to her tent. All happiness was erased when he repeated what Angus had told him.

"Are you certain? Is he certain?" Guda's wings lifted but didn't open.

"He is to be bait. I do not think they fully trust him."

"And they would be right, as he told you their plan."

That was true. He'd been so busy wallowing in his own stung heart that he'd missed that obvious truth. "Unless they wanted us to know."

"Or they are testing him to see if he is trustworthy, in which case, anything we do proves he isn't." Guda tilted her head. "Ellis has mentioned nothing to me, but she has been ill."

Ellis was a warlock of some regard. She worked for both the college and the underground. And while she shared information, it was useful to have more than one source. Saka didn't think Guda trusted Ellis completely. No warlock could truly be trusted.

CHAPTER 7

BEING BAIT was about as much fun as Angus expected. But Dentin seemed happy to swallow it without thinking about the consequences. Perhaps he wanted the glory of catching Angus and the power that would come from killing Angus's demon. And it was all going according to plan. The underground moved closer, though not fast enough, from where they had been waiting on the bridge.

His heart pounded from the chase, and he pretended to panic at being trapped—most of which wasn't actually pretend. If the underground didn't step in, he was off to warlock prison forever. The cold pinched his lungs with each pant.

Come on. Dentin had him trapped. They needed to step in—unless this had been a way for the underground to get rid of him.

Snow hit the edges of the circle but didn't fall within. He lifted his gaze to watch it slide down the outside of the invisible barrier. In Demonside the circle would be bright blue and crackling with energy. He could see it in his mind. His boot slid on the slick cobble, and he went down into a crouch.

Dentin summoned his demon to draw up the power that would bind Angus and make him safe to be collected and transported. The void opened, and the plan to catch Dentin unraveled in the space of three heartbeats.

Ruri, Dentin's demon, stepped through, closely followed by three others. Angus tried to bring down the circle with magic and force. But Dentin was strong and his circle stable. Angus swore. He'd told Saka, but he hadn't expected the mages to do that. Dentin struggled but was no match for the demons. Before the underground could arrive, Dentin was dragged across the void and the tear closed. There was nothing

Angus could've done because he was trapped. Even if he'd gotten free, he wasn't sure if he would've stopped the mages.

Angus bit his lip. Snow landed on his black coat. With no one to maintain the circle, it had fallen.

He got to his feet as the underground arrived. And he, like the other members of the underground, stared at the space where Dentin had stood not three seconds before.

Because no college-affiliated warlock was willing to be seen getting their hands dirty on the mission, the underground group was made up of only wizards. They stamped their feet in frustration.

"That's it. We'll never see him again." One of the men huffed out a breath. It formed a soft cloud.

Snow stung his face. Angus was cold to the bone after being out for so long. While he knew the mages would rather have Dentin in the college, Angus hadn't expected them to take the warlock from under the noses of the underground. He pushed his hair back and blinked, not sure what to do next.

Gradually Angus became aware of a change in the mood. Behind him the ice that had formed on the edge of the river creaked and cracked. The snow was crunchy underfoot, and he couldn't feel his fingers. None of which bothered him nearly as much as the look on some of the wizards' faces. They glared at him as though he were the cause of all their problems—which he technically was. If he hadn't told Saka, Dentin would be on his way to underground headquarters. He took a step back, only to have his boot slide again.

One of the men grabbed his arm and hauled him up. "You betrayed us."

He had. But they'd betrayed the mages first. "I did exactly what you asked. I can't help it if his mage took him."

Dentin would never leave Demonside. But even his death by sacrifice would not rebalance enough magic to lift the early winter. All they could hope for was that Spring would come and there would be a summer of some sort. If not, they would starve.

His companions didn't like him, and they trusted him less. He was bundled into a car. For a heartbeat he was tempted to open up the void and disappear so he didn't have to talk to anyone, especially not the underground leaders, but that would only make him look guilty. Was he guilty?

Maybe he shouldn't have told Saka, but when pushed, he put his faith in the demons and not the underground. Angus was a demon in human skin. He stared out the window to avoid the unhidden accusation in their glares.

By the time they reached the building, an old school, the driver had told the leaders what had happened and Angus knew he was going to take the blame. The underground should concentrate on the college. Dentin was nothing. He wasn't near the top—just a midlevel warlock who reported to someone else. The demons would extract that information and rebalance at the same time—wasn't that a better use of the resource?

He caught his thought as soon as it formed. A life wasn't a resource. Shouldn't be, and yet that's exactly what a warlock was right then. The faint marks on his arms and legs tingled from Saka's little blade, and his blood heated. *He* was a resource—one that would be replenished to be drained again. He was a willing participant. Fuck, he even enjoyed it. He stared at the ice-encrusted windows.

If he did nothing, two worlds would die so a few could have power, and he couldn't step away from that and forget. Though it would be nice if he could.

Terrance could.

If Angus were more like him, he'd push it all aside and focus on his training as though the world weren't freezing up around him. When they lay on Terrance's bed and watched a movie, Terrance had shown him how to watch news from other countries. It was different from what they were told about those countries. The Mayan Empire to the south *didn't* appear to be full of bloodthirsty demons who trained humans to die for them. They had priests who were very concerned about the storms and flooding of their farmlands. One priest wore the feathers of his demon, and his demon wore a bracelet of his human's hair. Their temples were vast, and they seemed to hold the demons in great esteem. Angus had never seen a feathered demon.

Why had Saka never talked of those demons?

It wasn't just the Mayan Empire. He'd seen snippets of news from other countries that plainly hated magic and were calling for the deaths of all who used it.

He'd had to turn off the TV at that point. But Terrance was excited. There was a whole world out there that had been kept from them—and maybe for good reason. Some of them wanted to kill all humans who used magic, even wizard magic. The night had ended with just a kiss, as though it had been a proper first date. It had left him wanting more.

He got out of the car. Someone kept a hand on him at all times, as though he were under arrest, and maybe he was. Could they really hold him accountable for something the demons had done?

While he would've liked to say no, he had a feeling they would.

The tall man who liked to be obeyed was waiting in what might have once been the principal's office. His mask was firmly in place. Must be nice to be able to hide behind anonymity. Angus would never have that again, not with the reward for his capture so public. What would it be like to be a no one and to just live his life?

He'd have to leave Vinland, but leaving was impossible. To the East was an uncrossable no-man's-land. To keep out the Nations people, as he'd been told, or to keep the Vinnish in?

To the south was the Mayan Empire, and some smaller independent nations that aligned themselves with the Mayans for the most part, assuming that his geography lessons were correct. If the people in charge were lying, why not lay false groundwork at all levels so no one would question anything?

"What did you say to your demon?" The masked man leaned forward.

There was no presumption of innocence. Angus did his best to sit still and not fidget, but he didn't answer. He didn't want to lie, but he didn't want to tell the truth either. He would've preferred to talk to Ellis.

"Answer, or I'll have someone go through your head," the man barked.

Angus didn't want any more warlocks to poke around in his head and give him a migraine. The first time had been bad enough.

"I don't know why the demons took him. I'm just as shocked as you." A truthful answer, though not the one the man wanted. "He was there, and then there were four demons, and he was gone."

"Did you recognize the demons?"

"Only Dentin's mage." It had happened so fast he hadn't gotten a good look at any of the others. He doubted they were mages, though. Demons were careful, and they needed their mages more than ever if they were to survive.

The man leaned back. "You need to think about your position, Angus. You want to help us overthrow the college?"

"Yes. Of course I do."

"Then you need to work with us, not against us. The demons are using you. You offer yourself in exchange for knowledge, but they won't share all their secrets with you. You're human."

He knew then that he'd skated too far to the middle of the river. The ice was thin, and no one would save him if he dropped through. "I know I am. We all want the same thing—to stop the ice age here and the dying of Demonside."

"We lost a valuable source of information today."

"Hopefully the demons will share their information." Angus wasn't sure they would when he didn't want to share what *he* was learning.

"Hmm. Hopefully they will." He looked at his paperwork. "You can go. You'll be returning to Demonside with the other trainees. You're to keep to their schedule. Am I clear?"

"Yes." He wasn't allowed to go when he wanted. They were watching him. And he would watch them. With college warlocks in leadership roles, could the underground really take down the college, or were they just planning a coup?

Or maybe he was thinking too much about it.

He reached the door.

"One more thing, trainee Donohue."

52

He wasn't a trainee. He was an apprentice. None of the other trainees had a demon. Because of that, he was still a warlock in training, or a rogue, according to the college. He turned and looked at the man.

"We have rules for a reason. If the college were to learn who we are and what we plan, we would all be dead. You don't think of others. You act carelessly. You're a danger. For his safety we've had to relocate Terrance Erikson. I'm sure you'll understand. It's for the best until this situation is over."

Angus fought for breath. His heart swelled and blocked his airway. "What have you done to him?"

"Nothing, at the moment. We're looking after him. Let's keep it that way." The man smiled. He was nothing but a warlock using any power he had to force others to obey. The warlocks hid their faces and names, so they were never in true danger. Everyone else was expendable.

Angus was numb down to his toes. They weren't protecting Terrance. They were using him. If he disobeyed the underground, Terrance would pay the price.

That was why mages didn't have lovers or families.

His fingers curled into fists, and his nails pressed into his palms and drew blood. Magic gathered. But there was so little to grab compared to Demonside.

The man watched him. "Is there a problem?"

He couldn't rip that stupid mask off his face or demand Terrance's release. He had nothing to bargain with, and he needed the underground to open the void for him so he didn't die in Demonside. That didn't quell his desire to do something.

They were waiting for him to react—to break. Then they'd leave him to die. They didn't need him, although they acted like they did. All they wanted from him and the other trainees was information on the demons and Demonside.

Angus unclenched his fists, but not his jaw. "No problem. I hope he doesn't miss the PRA tryouts. He's hoping to put magic behind him and do what he loves."

The man stared blandly ahead. "I'm sure we'll all be cheering him on next season."

They'd let Terrance play for as long as he was useful.

It only took one lie for his trust in the underground to crumble to dust.

CHAPTER 8

FOR THE next three days, Angus kept to himself. He needed to talk to Terrance and find out if he was all right. For all of the underground's pretty words, Terrance was a hostage because of him. But on his side of the void, he could do nothing. He needed Saka's help.

He used the time he had to learn more about the world. He logged into the network the way Terrance had shown him and accessed the news from beyond Vinland. It was fascinating and terrifying, as though he were looking at some other world. He struggled to believe what he was seeing. Was it really that different beyond Vinland?

The World Council of Demonology and the Institute for Magical Studies were both arguing for economic sanctions against Vinland. Angus had heard of both bodies. College warlocks sat on both, but what he'd been told didn't marry with what he was hearing on the news. Angus had always thought Vinland was leading the world in demonology, but that didn't seem to be the case.

The IMS was calling for a halt to all demon-based magic until the situation on both sides of the void was stabilized—something that New Holland and the Mayan Empire didn't want to do. The Mayans thought they could improve things, increase their efforts to prevent a full ice age from taking hold. New Holland had dropped out of contact.

There was talk of war between magic users and the countries who viewed all magic as bad. Countries that allowed natural magic but banned demon magic might side with those that outlawed all magic. The rest of the world laid the blame for environmental disaster in the laps of those who used demons—especially Vinland.

It was with great relief that he crossed the void back to Demonside with the trainees. But not all of the trainees shared that feeling. Some were reluctant. Did they not enjoy learning magic, or did they not like demons? He needed to make more of an effort to get to know them.

Saka stood to the side, and Angus couldn't help but smile when their gazes met. He got a small one in return. "You came back."

"Of course I did." Angus wanted to put his arms around his demon, but he didn't. That weird edge was there again.

Saka quietly assessed him. "I wasn't sure. You looked so happy when you summoned me."

Angus took a step back. "I was happy, but that doesn't mean I don't want to be here." It wasn't raining, so it was more like the Demonside he knew, only with an abundance of the blue-green plants everywhere. Shrubs and grasses grew in the sand, and trees stretched overhead. The lushness seemed to spill from Lifeblood Mountain and across the plains as far as Angus could see. He breathed in the familiar scents, and absorbed the new ones—the strong, ripe smell of the flowers and the darker, richer scent of the leaves. He'd never seen anything more beautiful.

Around him trainees reconnected with their mages. Angus didn't know why Saka was being prickly, and he didn't care. He put his arms around Saka. The relief at being away from the underground washed through him as his bones warmed in the desert sun.

Saka smelled of his favorite dry soap—sweet and salty. His skin was hot to the touch. Angus wanted to kiss him, but he refrained. There wasn't supposed to be anything between them but magic. Maybe Saka was trying to put their relationship back where it should be. It was the safe thing—the smart thing—to do. Angus resented the distance.

Saka waited a couple of heartbeats and then returned the embrace. When he did, it was a hard squeeze, as though he'd thought for a moment that he'd lost something he valued. Saka inhaled against his neck, and his breath tickled Angus's skin.

"We have much to talk about," murmured Saka.

"We do, but not here." Angus needed to talk about what had happened to Terrance and his fear that he'd never see him again or that he'd be hurt—fears he couldn't express on the other side of the void. Angus lowered his voice. "We have problems."

Saka drew back and held Angus's gaze. "You could've summoned me."

Angus gave a small shake of his head. He didn't trust any of the trainees. One or more would report back to the underground, a deliberate spy or someone who believed they were doing the right thing. Angus didn't know which, but the result was the same.

In a voice loud enough for all the trainees to hear, because they would all want to know, even if they weren't brave enough to ask, he said, "So what's happening with all of us? Are we to stay at Lifeblood or travel?"

"There will be three groups, and you will travel. The splits have already been made, based on discussions with the mages."

The mages separated out into the three groups. Jim was in a different group. Angus shouldn't be happy about that, but he was. He didn't want to deal with his traitorous ex. But Lizzie would be with Angus's tribe, along with her mage and another woman called Norah. Angus hadn't spoken to either of them much.

Jim didn't look happy with the split, and while Angus couldn't hear what he said to the mage responsible for training him, it was clear the mage wasn't going to tolerate the whining of a human trainee. Jim had never been good just getting on with things. If it got hard, he tended to quit. Had the mages already realized that? Were they testing him? If he hadn't remet Jim, he might've kept looking back fondly and imagining they'd had more than what they actually had. Angus turned away. He nodded to Norah and Lizzie.

Lizzie didn't seem to be bothered and was already chatting to Norah.

He glanced at the other team of trainees and nodded at the group of four. He'd spoken to Dustin a few times in passing. The groups had been split for a reason. By ability or by level of trust? Knowing demons, it would be the latter. He bit back a smile. Was Jim or Dustin's group the least trusted? He wished he'd made more of an effort to get to know the others while they were at Lifeblood, instead of clutching his stomach and being angry. He should've spoken to them after Terrance was taken, instead of locking himself away.

Angus turned to Saka. "When do we move on?"

"Tomorrow. We were only waiting for you to return. They will remain at Lifeblood." Saka pointed to Jim's group. "The rest of us will wander. We have a demon with an underground warlock now in our tribe so the underground will be able to open the void in the right place when it is time for you to go home."

That hadn't been his main concern, and Angus didn't want to think about going back already. Something must have shown on his face because Saka's eyes narrowed.

"You need to learn how to pack." Saka turned and walked away from the group.

Some things hadn't changed. He was still meant to do as he was told, but he didn't mind. Saka was safe and familiar. No one in Demonside wanted to kill him or hurt him, which made a nice change. Angus pulled off his shoes and socks, and his winter coat followed. Beneath them he had on his demon-style clothing. If his visits were going to be carefully timed, he would make sure he was wearing the right clothing. Then he followed his demon to their tent.

It was cool and shady, but the breeze coming through the open flaps was lazy and heavy with moisture. It was a different kind of heat, one that wanted to smother him. He folded up the coat and put his human clothes in a neat pile.

Saka sat near the table and the bready, fruit-filled thing. He'd missed the taste of the sweet water and the simple demon fare.

As soon as he sat, Saka made a circle. It wasn't the usual crystalline blue. It was darker, more purple. Angus frowned as he studied the structure. Visible magic made it easier to learn, but he'd never seen that kind of circle.

"It's not for containing magic." It lacked the resonance he was used to when making a circle for magic. His voice had an odd flat tone.

Saka smiled.

Angus touched the purple wall. It shimmered and bulged but didn't break. Then he glanced up. It arched over them, sealing them in. Sealing sound in. "No one can hear us."

Saka nodded. "You wanted to talk without being overheard."

"We could've walked along the river." Many of their lessons were near the river.

"You need to help pack up the village. We don't have time to walk."

"You don't have to help?"

"I am a mage. I have other duties."

How hard could it be to pack up? He glanced around the tent. He'd never seen it packed up, only unpacked, and it always looked the same. Everything had its spot.

"What is it you wanted to discuss?"

Angus didn't know how to say what he'd learned, and there was so much. He drew in a breath and paused. He didn't need to say everything at once. "We can't trust the underground."

"I know."

"No. We really can't trust them. After someone took Dentin, I got called into the leader's office, or at least I think he's the leader. He seems to be in charge of the trainees. I don't know who he is because he's always masked, but he's definitely a college warlock. They're watching me. I've been told I have to follow the trainee schedule. I'm not supposed to summon you at all."

"But you did."

"Only because Terrance knew a place we could go." They'd acted as though they were on a date, held hands, and gone to a part of the school that the underground didn't use—the science labs. If anyone was watching, all they saw for the first hour was two guys lying on a blanket on the floor talking about... well, nothing really. They just talked and kissed. They hadn't done any more than that

59

because neither of them wanted to put on a performance for the spy—if there was one.

Eventually they decided to risk the summoning. The kissing hadn't just been for fun. Sex magic was still the easiest way for Angus to draw up the energy he needed in Humanside. It took him two goes to make a tear in the void, and Terrance's hand down his pants. Saka didn't need to know that. The memory hurt, although it should've been pleasant. He hoped Terrance was all right. "The underground is holding Terrance hostage because they know I had some part in you taking Dentin."

Saka frowned. "Know or suspect?"

"Suspect," Angus conceded. "But they have him. If I do anything wrong, they'll hurt him. He wants to go back to his sport." He sighed. "He doesn't want any part of this."

"Except you." There was that pointed blade again, poking beneath his skin, even though Saka's expression hadn't changed.

"He's a friend."

Saka tilted his horns. "Be honest, Angus, to yourself and to me."

"Fine. I'd like more." Terrance didn't want him for his magic. As much as Angus would've liked Terrance to keep fighting, he also understood why he wanted to stop. Terrance could still have a life. He had a chance to not let magic consume him. Angus had wanted that once, but he was in too deep to back away, and he liked magic too much. Maybe if Terrance had a life, he'd tire of Angus always flitting between two worlds.

"Mages don't have families. They are a distraction and a weakness." Saka had told him that before, but the words lacked conviction and they were said by rote.

Angus took a moment to gather his thoughts. "I need someone at home. I can be a mage here, but when I'm there, I have nothing and no one." He had two very different lives and no idea how long he could keep going. He certainly wasn't able to keep them separate. He wasn't even trying to keep secrets from Terrance or Saka.

"You will always have me. We're bound until death."

"Here that may be true. There I'm forbidden from summoning you. If I'm being watched closely, I may not be able to even sneak away and call you." Angus blew out a breath. "I'm sure one of the trainees is meant to watch and report on me here."

"Who do you suspect?"

"Jim. Maybe. My father paid him to break up with me before." Saying it didn't hurt the way he thought it would. "If he's been bought once, he can be bought again."

Saka nodded. "He won't be with us."

"His girlfriend will be." Angus had no idea how close or committed Lizzie and Jim were.

"His girlfriend is a far better wizard than he. The separation was deliberate, Angus. I do not think Lizzie will be a problem. Norah, I don't know well enough yet. You will get to know them both better. Sometimes you will be taught together. Sometimes it will be as we have been doing. I want you to get better with a blade."

Angus stared at Saka. He didn't like the direction of the conversation. "I can do it now."

"Only on yourself."

Angus winced. He wasn't ready to cut someone else. He didn't even want to think about it. "Can't we work on sex magic?"

Saka smiled and gave a short laugh. It was almost a chuckle with an undertone of growl. "You need to learn to do other things. You know how to raise power. Now you must use it."

"To heal?"

"Soon."

Angus studied his toes. He couldn't look up as he spoke. "What about Terrance?"

"He is safe, is he not, as long as you appear to obey?"

"They could force me to do things. I'm a liability while they have him." Saka fixed him with a look that made him want to wilt. "I know. That's why mages don't have families."

"I will speak to the other mages tonight, but do not become hopeful. There are other, more pressing issues than one unhappy ex-warlock."

Angus got the distinct feeling that, if it were up to Saka, Terrance could stay locked up wherever he was. Maybe he wasn't imprisoned. Maybe he was fine… and would continue to be fine as long as Angus didn't screw up. Trouble was, he had a long history of screwing up. Especially when it came to magic.

CHAPTER 9

"THEY ACTUALLY took Terrance?" Guda sat at the top of Lifeblood Mountain as the sun set. It was the last night the mages would all gather. There were only two apprentices to test that year, and they wouldn't be ready until the moon was high.

"Yes. He is apparently leverage."

"Of course he is. They realized Angus needs to be controlled or he will be a threat."

That was true. Angus could see through their lies. Saka had been teaching him how to sense for untruths, but Angus seemed to be able to do it naturally. As much as he wanted to learn to heal, Angus's talents seemed to lie elsewhere. He was a leader, someone who could inspire others. People liked him.

People would always want to be with him.

"He wouldn't be a threat if they were being honest about what they want."

"We always knew that they were not truly on our side, but it is better to have some human allies than none." Guda flicked her wings. "We cannot leave Terrance in their hands. It will be easy for them to make threats and for Angus to feel pressured."

"He shouldn't have gotten involved with Terrance." Angus's affection for Terrance was a thorn that had worked its way deep.

Guda looked at him for several heartbeats. He wanted to look away like a guilty child, but he made himself sit still and hold her gaze. For all that he tried to hide it and deny it, his old teacher saw straight into his heart.

"Jealousy is just as damaging to a mage, maybe more so than having a lover," Guda said softly. That only made it worse. She should tell him it was wrong, not accept that he cared for Angus more than he should.

Saka glanced away. "I did not know what it was at first. Now I do not know how to get rid of it. He is human. My apprentice. And I am jealous of the time he spends with another man." It was a mark he could not scrub from his skin, no matter how hard he tried.

"We should try to get Terrance," Guda repeated.

"We should tell Angus to ignore their threats." Would the underground actually kill Terrance? Saka didn't know. If they did, he would no longer be a problem, and if they didn't, Angus could shake himself free of their demands.

"He will not. He has a human heart, and they are tenderer than ours. Not only that, but it would be a sign of our faith in him."

It wasn't the underground the demons trusted. It was Angus. No one had put that burden on his shoulders yet. For the moment, the underground was useful, even if they were not open. They had given Angus a chance to come and go and for him to find like-minded wizards. Some of the wizards were there because they felt they should be, and others because they genuinely wanted to help. The teams had been assembled with that in mind.

"It will have to be voted on." And he would vote against. It was too dangerous, and they didn't know where Terrance was.

Guda looked at him with sadness in her eyes. "Do not vote in a way that you will regret, just because you cannot contain the way you feel." She used his shoulder to get up, but didn't straighten immediately. "There is nothing wrong with falling in love, only when you let that love become a weakness. You would do well to think on the path you are walking, student of mine."

She stood and shuffled away, her age clear in her gait. She would stay to supervise the training of the humans they trusted the least. Jim was one of them.

Her warning rolled around Saka's skull. He could love Angus as long as it wasn't a weakness, but it was already tearing him open. He didn't know how to fix the wound or stop the poison from spilling. Seeing Angus had only made it worse. He'd wanted to embrace Angus, kiss him, and greet him as a lover when he stepped through the void. Instead he'd forced distance. That night, while Saka was with Guda, Angus was being shown how to pack up the tent.

There'd been a moment when it was clear that Angus hoped for something, but Saka had turned away. He hated himself for that, in part because he knew that the sex would help rebalance, but also because he wanted it too. He wanted to steal another moment where rebalancing and magic didn't matter.

He closed his eyes.

He'd promised himself that it would be only the once for pleasure. And before Angus had almost given his soul to Demonside, there had been pleasure. But in the days when death stalked, Saka realized what Angus meant to him, and pleasure had become a dangerous indulgence.

It was all right to love. He didn't doubt Guda, but most mages were told it was better not to. He'd had lovers, but he hadn't loved them.

Was it love that he felt for Angus?

He didn't know. He'd never been in love, and he had no idea how to stop it from turning him inside out. The tribe needed him whole. Angus needed him whole. He couldn't be the mage they needed if he acted in his own best interest.

The mages were gathering, and he got up to join them. They would vote on what to do about Terrance, and Guda wouldn't know how he voted.

But *he* would, and he didn't know if he should vote with his heart or his head. It would be easier if Angus tore Saka's heart free and left it in the sand for a scarlips, but Angus would never do that. If he voted against rescuing Terrance, he might as well carve a hole in Angus's chest. He couldn't do that either.

THE VOTE had been taken and the plan made in a rush. The tribes were about to leave, so any rescue had to be done immediately. Saka thought it rash, but people were desperate to do something, to fight instead of waiting. His vote had been lost in the deluge of affirmative votes. He watched the dawn, and with the other mages, he waited for the return of the rescue party.

Guda and her warlock met every morning. They used the tear in the void to get through. From there, Guda planned to reason with her warlock and encourage Terrance's release or, if the opportunity presented itself, grab Terrance.

The work should've been done in two stages—gain the information and then attempt a rescue or not.

It was midmorning when a tear opened and the mages and hunters returned. The group was smaller than it had been. His ribs tightened around his lungs and made it hard to draw breath. Where was Guda?

Then he saw his old teacher being carried. There was blood all over her and those carrying her. It splashed on the top of the mountain like rain.

He broke away from the other mages. There was no point in holding a circle for the returning demons. They were back—as many of them who were coming back. A mage and a hunter were gone.

Dead or captured? It would be better if they were dead, not used to drain more magic from Demonside in rituals.

"Guda." He dropped to his knees by her side, and people gave him space.

She wheezed with each breath. He put his hands over her wounds. There were too many. He'd seen the damage before—bullet wounds. The metal was still inside her. Why had no one bothered to heal her? They were easy wounds to heal but fatal if left.

"No," she whispered.

"It is not too late." He glanced at the mages who had brought her through and sought help, but no one stepped forward. What had she said to them?

"I asked them… to bring me… back so I could die on… Lifeblood. They have done that." Every word was a struggle.

Saka couldn't imagine a world without her. She had been a constant for most of his life, a teacher and friend.

"You don't have to die."

66

She stated at him with her dark eyes. "Let me give my soul. You do not need me."

But he did. He might be head mage for his tribe, but it was Guda that he spoke to when he needed guidance, when he needed to confide or be challenged. Was this her last challenge to him?

He would fail it.

His hands were sticky with her blood.

Terrance hadn't even been rescued. Bitterness roiled through him. "It was for nothing."

She gave a small shake of her head. "They wanted us to try. They were waiting, and we were too slow to realize."

"Ellis betrayed you." He'd thought Guda had a good relationship with her warlock. They had worked together for a decade.

"No. She was betrayed. She didn't agree with the changes. Now she is dead." She placed her great clawed hand over his. Her talons were no longer shiny. They were flaky, and some were broken. How had he not noticed that age had crept up and stolen parts of her? Or had he been blinded by his own need for her?

She drew in a breath. "Find a way forward, Saka. I can no longer lead you."

But he was lost and had no light. Already he was losing his footing and had nothing to grab on to. Her chest stilled.

"Guda," he cried, but her soul was gone from her body, back into Demonside.

He rocked back on his heels. Blood dripped off his fingers. He wanted to howl like a child, but he couldn't. He didn't know what to do. She could've lived a little longer—a year, maybe two. He wasn't ready to be alone, but he drew in a shuddering breath and pulled himself together. He couldn't come apart with so many watching.

No one said anything.

There would be discussions later about what had gone wrong. Though no word of it would spread beyond Lifeblood Mountain. What was discussed there was secret unless they agreed otherwise. The hunters had been sworn to silence on the matter before they left.

Their failure was something they would have to dissect. The brutality of the underground was a concern.

The hunters who'd accompanied the three mages hovered above the ground, unwilling to set foot on the sacred space. Their wings created a breeze that buffeted him, and for a moment, if felt as though he were going to fall off the side of the mountain.

The world would never be the same again.

His chin tipped to his chest. He would arrange the body and leave her there. Mages were left in the open so their bodies could be used by the creatures who roamed Demonside. Others were buried in the sand. It wouldn't take long for there to be nothing left. When he came back next year, Guda would be completely gone.

CHAPTER 10

ANGUS KNEW something was going on because Saka and the other mages hadn't come down the mountain. The whole tribe was packed and waiting and none too happy about the delay. He'd done his bit to help, or at least not get in the way or botch it up as he was shown what to do. Everything was folded and stowed away. Even Saka's little table had its legs folded so it became flat.

Most people didn't have as much as Saka or Miniti. It must be a status thing as well as a practical thing because every item had to be moved. What wasn't carried was loaded onto sleds or the backs of the animals that were tethered near the camp. He'd seen them from a distance, but never up close.

They weren't as big as horses, but their backs were broad, their feet were like dinner plates, and they were covered in scales. Their toes dug into the sand as their burdens were added. They reminded Angus of alligators—if alligators had long legs, a stubby tail, and could be tamed.

"What do they eat?" He didn't want to get too close and accidently lose an arm—not that anyone else seemed to be worried.

"Camp scraps, bark, bones, pretty much anything. They are scavengers," the demon who'd been very patient with him all morning said.

When the creature let out a bellow through its nostril flaps, the demon gave it a friendly nudge. "Are you scared?"

"No." A little. But he wasn't going to reveal that to anyone. "Curious." He reached out a hand, only to have it slapped away.

"Approach from the side. They have sharp teeth at the front for tearing and can give a nasty bite." She stared at him. "You would be very tender and probably tasty." She snapped her teeth at him, and Angus had the distinct impression that she wouldn't mind giving him a bite. She laughed as she walked around the other side of the beast to adjust the straps.

Lizzie stomped over with an armload of stuff that belonged to her mage. "This is the last of it." She wiped her forehead and pulled her shirt, which was stuck to her with sweat, away from her body. "It's not even midday yet."

"We should've left already," Angus said as his gaze drifted to the mountain.

"Nothing good ever comes out of a meeting that lasts this long." The demon clicked her tongue and shook her head. "No one wants to start a walk under the midday sun."

"So this afternoon?" Or had they packed up for nothing and would remain another day? If they had to unload, no one was going to be in a good mood.

"Miniti will say when we go."

Miniti, who had graciously allowed others to join her tribe as long as she was still in charge. Who'd already gotten a taste for his blood and who Angus tried to avoid as much as possible.

"Go humans, before you turn pink and pass out." The demon shooed them away.

He was never going to live the heatstroke down. Lizzie glanced at him but didn't say anything as they made their way to the shade of the trees. The buzzing insects had also retreated and were making the most of the fruits and the flesh available to bite.

As much as he wanted to squash the green-winged thing that landed on his arm, he settled for flicking it away. He already had a welt on his shoulder from where something else had bitten him. And while he knew he shouldn't, he missed the dry when the insects were dormant. Even the rain was better. At least it had been slightly cooler.

"Ugh." Lizzie brushed something off her ankle. "I'd sit, but I don't want them crawling up my pants."

The river was a glistening ribbon of temptation about ten yards away, but there'd be no relief there. Things that lived in there had woken up and were breeding and doing their thing before the river sank. Some of the things—fish, eels, he wasn't sure—sank with the rivers. They were pale and eyeless and apparently delicious. He might have eaten some for dinner. It was easier not to know.

"You okay with the split?" He hadn't spoken to either of the trainees in his group because they'd been too busy packing. While he didn't want to talk too much about himself, he could try to find out where Lizzie sat when it came to magic and demons… and Jim.

She shrugged. "Yeah. I guess. We're here for a few weeks, then home. It's not forever. Jim and I will be fine."

Angus nodded. "He didn't seem happy."

"He's not. He wanted us to stay together, and he hates that his mage is going slow. His words." She shooed away another bug.

"Ah." Angus wasn't about to share his suspicions. "And yours?"

"Good. Drawing up, rebalancing, the basics, I guess. What about you? You do other stuff?" She lifted an eyebrow as she looked at him.

"Yeah." He was being taught like a demon apprentice.

"I've seen you with him. You're friendly. Jim mentioned the marks on your arm. That's not just rebalancing." She pointed to a few faint scars that were visible.

What else had Jim been saying, or asking her to do? Angus glanced down. The scars were only the thickness of a hair and almost completely faded. He was hoping he'd learn how to heal himself soon, and then they would be completely gone. How much did she know about what he did? Some wizards used blood magic, but did they know about the emotion behind the cuts? "It is, but different."

She studied him for a minute. "You're learning other things. I heard whispers that your mage is your lover."

From Jim's lips to her ear, or had she heard something from the demons? Angus swallowed. No one thought twice about it. Back home, even the underground would be horrified, especially the college warlocks.

71

Lizzie pushed a strand of hair off her face. "I'm not going to say anything. I just wondered if it were true."

There was no point in lying about it if people were talking about it. He wanted Lizzie to trust him, even if he didn't trust her. At some point Lizzie would have her suspicions confirmed or she'd learn there were more powerful ways to rebalance than what she was being shown. "There are three ways to rebalance—blood, sex, and souls."

"Souls as in death."

"Yes. Although little bits can be given." He was sure Demonside had taken a piece of him when he almost died. A part of him never wanted to leave when he was there. He was accepted. Magic was as natural as breathing, and it flowed through him. He missed that when he was across the void.

Lizzie nodded. "So the people who were killed." She nodded at the mountain. "It wasn't just about their blood."

There would have been ritual cuts before their death. They would've been given a choice. They would've been offered either drugs or magical relief. It didn't make it any less distasteful knowing that they were criminals or volunteers who wanted their deaths to mean something. Their deaths had brought life to Demonside.

"It's complicated, and I don't fully understand what goes on up there." He'd been part of one power-raising orgy. That had been enough for him to step aside. He wasn't ready for that kind of magic.

"But you've been up there."

He nodded. "And I can't talk about it because I was there as a mage. What is discussed by the council of mages is private."

The trainees had been welcomed up there, like any apprentice, but the next time they went up Lifeblood, their training would be over. The next time he went up, it would be to be tested and admitted as a mage. That would take years. He would be between two worlds for… not just years but for the rest of his life, He didn't want to give up Demonside to live only with humans.

For a heartbeat his future unfurled in front of him. Never in one place for more than a few weeks. Always back and forth. Who would want that from a partner? How could he expect anyone to put up with that? He shivered despite the heat.

"Do you trust the demons?" Lizzie's voice yanked him back to the sticky shade of the trees and the droning of the insects.

"As much as I trust anyone." Which wasn't much. He could count his friends on one hand. And one of them was imprisoned because of him.

Lizzie stared at the river, and neither of them spoke. A small herd of tenga wandered over for a drink. While they couldn't be called cute and furry, they shimmered like gold in the sun, their tiny green horns like emeralds. They were also good to eat. He'd eaten more in Demonside in the last few weeks than he ever had. Members of the tribe were no longer thin. Saka's collarbone had vanished. It wasn't just the animals making the most of the abundance of food.

Lizzie kicked at a few fallen leaves. "I never realized how many warlocks are in the underground. I thought it was all wizards."

"Me neither." It didn't fill him with confidence, only suspicion.

She pressed her lips together, concentrated on the leaves, and pushed them aside to expose the sand. "So, if it's full of warlocks… how is it different from the college?" She looked up at him. "You're a warlock. How are you different?"

He hadn't thought of himself as a warlock for a while, but that's how humans saw him. He was a rogue warlock—the worst kind. He knew just enough to be dangerous. "I'm an apprentice mage. I don't share beliefs with the warlocks, and I can only hope that the warlocks in the underground don't share beliefs with the college."

"That's a lot of hope."

"Yeah." And he wasn't feeling any of it. Did the warlocks really want to bring back nondemon magic or did they want to steal power from the college? Were people like Lizzie just foot soldiers in the war?

And what was he?

How could he align himself with only the demons *or* the underground when he had a foot on both sides of the void? He wanted to save both worlds, and he didn't care about power squabbles. A brown bug crawled along his arm and bit him without warning. He pulled it off, tearing his skin in the process. The thing still held his flesh in its pincers.

Some days literally everyone wanted a bite.

Lizzie peered at the bug as it ate the piece of his skin while his arm bled. "We're the bug, at the mercy of whoever is holding us."

He put the bug onto the sand, and it scuttled beneath the leaves. "Then, who has the gentlest touch?"

"I guess that depends on who finds us the most useful."

He shook his head and pressed his shirtsleeve against the wound. "No, who do you want to help and who do you want to bite?"

CHAPTER 11

SAKA HADN'T said a word since he came down the mountain. He didn't know what to say. There was a fresh cut over his heart where he'd made an offering of his blood. Miniti had seen him coming and gotten everyone moving, but Saka was happy to walk at the back. They didn't need him at the front to look for water as they followed the river away from Lifeblood.

For the moment the tribe didn't need him at all.

That was a good thing. He couldn't be any use to anyone right then. He couldn't still his thoughts. He'd voted against going and hadn't volunteered to go. If he had, would he have been able to prevent Guda's death? He had more experience with humans than most other mages, simply because he was one of the few who'd allowed a connection to form with a warlock.

He should've gone with Guda.

Guda had been his family longer than his mother. He'd left her to become a mage as soon as he was old enough. When she died, it hadn't hurt like this. Pain was becoming something he was too familiar with.

Just like when he thought Angus was going to give his soul to Demonside.

Guda was dead because of Angus. Angus kept bringing pain to Saka's heart. He had slipped in and was tearing him apart. Saka didn't want to love if that was what it felt like. It was a weakness. Guda was wrong. It couldn't be a strength.

Even their last conversation had been about Angus.

Saka regretted the day he'd felt the pull and stepped through the void to get a new warlock. Demonside needed new information, an ally they could control in the college. Instead they'd gotten Angus, a warlock who wanted to save Demonside.

Now the underground had the means to make Angus do their bidding, because he'd let himself fall for Terrance. There would be no second attempt to get Terrance back. Saka would have to speak to his apprentice, but it was a conversation he didn't relish having.

The glare from the sand stung his eyes. He would not cry for Guda. She had lived her life doing what she loved and following the path she'd picked, and she had died on Lifeblood. How many could say that? He only wished she could've lived long enough to see Demonside restored and the college defeated.

He blinked and saw Angus to the side, waiting for the tail of the tribe to catch up. Saka clamped his jaw together. He was not ready. He had never wanted an apprentice. Maybe he wasn't a very good teacher. He certainly wasn't doing a good job with Angus.

As well as Usi and Saka, there were now two other mages and their human trainees in the expanded tribe. It wasn't unheard of to let an apprentice experience the teaching of another mage, especially one with different skills. Usi was very good with a knife and at causing pain. While Saka knew Angus liked neither pain nor the knife, he needed to learn.

It did no one any good to only practice the things they enjoyed. A mage needed to be multiskilled, even if some of those skills were rarely used.

Angus would learn how to hunt and kill and how to fight, which was exactly what he'd asked to learn.

Angus fell into step with him. "Miniti would like to talk to you this evening."

Saka nodded. He'd expected that. The mages had agreed that the failed mission wouldn't be discussed. Those who had hungered for action had brought the disaster, but all were chastened. Publicizing it would only damage the morale the rain had lifted. People would doubt the mages. There was no good outcome.

Being correct was no comfort. Anger and hurt simmered. He would not rage at Angus. He should've gone with Guda. Saka blinked and saw the bullet wounds again. No one could've predicted the betrayal.

"What happened this morning?" Angus's gaze darted to the open wound.

Saka would have to heal it that evening. There was no point in being foolish and risking infection, but for the time being, he wanted to feel the sting.

"Nothing." Nothing he could talk about anyway. Miniti would be unimpressed when he told her Guda was dead but he couldn't tell her how. "I want you to work with Usi."

Angus stopped walking as though he'd slammed into an invisible tree.

Saka didn't wait for him.

Angus hurried to catch up. "Why? Have I done something wrong?" Saka made the mistake of glancing at him. Beneath his hat his face was pinched with worry. "Do you not want me as your apprentice anymore?"

The horror in his voice was another twisting blade. Saka didn't know how not to let it pull him apart and leave him vulnerable.

Mages didn't have families, yet Guda had said that it was possible. Perhaps it was a modern thing to not get too close. He'd had lovers, but none had expected more than a happy joining when the need arose. He'd never felt more than a passing affection for any of them.

"You are still mine. And I will still teach you, but Usi is better with a blade."

"No... she is better at inflicting pain. You told me that. You once asked me what I preferred, and I told you pleasure."

"And I'm telling you, you must learn pain too." The words came out as a snarl. Saka drew a breath. "I will be there. I will be your subject to practice on." Usi would enjoy that.

Maybe if Angus cut into him enough times, Saka would stop liking the warlock.

CHAPTER 12

THE DELICATE set of bone-handled knives was too pretty for the job they'd been made to do. They were one of the gifts Angus had been given when he was unconscious after his father tried to kill him. While he'd handled them several times and had personally thanked all the people who left gifts, he'd never used the knives.

He'd made cuts on himself with Saka's knives as he learned how much pressure to use and where was safe. And he had learned that, beneath the skin, he looked like any other raw meat.

His stomach flipped and refused to settle. Angus glanced at Saka who lay naked on the floor of his tent as though nothing were amiss. He wanted to ask if Saka was sure he was ready. Angus wasn't sure. There must be other things he could learn.

Wouldn't it be better if he learned how to use magic instead of more ways to draw it up? But he didn't want to voice his doubts in front of Usi.

Usi was far too happy to be there. If it bothered Saka, he didn't show it. But it bothered Angus. She wasn't supposed to be in the space where he learned with Saka. And while he could see the logic in learning from other mages, Usi would enjoy hurting Saka and then expect Angus to enjoy it. Angus didn't know if he could cause Saka pain.

He'd never used a knife on anyone.

Saka had used it on him, and even though he'd been afraid, he ended up liking it because Saka had somehow combined it with the sex magic he was so good at. Angus would rather be doing that, even if Saka kept him on edge all night, until he was begging and broken.

Would Saka beg for it to stop?

78

"Ready," Usi said.

Angus's mouth was drier than the sand of Demonside after a year with no rain. He nodded. Around him the tent was dim and mostly empty, except for the bed and the orb-shaped magic collectors, of which there were only three. Everything else was packed for the walk. Few tents had been put up because they would move on the next day. Saka had asked for his tent so they could work, but Angus had hoped Saka would change his mind all day.

If anything, Saka had withdrawn further and given short, sharp answers to any question Angus asked. So he stopped asking. There was definitely something wrong with Saka, and this was not the way to find out what.

Usi passed her knife through the flame, and Angus copied with his chosen blade.

He still hadn't come up with a way to back out, and he didn't know what to say to stop it. Did he really need to learn how to cause pain? Saka was right in that he needed to be multiskilled, but it could wait. Couldn't it? Until he knew more? Until he was more sure of himself? What if he actually hurt Saka? His stomach clenched, and he almost threw up.

Usi watched him as though hoping to find weakness, and that was enough for him to keep his expression blank.

"You will make and hold the circle." She didn't have a conversation the way Saka did. Perhaps there was a reason why she didn't have an apprentice yet.

His hand was sweaty around the bone hilt. He had no idea what animal the bones had come from and had decided it was probably rude to ask. Maybe it was better he didn't know. That he held death in his hands was bad enough, but Saka had been impressed with the quality of the knives.

Angus drew up the circle around them. It crackled like lightning and shimmered crystalline blue. While he could hear the noises of the camp, they faded away as he brought his focus to what he had to do.

Get it done. Get it over. That was all he could think about.

Usi knelt on the other side of Saka. She ran through a basic list of places not to cut because death would follow, and that wasn't the aim. He knew those things. Was she just making sure? Or was she trying to impress Saka with her ability to teach so he would speak well of her and recommend that she take an apprentice?

Angus blinked and focused. She talked about pressure points, demonstrated with the hilt of her knife as she pressed into one on Saka's wrist and then several others up his arm. Each time she drew a hiss from Saka.

"There is no need to start with blood. Like lust, you want to build the pain. The magic will look and feel different. That is what you need to learn. Holding lust is easy." Her lip curled in the slightest of sneers.

Saka didn't challenge her the way he usually would've.

Angus's eyebrows twitched. He'd been caught up in lust, and there was nothing gentle about the energy during the orgy. He might not remember the details, but the disconnection and the hypersensitivity were echoes that he couldn't forget.

After that night Saka hadn't pushed any ritual sex and had instead kept what they did to a very low level. Angus missed the intensity—that moment when the whole world was reduced to what he felt and someone else was in control.

That someone was supposed to be him, but he'd much rather bring Saka to the edge of pleasure.

He tried to locate the pressure points on Saka's other arm, but it wasn't as easy as she made it look.

"You are using your eyes. Use your other senses," Usi said as though he should know better.

"Put your other hand on my arm. Reach out with magic to feel where the nerves run." They were the first words Saka had spoken to him since Usi arrived—a simple command with no emotion beneath the words, none of the reassurance he'd come to expect.

Usi dug the hilt in, and Saka's back arched, but not a sound slipped past his lips.

Angus did as Saka told him. He rested his palm on Saka's wrist. His skin was hot and rough. Angus brushed his thumb over the veins in a silent apology. Then he reached out to find the nerves. It took a few heartbeats before he could feel the life in his demon— where the blood rushed beneath his fingertips, where the deeper veins and arteries were, then the finer network of nerves, and the clusters at the pressure points. It was a map to pain... and pleasure. When he looked at Saka, he saw the nerves like golden roads over his dark red skin.

He swallowed hard and pushed the handle of his knife into a nerve cluster near Saka's elbow. Saka barely flinched.

"You will have to press harder," Usi said.

He didn't want to press harder, but he did. And he repeated it for each pressure point until Usi was happy that he could find them and apply different pressures—a hard, short jab, or a slower, more consistent, grinding pressure that built until Saka grimaced. All Angus wanted to do was apologize.

The orbs glowed, but not with the soft light he was used to. There was the familiar static of magic building, but it tasted different. It had a sour undertone—not one that tasted bad, more like tart lemon than sweet orange.

Usi nodded. "Now we move on." She ran her hand down Saka's arm as though she were caressing him.

Angus was very familiar with that stroke. When Saka did it to him, it usually signified a change. Saka would pause in what he was doing to give Angus a chance to catch his breath before he pushed harder. Angus still had his hand on Saka's arm. He hadn't moved it. He didn't need to touch him to know where the nerves were, but he wasn't ready to let go.

Usi turned the knife in her hand so she could use the blade. "All cuts hurt, but some hurt more. You can cut without making him bleed." She demonstrated by carving a line around the curve of Saka's bicep. "You don't want to cut tendons or slash nerve clusters."

81

She pressed on a pressure point with one hand and carved with the other. "Pain can be multilayered." She reopened the wound on Saka's chest.

He hadn't healed it yet, and he hadn't mentioned how it happened. Usi knew. She'd been up Lifeblood. The grunt of pain was different that time. Fresh blood leaked from the wound, but the cut was only deep enough to bleed.

She rested an elbow on Saka's thigh. Angus could see the golden cluster she was targeting, and he was sure that Saka had tensed. Usi's pointed teeth gleamed in the light. She looked relaxed as she twisted and applied more pressure. "Some people will ask you to stop. Others will stay silent. You need to read their body. Saka and I aren't that different." She moved again, and Saka's belly tensed. As the muscles bunched, she dragged the tip of the knife across his skin and lifted a delicate flap.

Angus closed his eyes, and his stomach leaped into his throat. He was going to be sick.

Saka breathed in short, sharp pants. The magic in the air thickened. There was no appealing scent of desire, just the tangible aura of pain. Angus closed his eyes to keep it together.

"Do it. Then we will stop for today," Usi demanded.

Angus forced his eyes open. His gaze clashed with hers, and he considered telling her where she could shove the knife and her lesson, but Saka had wanted this for a reason.

Maybe it was so Angus could see the ugly side of magic. Whatever the reason he didn't want more lessons like that. He didn't care if he only had a few tricks up his sleeve.

But he wouldn't always be able to rely on pleasure to draw up magic. Even on his side of the void, he used his own blood and pain. But how much could he do if he were in agony? Not much. Was the underground using Terrance in a similar way?

Anger burned through him at the thought of someone hurting an unwilling human.

Saka had volunteered. He knew what would happen. He understood more about magic than the college warlocks who liked to think themselves so smart. Not one of them would ever offer themselves up so a student could learn.

He wouldn't waste the opportunity Saka had given him. He considered his teacher's body for a moment. He knew it well, knew where Saka liked to be touched, knew the taste of his skin and the sound of his pleasure-filled groans.

Multilayered pain is what Usi wanted to see. Then it would be over.

His knife skills were not as good as hers, but he spilled fresh blood, and Saka's breath came in sharper pants. The magic in the tent crackled and swelled.

Usi smiled. "Now we clean the knives, and then you can tend your mage."

THE ORBS glowed with their sickly pain-fed light. Saka hadn't moved yet, though the circle had been dropped and Usi had left.

"Do you need me to get you something?" Was it time to have something to eat or drink to ground themselves? The work felt unfinished. Sex magic had an obvious end, but pain didn't.

"You can raise a circle and heal the cuts." Saka's eyes were closed. How much was he hurting?

"I've never healed anything." Not even himself. Saka had always done that.

"So now you learn." His voice was as sharp as a blade. "I have told you and shown you how. It is not good manners to leave someone in a mess."

Saka had always made sure that he cleaned and healed any cuts he made on Angus. When Angus cut himself, he either had to ask Saka or, if he was on the other side of the void, he waited until his body did it on his own.

He brought up a circle around them. It was smaller than when Usi had been there. "Shouldn't she have done the healing?"

"Mages have different abilities. Healing is not one of her strengths. I asked her to leave it for you."

That explained why the injured came to Saka, not Usi. It had nothing to do with him being head mage and everything to do with him being the better healer.

Angus's heart rate picked up, and while he hadn't wanted to hurt Saka, he was more worried that he might heal him wrong. "What if I screw it up? Shouldn't I learn on myself first?"

"It is harder to do on yourself." Saka opened his eyes but didn't look at him. "I will make sure you do it right."

It would be harder than growing a tree. And as much as he wanted to learn how to heal and help people, Angus was also terrified that he might make it worse. "I don't want to hurt you more."

He knew from experience that healing wasn't painless, though it was different from being cut. Healing pain came from within and tore its way out.

Saka drew in a breath but said nothing as he exhaled.

A trickle of blood slid over Saka's chest to land on the cloth beneath. The stain spread with each breath. He had to do something. "How do I start?"

"Gather the energy. Pick a cut and guide the skin to knit back together. You know what the process looks like and how it feels. I have shown you how it is done."

Angus didn't know how to use magic in that way. "You know what you're doing."

"And I can stop you if something is wrong."

Angus looked up at the orbs overhead. It was easy to release the magic into the circle. When they had sex, they usually just released the magic into Demonside, but there had been no rebalancing tonight. Using magic in Demonside did no damage. It was like any energy and couldn't be destroyed. It was only when it was taken across the void and not returned that problems started. And magic could only be returned by humans or animals from across the void.

The lemony magic whipped around the circle like a stray tornado until Angus got hold of it. Usi wasn't wrong. It had a different feel, but it was no harder to hold. He drew the magic into himself as he'd done before. It swelled within him, and he felt invincible. He had power and strength beyond what he normally had. The magic was in his veins and under his skin, and the static was in his soul. He breathed out and found the calm inside.

It was so much easier to use magic in Demonside.

Drawing the scraps in Vinland didn't give such a buzz. Whenever he'd had sex with Saka on the other side, Saka had taken the magic back to Demonside with him, so Angus didn't get to revel in the power they released. In Demonside, the magic was used to rebalance, so Angus never got to draw in the power to use. All his lessons had been about drawing *up* the magic. The crackle in his blood was the taste of power. He took another heartbeat to enjoy it, even though the taste in his mouth was sharp and the sensation under his skin was more like claws than a caress.

Angus looked at Saka and the numerous cuts and didn't know where to start. He bit his lip and fisted his hand to stop it from shaking. The magic wanted to spill from him. The need to release had been lit like a fuse. He wouldn't be able to hold on to all of it. It was far more than the tiny amounts he'd held before. If he weren't careful, it would slide away and leave him empty.

"I don't want to do this again."

"You will. And you will get used to it, and you will practice simple healing after." Saka turned his head and looked at him. "Do you think it would be easier on someone else? A stranger?"

Would it be? Saka had done it before. He knew what was coming, and he'd worked with Usi for years. How many times had he let her use him? Or did he use her? Or did they get a willing volunteer?

He had questions, but he wasn't sure he wanted to know the answers. It was no different from what the warlocks did across the void, only they used demons—often demon animals that had no idea what was going on. They didn't give their demons an opportunity to say no.

"I don't know." He selected a small, shallow cut and hoped he wouldn't make a mess of the healing. Saka was right. Angus had seen and felt healing many times. He took a breath and placed his fingertips over the wound. Saka flinched as though the area were suddenly tender.

85

Angus pushed the energy into Saka's skin, drawing it together and forcing the cells to multiply and close the cut.

It took only a heartbeat. The body wanted to heal. All he had to do was give it a nudge and the energy boost it required. It seemed too easy. He glanced at Saka. He would say something if Angus were doing it wrong, wouldn't he? But Saka had his eyes closed again. Angus moved on to the next wound and the next one and gradually moved on to the bigger, deeper cuts.

His hands never left Saka as he guided his fingertips to their next destination. Angus did nothing, but the magic changed texture and softened into something viscous like honey. It was a magic he was more familiar with.

"From the inside. You cannot heal the surface first. You do not need to be touching me either." At some point Saka had started to watch him. "I can see what you are doing."

"It wasn't my intention." He'd changed the magic to something he was more comfortable with. His lips curved.

"But it is the result."

"I like touching you." He healed the deeper cut from the inside, which was more complicated. The demons who'd healed his internal injuries must have really known what they were doing. If they hadn't, his organs would've attached in all the wrong places.

Angus slid his hand over Saka's thigh. Then he moved over Saka to heal the cut over his heart. But Saka grabbed his wrist before he could touch it. "No."

"You've worn the cut all day. It needs to be healed. You know that." There was some kind of rule that wounds must be treated when the tribe stopped moving, or more immediately if they were serious. Treat the injury before it becomes infected. It was a good rule.

Saka said nothing, but the hurt was clear in his black eyes. The pain was more than when Angus had carved into his skin.

Angus didn't pull back, and Saka didn't let go. "How did you get it?"

"I will heal it later." Slowly he drew Angus closer. "I think it's time there was some rebalancing."

Angus swallowed. He did not want to swap places with Saka. "How many times have you done this?"

"Enough to know you weren't even trying. You let your… affection get in the way."

Angus glanced at the tent walls and the golden sigils that shimmered in the light. It was true, even though he didn't want to admit it. Saka flipped him onto the floor, and then Angus was the one on his back. His heart jumped and slammed against his ribs. He couldn't read the look on Saka's face, but he was sure it wasn't good.

Saka pinned Angus's hand to the warm fabric of the floor of the tent. "Mages must do things they don't want to. They must find that strength. You must put aside your affection."

It was clear from the way Saka's body pressed against him that he hadn't put aside *his* affection.

"Affection has some uses." Angus lifted his hips.

"Affection is not needed to rebalance. It is a ritual. That is all." Saka's touch was hot as his fingers traced Angus's jaw and down his neck to the rapid pulse, where he paused and pressed lightly with his clawed fingertips. "You need to separate ritual."

The heat that usually existed between them became a dangerous creature that could tear him apart. "From what? Rebalancing is rebalancing."

"No, it's not. We have been playing." Saka lowered his head as though to kiss him, but he didn't. He brushed Angus's cheek with his lips and lowered his hips to press against his. "I should have been training you better."

It was easy to fall under Saka's spell—the way his lips tasted Angus's skin and the way he moved against him. Every action was designed for maximum result. And it was working. Lust bubbled through Angus's body, and he was almost fooled. He could nearly pretend that was how it should be or how it had been. But it wasn't a lesson in control, at least not for Angus.

He was tempted to push aside the doubts and let Saka have his way. Angus knew he'd enjoy it. Saka was a good lover—too good, too well trained in making sure the magic was right.

Angus closed his eyes as Saka's lips went lower. They brushed across his stomach, and then Saka eased his hands into Angus's pants. His dick throbbed with the need to be touched. But it wasn't like returning the magic those few times they'd been together across the void, or like the hasty coupling by the lake. There'd been no finesse there, but he'd glimpsed a part of Saka that had been buried so deep Angus wasn't sure if he'd imagined the whole thing.

He brushed the tip of Saka's horn with his free hand. It was cool and smooth. Saka's mouth was a whisper away from sliding over his dick. Angus wanted it, even though he knew from the way Saka was behaving that there would be no quick relief. While Saka wouldn't dole out retribution for what had taken place, Angus sensed something else there—something Saka had been avoiding all day. And that wasn't like Saka at all.

Before he could enjoy the delicious heat of Saka's mouth, Angus jerked Saka's horn up and forced him to look at him. It wasn't heat in Saka's eyes. Angus was used to looking into the darkness and wanting to melt into a puddle of longing. They'd always had that snap of attraction. But that snap had turned on him, and the whiplash was going to hurt if he didn't get out of the way.

"What's going on?" His voice betrayed the need that raced through him.

"We aren't done for the evening." Saka twisted away from Angus's grip.

Angus tried to tug his hand free, but Saka gripped him tighter.

Their gazes locked. For several heartbeats neither of them even blinked. Once Angus would've looked away and done whatever Saka told him. Not anymore.

He arched his back in an effort to throw Saka off, and an undignified wrestling match followed. They grappled, their hands slid over humidity-slicked skin, and their hips bucked. He wasn't going to submit when Saka was in such an odd mood. Angus's pants tangled with his legs, but Saka wasn't even trying, and Angus finally pushed Saka onto his back and straddled him to keep him there. He pinned Saka's hands the way Saka had pinned his.

Angus huffed out a breath, relieved that he'd won, even though he wasn't sure what he'd won or why. The curve on Saka's lips did nothing to quell the doubt.

"I did wonder how long it would take before you wanted control." Saka's voice was low and smooth, as though it were part of the seduction.

"I don't want control." In that breath Angus understood that he liked the torment when Saka controlled how much pleasure he got and when he got to come. "I want to know what's wrong with you."

Nothing had been right since Saka came down the mountain.

"There is nothing wrong with me." But Saka couldn't meet his gaze.

Angus put a hand over the wound on Saka's chest. "You're wearing your pain for all to see, even if no one knows what caused it." Had he done something? Broken some taboo? "Was it me?"

"Not every part of my life is about you." Saka threw him off with a snarl.

Angus landed on his back a yard away, gasping for the breath that had been stolen from him. Saka had used his full strength. Angus sucked in another breath and propped himself up on his elbow in time to see Saka walk out the flap of the tent, wrapped in the small piece of cloth that passed for a towel.

He lay back down, swore, and slammed his fist into the floor of the tent. "Fuck."

Whatever the problem was, he hadn't made it any better. Perhaps he should've let Saka do what he wanted. At least then he wouldn't have a hard-on, he could've rebalanced some magic, and he'd have slept well.

He stared at the collector orbs that hung from the ceiling, sure he was imagining the lingering, sickly yellow gleam.

The night had been well and truly fucked up.

For the first time, he looked forward to going home if that was what it would be like with Saka from now on. His heart felt like someone had rubbed it down with sandpaper. While they'd never been equals, there had always been something between them. He'd been wrong. All they had was magic.

What had Saka said? Affection had no place?

Fuck him. He didn't need Saka to get off or rebalance.

He created a circle. Then he wrapped his hand around his half-hard cock and closed his eyes. It wasn't the same as letting someone else take control, but he knew when to stop and take a breath. It wasn't the hurried jerkoff that he'd done in his room at college. It was something else.

The magic gathered, soft as velvet. He swept his fingers around the head of his dick, over the slit, and then down. His hand was slippery. He should let go.

A little more.

One breath.

Two breaths.

It hurt. He had to stop touching himself for a moment, but that didn't change the throbbing or the tightness. Come leaked onto his belly, and he ran one finger along his length.

Could he last longer?

Why was he doing this to himself?

Because he wanted to know if it was the same, if he could rebalance alone. So far, the gathering of energy was the same. He focused on the orbs and not the ache within him or the way his hand seemed to tremble or the tightness in his chest as his heart tried to break some kind of beat-per-minute record.

No one had ever died from too much lust, but he'd felt like dying more than once with Saka.

Angus reached the point where frustration became pain. He cupped his balls, needing the touch but not able to bring himself to touch his cock. Even the breeze on his skin had become too much.

One stroke… he had to think about the magic.

A couple more breaths… it was going to work.

His skin was slick with sweat. The shirt clung to him. Suddenly he realized that Saka could walk in at any time, and Angus didn't want that interruption. He wanted to do it alone and finish.

He wrapped his hand around his cock, and that was all it took. He groaned, and it was as though the sound were ripped from within him—not part of his soul, but part of him. Some magic that he'd carried for Humanside had been returned to where it belonged.

That was why Demonside killed humans. It literally sucked all magic and life from them. Even if he didn't have sex and shed no blood, it would happen, although much more slowly. And that was why there was no fixed amount of time that was safe for humans to remain in Demonside.

He lay on the floor exhausted, and the orbs glowed brightly. All he had to do was drop the circle and release the energy. For the moment, he was content to do nothing but stare at his success—and wish he had someone to share it with.

CHAPTER 13

SAKA STALKED through the camp as though having a wash were the most important thing he needed to do. No one interrupted him. Downstream from the camp, a wash area had been set up. It wasn't like the one they used when in a more permanent setup. Water had been gathered into several large pots, and there were small bowls for scooping it out. No one was meant to take more than a scoop or two because gathering the water was hot and dangerous work. Most would take only enough to remove the worst of the travel sweat and grit.

He longed for a shower, but a wash would have to do, and it gave him an excuse to not be near his tent.

He ran his hand over his chest. The wound was raw, and the pain radiated deeply, but not all of it was from the injury. Usi had known that reopening it wasn't just about physical pain. She'd played her role, and even though Angus had been an unwilling student, he had applied himself to the job as he always did. As an apprentice, Angus couldn't be faulted. It would be easier if Saka could find a reason to dismiss him.

Saka kept his palm over the wound. He should've let Angus heal it. He should've let Angus kiss him and hold him. He could've pretended for a little while that everything was as it should be, and when he woke, it would be a dream and nothing more. He would change his vote and volunteer. Terrance would be free, and Angus wouldn't be beholden to the underground.

Guda would be alive.

By the river and alone for the first time all day, he let himself grieve for his lost mentor—the mage who'd guided his magical

92

studies and been his friend for more years than he cared to count. He hung his head and let the pain wash through him and the tears fall on the grass. His shoulders lifted with each breath.

He needed to calm himself. No one could see him so broken. Saka blinked and lifted his head. The ache was still there.

No amount of cuts could distract him. No magical working could push the pain aside or bury it deeply enough. He'd hoped that he could lose himself in the sting of each fresh cut, in the bruise that bloomed on each new pressure point. He'd wanted Angus to fail.

Guda would be horrified. No mage should want his student to fail. If Angus failed, it was clear Saka was failing as a teacher. But unlike a demon apprentice, Angus couldn't leave Saka because they were bound, warlock and demon, until death.

Saka did not wish Angus dead.

He dug his nails into his chest. That was the problem. He couldn't imagine a life without Angus. Like the larvae of the pela, Angus had burrowed his way in and made himself at home, and Saka didn't want to cut him out. It would destroy him.

How was he supposed to not let it be a weakness? It already was. His jealousy had caused Guda's death. He was to blame, not Angus.

He hissed as he healed the cut. The heat in his skin was almost as bad as when he'd made the cut, but he left the scar. He wasn't ready to erase everything. Not yet. Then he washed in silence, daring a riverwyrm to come and take him. Behind him there was enough noise from the tribe to scare away any predator. Hopefully Angus would be asleep when he went back to their tent.

He dried and rewrapped the towel around himself. As he turned, a light flickered in the corner of his eye. He didn't need to study the light to know what it was. He was very familiar with that color and feeling. But he was here and Angus was there.

Saka turned to stare at his tent. There was only one... no, there were two rational explanations, though he doubted Angus had taken a demon as a lover or one of the human women in the time

Saka was out of the tent. Even the thought was enough to twist his gut. He'd rather have Usi dig her knife in and reopen the scar on his chest. But if Angus had no lover, that meant he was experimenting by himself.

Because Saka had walked out instead of accepting the tenderness Angus had shown him while he healed the cuts. He was no great teacher... or friend or lover.

Slowly he made his way to his tent. The vegetation was cool beneath his feet. Soon the plants would dry and return to the sand. Someone left his tent and walked straight toward him. Angus stopped a few paces away and jerked his chin as a greeting, as though he had nothing to say.

Saka deserved nothing but the coolest brush-off, but he had to say something. "You rebalanced."

"I did."

Saka didn't know what else to say, and he wasn't ready to talk about what had happened on Lifeblood or after the training. Angus didn't elaborate, so Saka stepped to the side and let Angus go past, but he turned to watch him go. For a moment he wanted to go with him to make sure he was going to be all right by the river. But he didn't. Angus had been there long enough to know what to do, and he hadn't asked for Saka's company. Or maybe he didn't want to be shoved aside.

In the tent Saka lay down, but he didn't fall sleep, even when Angus returned and lay next to him without touching him. The distance was so great Angus might as well have been across the void. Saka wanted to feel Angus's touch. He needed the kindness after tonight, but he couldn't make himself reach out, no matter how much he craved comfort.

When he did fall asleep, his body betrayed him.

Saka woke curled against Angus, his arm draped over him and their legs tangled. There wasn't even a sheet between their skins. Once he wouldn't have cared. He would have enjoyed the moment for what it was. But he couldn't fall in love and certainly not with a human, with a warlock.

94

Was he no longer fit to be a mage?

Saka eased his legs free. He should get up, get ready for the day, get away. Angus stirred and clasped Saka's hand to his stomach. Saka felt the smooth line of scar tissue beneath his fingertips. He froze.

"You don't have to pull away." Angus's voice was soft and muffled with sleep.

Saka closed his eyes. He didn't want to. He needed to. Angus rolled over and pulled Saka close so his head rested on Angus's chest. Saka didn't even resist.

He didn't need to worry about falling in love. He was sliding into it heedless to the danger and despite the warnings. Whatever happened to him was entirely his own fault.

No one could know. Miniti would demote him. Usi would take over, and he couldn't bear that. He'd have to change tribes, but he'd be stuck until the next gathering.

"Whatever it is, you don't have to tell me. Just don't be a dick." Angus's fingers smoothed over his skull and up one horn. His heartbeat was a drum in Saka's ear—constant, reassuring. As long as there was music, there was life.

Don't be a dick. He knew that was something akin to "Don't shut yourself off" or "Don't push me away." But if he let Angus in, everything would crumble. If Angus died, there would be nothing left inside Saka.

Watching Angus fight for life had tied him in knots. He couldn't do it again. But he didn't want Angus to sleep on the other side of the tent, and he couldn't teach him if they were barely talking.

Saka couldn't talk about the failed rescue—which was his fault. He had let jealousy blind him. He should've been there—but he could talk about Guda, Her death was no secret, but the way it happened was a secret. He needed to be able to share his grief. Angus had known Guda. He knew what she'd meant to him. He'd understand. But the words remained trapped in Saka's throat. They closed it up and made it hard to breathe.

Beyond the tent, people were waking up and making breakfast. They needed to pack the tents and eat. He needed to get ready to face the tribe as though nothing were wrong. But he couldn't move.

Angus kissed the top of his head, seemingly preparing to let him go.

Saka wasn't ready. He forced the words out. "Guda is dead. She gave her soul on Lifeblood Mountain."

"Dead?"

Saka nodded.

Without her, the whole human-trainee experiment would never have gotten a chance. They'd be at war with the humans, and many more demons would be dead or dying. Her death was so much more than the loss of his mentor.

"I'm sorry. I shouldn't have been angry at you." Angus's lips brushed over his skin.

"You didn't know."

Angus tightened his embrace. "I should've realized you were upset. Usi knew?"

"She was there."

Angus cupped Saka's jaw as though to force him to look up, but he didn't apply any pressure. His fingers rested along Saka's skin. "Why did you do that lesson last night?"

"Because I wanted to block it out. Because it needed to be done. Because I wanted you to hurt." Which was very petty of him.

Angus didn't speak, but he didn't push Saka away either.

"You did well." As always when it came to magic, Angus did well. He did what had to be done.

"That's not a compliment," Angus said.

"It is. And it will happen again." Saka glanced up.

Angus squirmed beneath him. He seemed to want to get free. "There are other—"

Saka kissed him. He didn't want to hear Angus's objections. He knew Angus didn't like it. He'd be worried if he did.

They both liked the same kind of magic. They were well matched. As the warlocks said, the kind of demon they got said a lot about the warlock.

What did it say about the demon, especially when a mage could turn away the seeking connection? He'd actively sought it that day.

"We need to get up," Angus said against his lips.

"I know." He didn't want to. He liked the steadiness of life at the foot of the mountain, instead of the endless routine of walking and setting up. He didn't want to see Usi and her knowing gaze.

He needed to take his place at the front and be head mage, even though he didn't feel as though he could. He moved and covered Angus's body with his. He threaded his fingers into the soft, red-gold strands of Angus's hair. He didn't want to leave his bed.

Angus gazed up at him, his blue eyes wide and all traces of sleep gone. "We can rebalance tonight."

"I don't want to rebalance." *I want you.* While he'd promised himself it would only be the once, it was too easy to let himself be consumed by need instead of holding back and doing what was right. There would be other times, and they had days until the void would be opened. "I think you did a good job on your own last night. Maybe I should have stayed to watch."

"I think you would've given in." The wariness was gone, replaced with challenge.

Saka had heard other mages talk about their apprentices and how there would be a moment when they stopped blindly obeying and started to question. He hadn't expected it to happen so quickly.

He gave Angus a small smile. "I don't think so."

Was Angus ready to be the one in control? He had started to push the boundaries. Saka drew in a breath as he imagined being at Angus's mercy, imagined Angus keeping that delicate balance to make sure neither of them tumbled over until just the right moment. Saka hadn't been in that position since he finished his training. He'd always been allowed to lead.

His body liked the idea of relinquishing control.

"Tonight, then," Angus said. He moved his hands over Saka's hips.

97

Saka kissed him. "Yes, tonight for rebalancing." He moved his hips and enjoyed the length of Angus's erection against him. He should move away and let Angus remain unsatisfied. It would be better that night. All day to think about the ways Angus could torment him. "This morning is for us."

Angus gave a small nod. Their lips met, and lust tumbled through Saka. He didn't bother to try to control it. Didn't want to. He could take a lover—someone he could be with separate from all magic—but he didn't want one. He didn't have time for one. And Angus was there and willing.

Angus slid his leg over Saka's and hooked it over his hip. "They will be waiting to pull down your tent, and I don't want to get caught like this."

"Our tent," he corrected. But Angus was right. They didn't have time to luxuriate in every sensation.

Saka rolled his hips and pressed closer. They moved together. It was almost enough. He wanted to find the oil and thrust deeply into Angus's ass, but the oil was packed because he hadn't planned on having sex. For a couple of heartbeats he thought about forgoing the oil, but then Angus slid his hand between their bodies.

Angus wrapped his hand around both their cocks, and groaned. Saka smothered the sound with a kiss. He put aside all other thoughts and worries, and for that morning, they were simply two men in desperate need of each other. Angus raked his teeth over Saka's lip. Saka shifted position, so he could watch as Angus stroked both lengths—dark red and pale together.

"Both hands," Saka ground out.

Angus obeyed. Come beaded on the heads, and Angus slicked the fluid down the shafts. Hot need gripped his balls. He thrust into Angus's hands, messing up Angus's rhythm.

He would enjoy watching Angus tonight. Then, when Angus thought he was done, Saka would make him realize that he wasn't. He wanted to watch as Angus tormented himself. The stroke of his hand…. But Angus was right. He would give in and want to touch him. Even then he needed more. He slid his tail around Angus's hand and teased the slit of Angus's ruddy head.

Angus drew in a shaky breath, and his chest lifted, but he kept control. Saka let him claim the victory, and succumbed first, giving in to the release he craved. His body jerked, and the heat rolled down his spine as he came on Angus's hands and cock. He gave a couple more thrusts as lust continued to ripple through his body and the last of his pleasure splashed onto Angus's skin. Angus's back arched, and his eyes closed.

Stop him now and make him wait.

But he didn't. He watched as Angus stroked and the head of his cock darkened. His breath caught the moment before he came, and the thick white fluid mixed with his own on Angus's belly and chest. Saka leaned down for a taste of the salty-sweet mess.

Angus cracked open his eyes. "There's nothing wrong with a morning quickie."

"Quickie?"

"As in just get on with it." A smile curved his lips. "For someone who's all about sex magic, you seem to have forgotten what it's like to do it for fun."

Maybe he had. His last lover hadn't even been part of the tribe. He'd been a trader, moving from place to place. They'd gotten together a few times a year until he vanished. Either Kitu had died in the desert or been taken by warlocks. For most of Saka's life, sex had been about magic.

Angus placed his hand on Saka's cheek. "It's okay to have fun."

It was almost a question, as though Angus weren't sure if it *was* okay.

Saka kissed him, and Angus slid his tongue over his as though seeking out the taste of their pleasure. "Yes. It is okay to have fun."

In those few words he gave himself permission to enjoy what he had. Magic couldn't consume his life or he would forget what he was fighting for.

It wasn't the fact that Angus had lain with Terrance that stung him. It was that Angus liked the human man the way Saka wanted to be liked by Angus. Angus had once questioned what Saka and he had, and Saka had said all the right things—that they were mage and apprentice, warlock and demon. They had something that was unbreakable. But it was more than that. He'd been lying to himself even then.

They were friends.

They were lovers, and he was in love.

CHAPTER 14

THE DAYS were full and tiring. They packed, walked, and set up in the evening. But even when the sun set, Saka kept him up and trained him until late every evening. Angus began to feel that he could walk and sleep at the same time. He would dream that he was holding the knife in his hand and that he could feel the cool, bone handle against his palm. Then he'd wake, and his hand would be empty. He wished he wasn't so familiar with the knife or that he couldn't tell from the tiniest change in Saka's expression when something mildly hurt and when it really hurt.

At least he was getting better at healing the cuts, even the deeper ones. Afterward, they'd lie together. Some nights neither of them could be bothered with any rebalancing. Instead they simply had fun. Saka was rediscovering fun, and Angus liked to see that other side of his demon—the part the rest of them never saw.

To the tribe, Saka was the head mage and healer. While someone else made them dinner each evening, Angus would help Saka as he dealt with the day's ailments. The walking caused blisters or strains. There were burns from cooking and one bite from a pack animal. People came to Saka, and gradually Saka let Angus do more than watch. Despite Angus's initial reluctance, the demons didn't seem to mind him testing out his new skill on them.

Norah and Lizzie would sometimes watch. While he spoke to them during the walks, they didn't talk about anything much. They needed to work out what they were going to tell the underground. Soon the void would be torn open, and they'd go back for a few days. Angus didn't know if he was excited or if he dreaded it—or a combination of both.

Angus ate something that was wrapped in leaves and eaten like a sandwich. He was glad to sit by himself for a little while and do nothing. In a few moments, he'd have to get ready for whatever lesson Saka had in mind. He stretched out his legs. His calves no longer ached at the end of every day, but sitting down was still most welcome. The soles of his feet were hard, and his toenails chipped. He needed a bath.

Before him the stars glimmered on the river and made it shine like ink dotted with diamonds. He'd love to strip off and swim, but he didn't dare. So he washed with a small scoop of water and still felt gritty—the same as every other night. With luck Miniti would've decided on a site by the time he came back from Vinland, so there'd be no more packing and walking. There'd be real showers.

He took a drink, but the thirst was deeper than he could quench. He'd woken up thirsty, but it wasn't heatstroke. He wasn't even sunburned. His hands were golden, and there were clear tan lines where his shirt protected him and where skin was exposed. He had no idea what his face looked like—probably like his hands, but with even more freckles. That didn't fill him with joy, but not all the changes were bad. He was fitter and stronger.

From where he was sitting, he could see across the desert until it disappeared into the night. They'd already gone beyond signs of civilization. All the tribes had headed in different directions. Years ago some tribes had decided not to return to Lifeblood each year and had set off for the ocean. Where exactly was that?

Where were the feathered demons that he'd seen on the news from beyond Vinland?

Footsteps reverberated through the earth as someone walked toward him. He was used to tapping into Demonside now. Saka had made him reach out until he could feel the footsteps of every tribe member, the eels in the river, and the herds of animals as they were stalked by scarlips. The first time he tried, he became so dizzy he stumbled and fell.

Saka sat next to him. He offered Angus a small piece of some delicacy, and Angus accepted and ate without even asking what it was made of. He'd stopped being cautious about the food long before... yet it really wasn't that long. The college year hadn't ended yet. It had barely been six months since he'd first arrived in Demonside.

"I told Usi not to come to our tent tonight."

Angus sighed, and tension slid from his body. He hadn't realized how much he'd been dreading another night of knives and blood.

"Good." He didn't want to do any more of that, but he could see how it was possible to use someone's pain to heal them. That was useful. He gave his arm a scratch and then had another drink and finished the water he'd brought with him. "I'm thirsty all the time, but I think it's more than that."

Saka was silent for a moment. "It is the beginning of Demonside sucking the life out of you. I saw it in your eyes today. That's why Usi isn't coming. You're putting too much of yourself into what you do, instead of using what is around."

"Too much rebalancing." His lips twisted into a smile. There'd been less of that and more being together because it was fun.

"Maybe. It is something we will have to be aware of. Something you need to work on so you do not exhaust yourself."

"Yeah. Use the magic around me, not what's in me. But it would leach out anyway. It's what Demonside does." He swallowed, and his throat felt dry. What if the underground didn't open the void? What if something happened and the college wiped out the underground? He exhaled and released those fears. There was no point in dwelling on them, even though he was tempted to start the useless circle of what-ifs.

Saka nodded. "So why are you here alone, temping the predators who are brave enough to get close to camp?"

"None are close."

"You cannot reach out far enough. There is a pack of scarlips following a herd of parrils." Saka pointed to the left.

Parrils—they were the spotted things that looked like a cross between a guinea pig and an elephant but with a hide as thick as his thumb. They grew to just above knee height and were quite tasty, kind of like duck.

"Then they won't be after me." Angus stretched out his legs and leaned back. The sky was a deep purple, dotted with stars. So many stars. Some people back home believed that there were aliens on other planets. Were there aliens on other planets in Demonside too? "Have you ever seen a feathered demon?"

Not even the birdlike creatures he'd seen had feathers. They had wings of skin for gliding or were more like giant insects. They weren't birds at all, but they seemed to have the same role as birds would have.

"No. Have you?"

He should've talked to Saka about it days before, but between walking and cutting, he'd kind of forgotten. He'd forgotten about Terrance too, which made him feel like shit. Demonside was all-consuming, and it had started to consume him. His heart beat a little faster. The void would open, and he'd go home to recharge. He would be fine.

"Terrance showed me how to…." How did he explain computers and hacking into news from other countries? "How to access news from other places around the world."

He'd never realized how restrictive the media was and how much the college controlled. But then why would he know unless he'd been shown there was more?

Angus drew the continents in the sand between him and Saka. He dug his finger into the place where New London was. "This is where I live, in Vinland." He pointed to the southern continent. "Here is where the Mayan Empire is." He didn't bother pointing out the smaller nations.

He pointed to a few more countries and indicated the ones that banned all magic and killed wizards and warlocks by dragging them through the streets so everyone could see what evil looked like and then burning them. Angus didn't feel evil, but he could understand how one run-in with a bad warlock could make people think they were all up to no good. And then there were the people who hated that someone else had magic when they didn't.

"So people pray for magic to happen in that place, but they will not actually allow the use of magic?"

"They have this religion that says demons are bad." But that wasn't the point of the conversation. "In the Mayan Empire, they work with demons. They offer sacrifices and were one of the nations who started up the World Council of Demonology. They're worried about the changes on both sides of the void. There was a feathered demon in the news. Where are those demons? The ones who work with the Mayans?" If anyone would help break Vinland free of the college it would be the Mayans.

Saka was silent for what felt like an eon. Stars died before he finally spoke. "I don't know." Saka always knew everything. "Why do you want to find them?"

"I think it would be wise to have an ally beyond the underground." He wanted to know about the world beyond Vinland and to learn what other countries knew about demonology.

Saka brushed Angus's back with his tail. "You worry about Terrance."

"I worry about me. About us. About here. About there and yes, about him. I think it would be a good idea to find the feathered demons. I don't know if the Warlock College can be stopped from the inside the way the underground thinks it can. There are too many warlocks in what was once a place for wizards to train."

"Or you are seeing shadows where none exist."

Lizzie felt the same way, or she'd been lying so she could report on him. There was no way to know until he went back—until he got in trouble, and Terrance paid the price.

"Are you not curious? How far does Demonside stretch? Does it match the continents? Where are we?"

Saka looked at the map Angus had drawn. "How long would it take you to walk across here?" He pointed from New London across to the west coast of the Nations.

Between the Nations and Vinland was a no-go area. No one traveled between the two countries. Not that the Nations was a country, not exactly. It was many nations that operated under one political body. At school he'd been told that they hated Vinland and sought to make war at every opportunity. And he'd been told the Mayans were brutal. But he was beginning to think his entire schooling was little more than propaganda.

"I have no idea. Months."

Saka scowled. "I will have to talk to Miniti. Study her maps. It won't happen while we are traveling."

"But you think it's a good idea?"

"I did not say that. I said I would investigate."

And he'd do the same when he was home. He'd get better maps and pictures, and he'd bring them back.

Saka lay back on the sand. "Perhaps tonight we do nothing. I don't want to see more color bleed from your eyes."

Angus stared at his demon. "What?"

"That's how I could tell that Demonside had started to drain you."

That was why Lizzie and Norah had been looking at him like he was some kind of freak. It wasn't about his magic at all. He was going to have to bring a mirror to Demonside to monitor the change in his eyes. Although Miniti seemed like the kind of demon who might have one—not that he was going to ask.

WHEN THE void opened for the trainees to go home, no one was ready. They'd barely stopped walking, and the underground was a day early. Even the demon who had the connection to the underground was surprised.

Angus carried his winter clothes in his arms, and his face echoed the shock on Norah's and Lizzie's faces. He wasn't ready to go—even though he needed to. The thirst hadn't gone away, and he'd stopped doing all magic, and having sex of any kind. Which wasn't any fun.

He wasn't sure Saka was ready for him to leave either. They hadn't spoken about Guda again, but when Saka was out of sight of the rest of the tribe, he appeared to be made of glass. Guda's death had taken something from him that couldn't be replaced. Angus hoped the internal wound would start to heal while he was away.

He didn't know what Guda's death would mean when he got home. She'd been Ellis's demon, but also a voice of reason. Angus was pretty sure that, without Guda, he'd have been sacrificed on Lifeblood Mountain. But her death didn't hurt him the way it did Saka. Instead it filled him with dread.

He clasped Saka's hands. "It's not that long."

"I know, but you need to go." Saka's face was unreadable. He was very good at looking as though nothing were the matter. "Be careful."

Angus nodded. One wrong misstep and Terrance would pay. It was too easy to forget about Vinland when he was in Demonside. There were other things to worry about, more immediate problems, like learning how to feel the magic in the ground to find the herds so the hunters would know where to go, or squeezing one more drop of rain from the sky. Would they still be able to do that when he came back? How fast would the rivers sink? He glanced around at the blue-tinged leaves and shrubs. Demonside had never looked so alive. And Saka's eyes had never looked so dead.

His own eyes were pale. He'd studied his face in a bowl of still water. It was clear enough for him to see the changes—the sharp edge to his cheekbones and the darker freckles. He hoped that the blue would return to his eyes. Or would they forever be like blue-tinged snow?

On a whim he embraced Saka, even though they didn't usually touch so intimately in public. Angus wasn't sure why they made that distinction because he was sure everyone knew exactly what was going on behind the thin cloth walls of the tent. "Don't let Usi cut you up while I'm not here."

"I will do what needs to be done."

Angus shook his head. "What's wrong with working with Lizzie's mage? He'd be happy to help you out."

Lizzie's mage had let it be known he liked sex magic.

Saka drew back. He didn't say anything, but he didn't have to.

"It's okay. I'm okay. I get it." And he knew that even if Saka did work with the other mage, they wouldn't have what he and Saka had. At one time, even the idea would've worried him.

He wanted to say more, but he didn't want anyone from the underground to see him kiss Saka. It was enough that the warlock standing near the tear had seen them hug. They would assume. He would deny.

No one needed to know. He would tell them that he'd learned blood magic. They'd approve of him cutting his demon. The lies were already starting to form, and he hadn't even crossed the void.

Angus had two separate lives. Neither would approve of the other. Demons didn't like lying. It was one of the worst things a demon could do. Yet he was becoming an expert.

It was for the best, for both worlds—for Saka and Terrance and everyone he cared about. He pulled his cold-weather clothes over the top of his lightweight demon attire and immediately started to sweat.

With a final glance, he stepped across the void.

The cold was a slap in the face and a pinch to the lungs after the heat of Demonside.

Lizzie hissed and stamped her feet. Norah swore.

One underground warlock stood in front of them. They were in a snow-covered backyard. Angus had no idea where they were—not the main building, the old school. Was that how it was going to be? Always moving and no place to truly call home?

The soft crunch of snow behind him was the only warning he got. He half turned, but before he could do more, he was pushed to his knees and a spell dug into his brain. It clawed through memories that he couldn't hide fast enough. It was not the first time a warlock had torn through his mind. Last time the college had tried to erase his memories of Demonside. They'd failed, but only because Miniti had anchored them.

Angus didn't want to lose anything he'd learned or seen. The first time he'd been in Demonside, Saka had carved a mark into his skin. Now it heated as Angus anchored everything he knew. He couldn't stop the warlock from looking but he could stop him from taking.

He was released, and he tipped forward. The snow bit into his hands and was already wetting the knees of his pants. He drew in several breaths before he even looked up. It wasn't just him. The underground had invaded the minds of Norah and Lizzie too. But the warlock hadn't tried to take his memories.

"Skitun," the warlock behind him spat. He had seen exactly what kind of magic Angus had learned in Demonside.

Angus looked up at the warlock in front of him, and the warlock's lip curled in disgust. "Maybe you shouldn't go poking around in people's heads if you don't want to see certain things."

"She's clean," another voice said.

"This one too."

Whereas he wasn't. He was unclean—a demon fucker. That was not acceptable in any of the books he'd read. Sex magic with a human was one thing. Screwing a demon was another. "Magic has to be rebalanced. What is taken here must be returned, or we will freeze in an ice age of our own selfishness."

Angus sensed the kick behind him before it could connect. He rolled to the side and stood in one smooth motion.

"We sent volunteers and criminals for rebalancing. Your demon has tricked you," the warlock in front said, so brave behind his mask.

"Blood, soul, and sex. Three ways to rebalance. But I'm sure a warlock of your standing knows that." They just didn't like anyone to practice it. He tilted his head as though in respect. Lizzie made eye contact. She'd want to talk to him later. He didn't know if he could be bothered.

"We had to search your minds to see if you were part of the attack. Was Angus involved?" the warlock demanded.

"What attack?" Angus glanced at Norah and Lizzie. They looked as puzzled as he felt.

"It's none of your concern. You'll stay here, under guard for your own protection." The warlock acted as though he believed that was true. Angus thought it was so a closer eye could be kept on them.

Angus put his cold hands in the pockets of his coat. He was still cold. He needed a hat and a scarf. "What progress has been made? It doesn't look like the early winter was halted." If anything, it had settled in. It wasn't a dusting of snow on the ground. It was a couple of inches.

"These things take time. We can't rush and kill every warlock loyal to the college. Some know no better and don't question what they're taught," the warlock said, defending the college.

"Doing nothing lets those in power gather more magic and do more damage," Lizzie said as she picked herself up from the snow. "We need more trained wizards. We need to show them that demon-free magic can be powerful." It was almost a convincing argument.

Angus nodded. "And what of the Institute of Magical Studies? Surely you can look to other countries to back up that claim? Not all magic users have demons. We have become too dependent on demons for magic, instead of using what we have." Textbooks from a hundred years ago had talked about the increasing laziness of magic users. That was true. Being a wizard required more effort, but it was also less dangerous.

The warlock took half a step back. "It's not your concern."

"Then what is?" Norah ventured.

"To learn demon magic from the demons. So we can prove that we can work together without the bond," the man said, as though they should be grateful.

Or was it to learn the demon's secrets? Angus couldn't be sure. Where were the wizards in power? Had they all been removed and replaced by warlocks? He didn't ask. He wouldn't get a word of truth from this man. How nice it would be to look in his head and rifle through his memories to get to the truth.

A headache bloomed at the base of Angus's skull, but the thirst that had plagued him for the last two days was gone. His tongue didn't feel like it was swollen and coated in grit, but he was still tired.

He planned to do very little walking—or anything—for a few days. But he did need to study. He wanted to get the old books, the ones that talked of giving demons a gift like a rabbit or goat after using their magic. He wanted to read about the Mayan Empire.

He wanted to see Terrance.

"Your personal effects are inside. I'll talk to each one of you later. Eat and rest. I'm sure you need it." The warlock in charge dropped his gaze to Angus, and he could almost hear the man say "Skitun."

CHAPTER 15

THE FARTHER the tribe walked from Lifeblood, the smaller the river became. It was still too big to step across—big enough that Saka didn't worry that it would dry up or sink overnight, but not big enough that he thought it would last until the next gathering, the way the rivers had when Guda was young.

She'd never tell him anything again.

He was still angry about her death. But the anger was at himself for not doing what was right. With Angus at home, and no doubt with Terrance, jealousy poisoned Saka's sleep and gnawed at his days. It wasn't pleasant.

Part of him hoped Angus would summon him just so he could see him. He wanted to know what was happening across the void. Was the college close to being defeated? What was the underground planning? Without Guda, he had lost the source of his knowledge.

He dropped back to fall in step with Miniti. He would wait for her to speak before he raised the question that Angus had driven into him like a thorn. Where were the other demons?

Miniti had local maps, and he had them memorized. Part of his job was to know where they were and where the wells were. But did she have others? Ones that covered more distance? He had no idea what the tribal leaders discussed at their meeting, and he wouldn't until she decided to share... if she ever did. There were probably things she couldn't reveal.

"How goes it with the humans?"

"They are learning." He'd spoken to Tapo and Wek, the two mages who had joined his tribe with Lizzie and Norah. Usi had been left out of that meeting because she wasn't teaching a human. But she had not been impressed. He'd hoped the humans assigned to Lox and Becha would come with him, but sometimes it was better to have friends elsewhere.

"Good. They are not demons. Angus isn't a demon." Miniti glanced at him as though she expected him to disagree.

"I know. But we fight for two worlds."

"Do *they*?"

Angus did. "Yes."

"And now you have a few days with no humans. Your skin will be glad for the rest." She glanced at him, and he inclined his head. She knew that he'd been teaching Angus blood magic. "Will the others get so advanced?"

"Not unless they prove themselves. They will learn basics." He wasn't going to explain to Miniti, and she wouldn't expect him to. The humans would learn how to draw magic from their surroundings and how to heal, how to hunt and how to find water. "It is more important that they learn about us and see us as equals and not things to be used."

"Or they learn ways to destroy us."

"And we learn about them as they learn about us." It was time to raise Angus's revelation. "Their world is more complex than we suspected. Different countries... giant tribes... treat the use of magic very differently. Some countries ban it and kill users. Some ban the use of demon magic and only use what they call natural magic."

"So we are unnatural?"

"We are not of their world, so perhaps that is true in a sense." He paused to see if she had anything else to say, but she only nodded for him to continue. They had been working together for long enough that she would know there was a point to the information. "But there are countries who also support demon magic and who practice the old ways."

"The old ways?"

"When Guda was an apprentice, humans would give demons a creature from their side of the void in thanks, to rebalance after a magical working. Some countries still do that. They honor their connection with demons." He didn't know much more than that. "They are called the Mayan Empire, and their country borders Angus's. But they aren't friendly. There was a war." Vinland seemed to not get on with anyone, from what Angus had said. That was no way to exist.

"And what does this have to do with our current situation? The humans there must be in winter too?"

"Yes. If their whole world is affected by the cold and ice, all of Demonside must also be affected." He looked at Miniti. "It would be useful to talk to the tribes who work with these other countries."

"Why?"

"To see how their area of Demonside is faring. To learn about the humans they work with."

"How does that learning help us now, when we must deal with the humans we work with? We clearly cannot change which *country* we work with. That must be set somehow."

He thought of the map Angus scratched in the sand… and the way the moonlight had illuminated his skin and the paleness of his eyes. He needed to protect Angus better, teach him how to avoid rebalancing when he wasn't willing. That was something he had never wanted to teach, especially not when Demonside needed as much magic returned as possible. But he knew it would take more than one warlock.

"I don't know." He knew it was the wrong thing to say as soon as the words left his mouth. "Finding other demons might answer those questions."

She shook her head, and her white skin glittered in the sunlight. Her mouth was too wide for her face, and her dark gaze turned on him. She wouldn't eat his soul, but she was clearly unhappy.

"We have enough problems without uncovering more. What? Would you propose that we walk until we run into strange demons? Who is to say they even have the answers. We must concentrate on doing what we can. Destroy those who would destroy us."

How could she be so blind? "Those strange demons could bring their humans into the fight. We wouldn't be so dependent on the goodwill of the underground."

He was very close to arguing with her, but she hadn't given him a direct order yet.

She stopped and faced him. "If their world is in trouble, why are they not already in the fight? You will not chase this idea. Find a better way to help us." She started walking again. "I want to see Angus when he returns. Alone."

Saka kept pace with her, unwilling to let Usi or the other mages think there was a problem. "Very well."

Teaching Angus to not give up the magic within him wouldn't help Demonside in the short term, nor would ignoring his knowledge. It opened doors and Saka thought they needed to tear down the whole tent, one panel at a time, until the structure was revealed. Only then would they be able to fight back and heal both worlds.

"How many days are we from the blue pool?"

Saka slid his mind to the river and away. The last time he'd seen the blue pool, it had been a muddy puddle surrounded by brilliant blue rocks. Metal workers liked the site because it was rich in ore. There was also enough space to plant and grow crops. He sensed it, cold and clear. And brimming. He blinked and realized Miniti had her hand on his arm to stop him from wandering in the wrong direction. It was easy to accidentally walk into the river when following it. "About four long days."

"And how long until the humans come back?"

"Five." Five in Vinland and ten in Demonside.

He hoped Angus's eyes were as blue as the lake when he returned, that it was easy for a human to reabsorb what Demonside had taken, but he had no idea.

He had no idea how he was going to find the other tribes either. But he would.

115

CHAPTER 16

THE DEBRIEF in the snow-covered yard was mostly Angus half lying about what he had learned. Yes, he had sex with his demon. Yes, he was learning sex magic. The warlock who'd ripped into his mind, without any lube or permission, had passed on everything he'd seen to the man in charge. A headache still pulsed at the base of Angus's skull. He wanted to learn how to block such magic and turn it on the user, but he bit back on the anger and the blatant lack of trust. He needed the underground or he had no way to get out of Demonside.

Without the underground's protection he was a wanted criminal in Vinland.

It was only after the debrief that Angus was allowed to go inside. Norah and Lizzie were kept away from him until they were spoken to. When he walked into the house, a light pressure formed on his skin. He hesitated in the doorway.

"Is there a problem?" the warlock who'd called him a skitun asked.

"Yeah. I didn't ask where my room was or where the bathroom was. I'm dying for a shower." He smiled as though he hadn't noticed there were magic dampeners in the house. It was clear the underground didn't want them using magic or summoning demons. Were they the underground anymore or just an offshoot of the college?

He didn't know, but concern had blossomed into full-grown distrust and suspicion. The original aim of the underground had been to promote learning among wizards and to push back against college propaganda. Now it wanted to take control from the college, and while Angus had no problem with the fall of the college, he cared about what replaced it. There would be a power vacuum to fill, and it didn't appear that trained wizards would take over. It would be more college-trained warlocks.

"Turn right at the kitchen. Both are down the hallway." The man studied him as though he were trying to work out which part of Angus was defective.

Angus turned away. He would not be made to feel shame or embarrassment. But it was there just beneath his skin, threatening to rise and stain his cheeks red. Soon they would all know, and they would all look at him with barely hidden revulsion.

It's not wrong.

It didn't feel wrong, but maybe it was….

And yet it must have been practiced at some point. Or had it always been forbidden? Was it forbidden everywhere? He had no idea and no one to ask.

He made a mental list of things he wanted to do. At the top was a shower—a long one so he could get the sand out of his hair and have a shave. When he was in Demonside, the beard didn't matter, but in Vinland, it itched, and he wanted the scruff gone.

He collected clothes and toiletries from the wardrobe in the room that was clearly his—the things Terrance had liberated from the college were on the desk—and went to the bathroom. Two steps in, and he stopped and stared. The man in the mirror wasn't the way he remembered himself. The bowl of water in Demonside had not revealed the full extent of the changes.

His hair had taken on a life of its own. No longer neat and styled, it was long and messy. His skin was no longer pale, and his freckles had darkened accordingly—there was no escaping them apparently. One step closer. His cheekbones were more pronounced. There was an edge to his face, as though it had been carved and not sanded down to give curves.

But it was his eyes that were the worst.

Another step closer.

His eyes were still blue—barely. Coupled with the half-grown and unimpressive beard and his hair, they made him look more than a little unhinged. He wasn't sure he'd trust a man who looked the way he did right then. It would take more than a shower to even come close to respectable.

As much as he loved the shower—there was no time limit, unlike in Demonside—he eventually dragged himself out of the warm water. He shaved and was glad there wasn't a tan line on his face. If he'd stayed longer, no doubt there would be. His body was pale, but his hands, face, and lower legs were tanned. It wasn't a great look. Dressed in clean human clothing and with his hair washed and brushed, he looked better.

But he didn't feel it. The magic dampeners pressed on him as though trying to smother him. They were common in public places, for security reasons, but he'd never been able to feel them before. Suddenly he could, and he didn't like it. How long until it became unbearable?

Maybe there were weak spots in the house, places he could claim as his own without explaining why. So he wandered through and noted how many bedrooms there were. Only three. It looked as though the underground planned to keep the groups of trainees separate so they couldn't compare notes. Some of the rooms had closed and locked doors. Lodgings for the people who would stay to supervise them? Angus didn't think for a moment that they'd be left alone.

In the kitchen he helped himself to bread and made a sandwich full of meat and cheese and relish. Still hungry, he made another and ate it over the chopping board. There was no point in using a plate when he ate them so quickly. He looked in the fridge again and helped himself to milk. At least he remembered to get a glass just before he took a drink from the carton. Was he expected to cook, or would meals be provided? Were Lizzie, Norah, and he under house arrest or being protected from those in the college who'd like to make sure no one went to Demonside to learn?

Lizzie wandered in and made herself a cup of tea. She took the carton of milk from him without a word.

Next time they would need to make sure they spoke before they returned. Assuming they were allowed to go again. Nothing was certain, and Angus didn't like that at all. He suspected the underground wanted them off-balance, which made him like it even less. He needed a new plan, one where he wasn't dependent on the increasingly unreliable underground.

He couldn't linger in Demonside—that was painfully clear— but he couldn't stay in Vinland either. Certainly not New London. Too many people would have seen his image, and reward money would sweeten the deal and make them ask fewer questions about what he'd done. His father's threats and promises were still causing him problems. For a horrid moment, he thought he'd never be free. His whole life would be running and hiding.

Too many people bought into the lies that wizards and rogues had caused the cooling climate. Not enough people were able to access news from around the world before it was heavily filtered. He'd read pamphlets put out by the underground when he was with Jim. Did they still do that?

Lizzie watched him from beneath her lashes, though she was clearly trying to be very busy stirring her tea.

He couldn't take it any longer. "Just ask."

He ate the last piece of bread crust. He'd missed fluffy white bread. And butter. And milk.

She put the spoon down and let a few more awkward seconds slip past. "So it is true? I mean, I thought something was going on... especially as that other demon with the green skin...." Lizzie took a sip of tea and gave him a pointed look.

"Usi." That other demon had a name, and he would make her ask.

"Yeah, her, was always going into the tent."

"That was for something different." He wouldn't share that either. It had been hard enough trying to explain that to learn blood magic there had to be a volunteer willing to bleed during the debriefing. The warlock asking the questions didn't seem to believe that mages would put themselves in that position. It didn't surprise Angus at all. Warlocks didn't teach the way mages did, and they didn't encourage curiosity. At least the man asking the questions hadn't asked for details about the sex magic, which was a small relief.

119

Angus glanced up at the dampener. Was it also a camera or a microphone? Until he discovered otherwise, he would be careful. Somehow he'd advise Norah and Lizzie to watch what they said and did. They were stuck there together, so they had to be on the same side.

"Usi has nothing to do with that. Saka...." He shrugged. "It's what Saka is good at—raising power with lust—so it's what he started to show me."

"And you like it?"

Lie or truth? When they got back to Demonside, he wouldn't be able to hide it. Besides, Lizzie might be the only human he could trust... sort of trust. "Yeah. What's not to like? He's a good lover."

"He's a demon." She sipped her tea and raised one eyebrow.

He crossed his arms. "Truly? I hadn't noticed, though I did wonder about his horns and tail."

She rolled her eyes. "Does it work?"

"What?" He wasn't going to hand over everything he knew. If she wanted details, she would have to dig.

She lowered her voice. "Can you raise power that way?"

"Yes." But he needed to learn to not put himself into it, to raise the power but keep his magic separate. That was going to be difficult when rebalancing the magic was part of the point. Or was that merely a side effect? He didn't know.

And he had no way to learn while he was stuck in this house.

He needed books that were in use before the college became the one and only way for warlocks to train. He needed to see old wizarding texts—or better, books from beyond Vinland. How did other countries work with their demons? His chances of acquiring anything except college-approved texts were extremely small, but that wouldn't stop him from asking. Then he had a better idea. "If we're trapped in this house, we should do something useful."

"Like what? Practice?"

Lizzie hadn't realized there were dampeners, and he didn't want to let it slip that he'd realized. "No, we should ask for old textbooks. I'm sure the underground must have saved some from destruction."

She frowned. "Is magic all you think about?"

It was most of what he thought about because it was tied intimately to his survival in both worlds. Meeting Saka had made his life dangerous and interesting, and it could only go back to how it had been if the warlocks erased all his memories. Losing Demonside would be like carving out a lung and a kidney and half his liver. He could live without them, but life wouldn't be the same, and he'd know something was missing.

"No, I think about Terrance, and I hope he's okay." He drew in a breath and then took the chance. "The underground took him hostage to make sure I behave."

If there was a microphone, he wanted the people listening to know there were some things he wouldn't keep quiet about.

"They wouldn't do that." Lizzie shook her head, and her expression shuttered.

"They did." He lowered his head as though beaten. "They don't trust me." He even managed to sound like he cared that the underground didn't trust him. "But how can I trust them when they'd do that to my boyfriend?"

THE FOLLOWING morning there were some books on the breakfast table. While Angus was sure they'd all been vetted and deemed suitable, he didn't care. They were all from before the Warlock College became so powerful. He ate cereal as he flicked through them. He noted that some pages had been removed.

It didn't matter. Something was better than nothing, and he didn't want to sit around and watch the lies that passed for news. He didn't want to hear about demons breaking through the void and killing when he knew that someone had to have summoned those demons. No one could open the void from Demonside.

Nor did he want the filtered news from the outside. He knew about the proposed trade sanction and the envoys from the World Council of Demonology, but he was sure Vinland's media would spin it as though they wanted to help, not that Vinland was the problem.

He heard the guards talking about magicless countries threatening war. War wouldn't make things better. The college would probably just draw more magic. Countries that didn't use magic didn't seem to understand that the solution was to rebalance. The college needed to release the magic it had stored. It wouldn't help the situation to starve the citizens or wipe out the people who knew where the magic was stored.

There was a knock on the front door, but he didn't bother to get up. One of their friendly guards would get it. The one who looked at him and sneered and muttered, or the one who wouldn't look at him at all? There was a third, a man who spent most of his time outside with a pipe.

Voices drifted from the foyer, and Angus looked up. His heart already beat a little too fast, but his head told his ears they were wrong. It wasn't Terrance's voice at the front door.

It couldn't be. Angus glanced at the books.

Maybe it was, and the people in charge wanted to look like they cared or at least like they weren't complete assholes. Or maybe they just wanted to keep Angus on their side. Give him the books and his boyfriend. What could go wrong?

It proved that someone was listening to everything.

He stood, quietly easing the chair back, and made his way through the dining room. He stopped in the doorway. A smile formed, and he didn't know what to say.

Then Terrance noticed him. Shock flickered over his face, and a smile arranged itself on his lips. Angus rocked back on his heels as though he'd been pushed. Had he changed that much? A full night of sleep had left him rested, if not relaxed. The guard with the sneer grabbed Terrance's arm and murmured something in his ear. Angus didn't need to hear the words to understand what he said.

"I know," Terrance said as he shook off the grip.

A few steps and he stood in front of Angus, who still hadn't managed to move and wasn't sure if he should. He'd never considered how his changed appearance might affect Terrance. Angus hoped his eyes would go back to normal. He still startled himself when he looked in the mirror, so he had to forgive Terrance his shock.

Terrance studied him for a moment longer. To decide if he wanted to stay or leave? "Did you learn heaps?"

"Yeah." What else could he say?

Terrance hugged him. His lips brushed Angus's ear. "I'm wearing a dampener. I can't open the void and escape."

Angus returned the embrace. He didn't need to act as though it was a welcome reunion. It was. He leaned in, smelling the cold on Terrance's skin and the faint musk of deodorant. "How long are you here for?"

"Not long enough. An hour at most."

They drew apart. They needed to talk away from the dampeners and the microphones. "Do you want to go outside? Maybe we can build a snowdemon."

"What?" Terrance and the guard asked simultaneously.

"I've been in the desert. I want to be in the snow. It'll be fun." He gave Terrance a nudge and a look that he hoped Terrance would understand.

"As long as it's with you, I don't care." That sounded almost genuine, but there was something else there.

"You can't go outside," the guard said, suddenly on alert and acting as though Angus had suggested blowing up the house.

"I can't sit out and enjoy the cold after baking my ass off for ten days? Do you know how hot it is over there?" Angus walked toward the back door. He doubted they'd admit to the dampeners, but what other reason could they give for not wanting him to step outside?

"It's too dangerous. What if someone sees you? You're still a wanted criminal." The guard appeared just a little too happy to say that.

Yes, that was a problem, but he was sure the house had been selected because it was in a secure location. He hadn't paid much attention to the neighbors the day before. Getting his memories inspected had scattered his thoughts and given him a headache that lasted most of the night.

"I'll keep my head down and hood up." Angus swiped his jacket off the hook by the back door. He paused for half a second to give the man time to react, but he did nothing except call his superiors.

They had a few minutes at least.

As soon as he stepped out of the house, the pressure on his skin eased. As he got ready for bed the night before, he thought sleep would never come, but he was so tired from the walking and the late nights of learning that sleep dragged him under before he had time to worry about it. He woke up aware of the pressure before he fully realized it was well past dawn.

In the middle of the yard, he rolled up a ball, as though all he wanted in the world was a snowman. The snow wasn't thick enough, and it would be a pathetic snowman, but he didn't care. The man followed them outside but remained on the porch, still on his phone.

"Stay close," Angus murmured. Then he brought up a circle that wouldn't stop a fly from crossing, but it would contain sound. He hoped he'd done it right. It had the right feel, and it was the right color in his mind. "Smile like I'm amazing or something."

"You're amazing and… what happened to your eyes?"

Angus studied the snow as heat colored his cheeks. "Demonside started draining me." One good sleep hadn't been enough to return the color.

"Shit."

"Yeah. I'm fine." He reached out a damp glove to touch Terrance on the shoulder. "And you?"

"I'm training with a team. Aside from the dampener, it's all good." But he didn't sound entirely sure that everything was good, and he glanced back at the house with worry in his eyes.

"No one can hear you. The house is full of dampeners and surveillance. I can only do stuff out here."

Terrance was quiet for a moment. "I want to play, or I thought I did, but it seems so stupid now. I know how bad things are. I've seen what's happening in other countries. I can help the underground, but they won't let me. My only value is to keep you in line." He glanced at Angus. "Not that they've said that. The underground has changed from when I first joined. Maybe I didn't want to see it." He patted the ball he'd been making, and it fell apart.

Angus put his hand over Terrance's. The guard was still watching them, so they had to act as though they were just rekindling. That would actually be nice, but he didn't want to do that under the watchful gaze of a man who hated him. "Too many warlocks?"

"We're both warlocks." Terrance smiled the way he remembered from when they first got together in a heady rush of lust. For a moment Angus was weightless. Terrance had the power to make him feel as though he were the sun and bursting with life. He was dazzled and willing to slip into the fantasy that someone could like him for being who he was and nothing more. Then the smile dimmed. "But yeah, too many senior warlocks. The guy in charge goes by the name Risely. I doubt it's his real name." He sighed. "It gets worse. While you were gone, new security measures were put in place. No one can see external news."

"What?" He hadn't heard that, but he hadn't tried to access it either.

Terrance held his hand. "Don't try. There have been some arrests. I don't want to believe it, but I think someone in the underground reported it to the college."

"They couldn't bring the underground down, so they corrupt it from the inside." It was bitter news to hear his suspicions confirmed. "Others must feel the same? What about other wizards?"

"He's looking at us. I'm going to kiss you. Maybe that's what he's waiting for."

"Is it what you're waiting for?" It was what Angus wanted but had been too scared to take.

Terrance didn't reply. His lips brushed Angus's as though he'd planned only a gentle kiss, but something changed the moment their lips connected. A hunger that was clean of magic and filled only with need broke free. Angus gripped the collar of Terrance's coat and drew him closer. He overbalanced, and they fell back into the snow.

Terrance came with him, and his body pinned Angus to the ground, his lips still there, still offering that taste of perfection.

"This new arrangement is going to make it really hard to see you."

Maybe that was the point. "Your life would be safer, better, without me."

"Nah. I don't believe that. I was already walking into trouble before you crossed my path."

The cold seeped into Angus's pants. The backs of his legs were wet, but he didn't want to throw Terrance off. He liked the way he felt, heavier and more solid than Saka, though the demon was far stronger. He also liked the way Terrance stared down at him as though he wanted so much more.

He toyed with a strand of Angus's hair, and his lips parted as though he were going to speak, but instead Terrance took another kiss. "We'll find a way. I'll make sure of it."

"I want that." Angus wanted many things, but most of them were out of reach. He wanted to ask why Terrance would still be interested in him after everything that had happened. But the words wouldn't form. For once he didn't want to understand. He just wanted to feel. "So what now?"

Terrance nuzzled into Angus's neck as his hips pressed closer. His body demonstrated how much he wanted Angus. "Now I get to wish that we weren't wearing all these clothes."

"It's a bit cold to strip." And there was the audience.

"Next time, we'll get to be alone."

"Yeah." Alone, but not free.

The smile left Terrance's face. "For the moment we just stay alive. The underground has been attacking the college. Several wizards have died. They haven't asked me to go on any runs yet. I doubt they will, but they might get your group to go."

"In the hope we die?"

Terrance inclined his head. "Why did the demons attack?"

"I don't know. But Guda and Ellis are dead." He'd have to ask Saka about the demon attack. "How do you know about the attack?"

"Because they came to the place I was staying. I thought… I hoped that they were going to free me and take me with them. But I wasn't sure. They killed two of the guards before they were stopped."

The cold wasn't just on his skin. It was in his bones and in his blood. It wasn't an attack. It was a failed rescue. He'd told Saka about Terrance being held captive, and the mages had taken action—action that had resulted in Guda's death. Why had Saka not told him?

"Would you have gone with them? Do you want to be rescued? If you leave, then you'll be a rogue. A criminal." And everything Terrance wanted would be gone. He'd never get to play rugby. At the moment he could still reclaim the life he'd wanted before he went to Warlock College and before he tangled with the underground. Angus understood why the underground was being nice to Terrance. They wanted him to have a good life so he wouldn't muck it up, so he'd have something to lose if Angus fucked up.

So Angus would know he was ruining lives.

Terrance pressed his lips together. Grim and ready to fight. "If I refuse to do anything they want, that's the stick they threaten me with. They won't be content to threaten me forever, Angus."

CHAPTER 17

SAKA WALKED around the blue pool in ever widening circles as he looked for suitable stones. Angus had three in his bag already. He tended to go for the pretty ones, but they didn't always make the most functional telestones. He needed to know if Angus could make and use a telestone. As far as he knew, no human had even been taught. Maybe it wasn't possible. Their minds, or magic, might not be up to the task.

They were on the farthest edge from the camp. The bells around Angus's ankle chimed with every step. Not all demons wore them. But some did as they were meant to ward off riverwyrms. They were among the gifts Angus had been given to tempt his soul into staying. Saka's tent had been too quiet when Angus was across the void, though he'd returned with bright blue eyes which lifted Saka's heart.

"May I ask what Miniti wanted to know?" Saka had taken Angus to see her as soon as he arrived, so she could see that he wasn't interfering with her orders.

He'd already contacted a few trusted mage friends to see if they knew about other demons. So far the news was not encouraging, but they agreed to set up a network of telestones in the hope of contacting demons elsewhere in Demonside. Another demon had made the suggestion, and that had saved Saka from breaking Miniti's edict.

"She wanted an update on the college and the underground." Angus lifted his gaze from the sand and the tough, flowering grasses that grew around the crystalline pool. "I didn't mention that *I* no longer trust the underground."

Saka nodded. "That was wise. I do not want the leaders to revoke the agreement that I fought for. War will not help us."

"Agreed. But in my world, it is coming. Vinland is preparing. Sanctions are already hitting food supplies. It's not looking good." He pressed his lips together and shook his head. "I don't understand why."

"Some people love power at any cost. It eats at them that other people might also enjoy the benefits. Will they use their magic as a weapon?"

Angus shrugged. "I don't know if there *is* a weapon or if they're just hoarding magic." He took his hat off and pushed his hair back. The red strands were dark with sweat. Saka knew the salty taste of Angus's skin too well. "You were there," Angus continued. "What did you wring out from my father's blood?"

There was only the slightest hint of bitterness. Given that Angus's father had tried to kill Angus, Saka expected more anger or rage, but Angus had returned from Humanside with his eyes blue and his heart shut up tight. He had only been back for a day, so Saka hadn't pressed. He let Angus think on it, alone and untouched on his side of the bed.

Saka was wary of rebalancing or even having sex for fun. He'd forgotten what that was like, but maybe it should stay forgotten. Then Demonside wouldn't take another part of Angus.

But he wanted Angus, and Angus needed to learn how to hold on to what he had and refuse to rebalance. Saka craved Angus's embrace and hungered for his kiss, but he hated that need. He couldn't indulge it until Angus knew how to separate himself from the magic of Demonside.

"I wasn't there. I was with you. But I was told your father was not forthcoming with his answers." Angus's father had screamed at the demons before finally begging for his life.

"He couldn't even do the right thing when on the end of a blade and at the end of his life." Angus put his bag down and used his shirt to wipe his face. His belly was pale, and the scar was no longer an angry red, but a soft pink. When he lowered his shirt, his face was set.

Saka put his bag down. They probably had enough stones to sort through. Some would be useless, but some would resonate with magic. He planned to teach all the trainees how to transform them. He needed to disguise his actions as lessons to avoid displeasing Miniti. The prickle of the deception clawed beneath his skin, even though he knew he was doing the right thing by seeking out other demons.

"Why didn't you tell me you tried to rescue Terrance?" Angus rubbed at his forearm as though to relieve a tired muscle.

Saka didn't expect the question and didn't know how to answer. He hadn't tried to rescue Terrance. That was why he'd said nothing about it. Not helping was a stain that would mark his conscience for as long he lived.

"I told the mages what had happened to Terrance and the effect on you. Some wanted to spill warlock blood. They wanted to strike against the humans." He swallowed. "I didn't agree. The plan was rash and rushed because it was our last night as a whole."

Angus didn't say anything, but he watched Saka as though he were searching for a lie in his words.

Saka forced himself to hold Angus's gaze. "I voted against the plan. I didn't go with them to find Terrance. I should've. Then maybe Guda would be alive."

Angus stood frozen, and Saka fully expected him to turn and walk back to the camp. But Angus only nodded.

Finally he spoke. "It was rash. They should've waited until there was more information about where Terrance was being held. But I appreciate the effort." Saka couldn't discern the look in his eyes. Then a smile turned the corner of Angus's lips. "That wasn't the reason you voted against, though. You wouldn't be jealous at all? You being a mage who's told me often enough that mages shouldn't have commitments or affections for others, lest it be a distraction from their duty to the greater tribe."

Saka stepped back. He could deny, but lying always came back and caused greater injury. Sometimes it was worth that risk, but this was not one of those times. "You are correct."

How petty he was. He was trying to teach when he couldn't control his own feelings, couldn't put them aside to best serve the tribe. Maybe Miniti was right, and he should focus on his little area of Demonside, not the whole world. But if Angus's world was affected, then Demonside would be as well. His responsibility was to the greater tribe. Not just his little corner of the desert.

Angus's smile became a grin. Then he nodded and picked up his bag. "You could've told me all that before." He stopped and toed at a rock in front of him. It was darker than the blue-tinged rocks around them and glittered in the sun even before Angus dusted it off with his shirt. "This is the one I want."

Saka sighed. Humans and their attraction to shiny things. "Bring the others anyway. That one may not work."

"You just want me to lug rocks around the desert." But he slung the bag over his shoulder and added his new rock to it.

"There is always a reason I make you do things. You are better at choosing rocks for the trainees than I am, because you are human."

"And the reason you're jealous?"

"Was jealous." He wasn't anymore. Angus would be forever his in a way that Angus would never be Terrance's. It was better that Angus had someone back home. He would never truly be a demon mage, but he could be a strong ally and a voice for Demonside. "I like you."

Angus gave him a sideways glance. "It's not that hard to say 'I love you.'"

But Saka had never said those words to anyone. Angus was the first person he'd ever loved.

THE MAGES and their trainees made themselves comfortable in Saka's tent, and it went from spacious to cramped. Until Angus, he had all the space to himself. Now it was too big when he was on his own. He risked a glance at Angus, who finally knew how Saka felt about him. How was Saka supposed to teach impartially when he wanted to protect Angus from error? Sometimes the best way to learn was to fail and try again.

"Do you think it's wise to teach them how to make telestones? They may not even be able to use them." Usi's voice was low enough to be private but loud enough that everyone could hear if they were paying attention—which they were.

He shouldn't have to defend himself to her. He was head mage. How he taught was up to him. Neither of the other mages had been bold enough to raise any concerns. Did they secretly agree with Usi that he was going too far? They'd all been happy enough to accept his offer to teach.

"True. They may not be able to use telestones at all. They may not be able to use the ones that we have made, as our minds are different. Magic is of our world, not theirs. So why not start at the beginning and see if they can even make one?" Saka spoke at the same controlled volume as she had.

While many mages taught use before creation, he'd been taught the other way around, and that was how he taught. It also made more sense for humans. If they couldn't make it, they probably couldn't use it.

Usi's eyes narrowed. She didn't have a response, but she didn't leave either. Instead she took a seat. How much of what was said and done would she report to Miniti or the other mages who'd voted against teaching humans anything?

For the moment he couldn't worry about it. There were humans to teach, and they had already picked up and examined the palm-sized rocks that Angus and he had gathered that day.

Communicating via telestone wasn't complicated magic, but Saka did hold doubts that humans could maintain the focus required. The stone held magic and became attuned to the user. It was the tuning of one's thoughts that required time and patience to learn. A telestone was a focal point and an amplifier, but concentration had to be precise and unwavering.

Angus hadn't given up his glittery rock. It was pretty when it was clean—like sunlight on the blue pool. And like any good mage, he handled the tool he intended to use to get a feel for it.

He glanced up and then put the rock in front of him, the way everyone had—even Usi.

Saka brought up a circle and blew out a breath. It would be interesting, if nothing else. He hoped that Angus was able to work without drawing magic from himself. While it might be okay for Angus to do across the void, it could be fatal in Demonside.

It was dark when Saka called the session to a halt. The humans hadn't managed to turn a rock into a telestone. Angus scratched at his arm, his scowl fixed in place.

Saka put his hand over Angus's. "Enough for today."

He'd watched Angus try and fail, without reaching to the magic within him. Angus probably could've made the telestone, or at least gotten close if he had, but the cost would have been too high.

Something writhed in Saka's mind—an image as though from a telestone. His arm itched, and he pulled his hand away, breaking the contact. The image faded.

"What?" Angus's concentration broke, and he looked up.

"You're close." Closer than Saka had thought. He studied Angus's eyes and looked for a fade, but there was none. But there *was* something wrong with Angus's arm.

"Close but unsuccessful." Usi smiled. "Perhaps humans don't have the mental capacity."

Saka flicked her a sharp glare. A mage shouldn't demean students. Not everyone learned at the same rate or had the same gifts. He'd heard of demons who took days even to learn to use a telestone. But once the skill was gained, it became easier.

Lizzie turned to Usi. "Perhaps it would help if you weren't heckling in the background. What exactly do you have to lose if we learn?"

The air in the tent stilled.

Usi stood. "I will not be insulted by a trainee of a guest mage."

Saka glanced at Lizzie's mage, Tapo, who gave a slight nod.

It was Saka's tent, and they were all there because he had welcomed them. It was his job to keep his guests happy. "Then you are free to leave,

Usi. Perhaps if you do not wish to be insulted, you shouldn't throw the first insult."

Usi swept out of Saka's tent. He was sure there would be repercussions, but he'd worry about them later. He refocused on Angus. "Pull up your sleeve."

"Why?" Angus said as he pulled up one and then the other. The arm he'd been rubbing looked red and was possibly a little swollen.

"What happened to your arm?"

"Nothing. It started to itch when I came back."

Saka sniffed Angus's skin. The faint scent of urine clung to the red area. "Have any of you ever seen the bite of a pela?" He used magic to heat his hand as though he were about to start a fire and then held it close to the redness on Angus's arm. Something beneath the skin moved, confirming Saka's suspicions that it was indeed a pela larva.

"Did you see that?" He glanced up at Angus, and from the paleness of his face and the width of his eyes, it was clear he had and that he was not thrilled.

"What is it?" Angus's voice betrayed his fear. "There's something alive in my arm, isn't there?"

"Is that where the beetle bit you last time we were here?" Lizzie peered at Angus's arm.

"Maybe? I don't know. Can you get it out?"

The other two demons moved closer. There was definitely a larva in there. Saka didn't want to warm it up and make it too active. He needed to get rid of it. There was only one way to do that.

"I've never cut one out," Tapo said.

"I saw a big one a few years ago." Wek looked at Angus. "They eventually eat their way out and drop into the sand, where they make a burrow and wait for the next rain."

"Where they then come out as those brown beetles, ready to bite the next person. That's cool." Norah grinned.

Angus did not. "Not helpful. I don't care about their life cycle. I want it out."

"It won't kill you. But it will become a rather unpleasant and painful lump. We usually cut them out and drop them into the sand so they still have a chance."

Angus gave Saka a pained grimace. "I'm so glad you care about the bug."

"Wek, will you help?" He could've called Usi back, as she had done it before, but he didn't want to work with her, even though she was the second mage to the tribe.

Wek nodded. It would be an honor for her to assist.

"I'll hold your hand... the other hand," Lizzie said. It was clear to Saka that Lizzie and Norah had been put in a group with Angus because they grasped ideas quickly and were not afraid to give things a try. They also helped around the town without complaint—or at least they didn't gripe within earshot of their mages.

"We're doing this now? Don't I get to prepare?" Angus brought his arm close to his body.

"How would you prepare?" Saka tilted his head.

"I don't know. Buy new pajamas and have a nice dinner before I let you pull the thing out of my arm?"

Norah laughed, and Lizzie bit back a smile.

Angus shook his head. "You two haven't experienced the pain of magical healing. It's not pleasant."

"This is a simple cut." It was only a risk if the pela burrowed deeper into Angus's muscle. Then there would be muscle damage. While Saka was sure Wek knew that, neither of them said it. There was no point giving Angus more to worry about. Besides, if there was damage, it could be healed, but it wouldn't be painless.

"Like I haven't heard that before." Angus lay down. "Just get on with it, then."

Saka pressed his lips together in a narrow smile as Angus surrendered to the inevitable. They could let the pela grow in his arm until it was done, but that had its own risk. "Relax. We will remove the larva."

Saka glanced at Tapo, who placed his hands on Angus's shoulders.

Angus closed his eyes, and the tension left his face. Tapo had put Angus to sleep without being asked, and Saka nodded in approval. It was always better to give relief before a procedure. And if the patient moved at the wrong time, the larva could burrow into the muscle to escape.

Saka gathered his knives and brought up a circle. True to her word, Lizzie took Angus's other hand. Saka pinned down the arm with the pela inside. Wek moved closer, ready to assist.

"You will be ready to draw it out?" Saka asked Wek. There could be no delay, or the pela would go deeper, and things would get decidedly messier.

"I've never actually drawn one out before," Wek said softly.

Maybe he should've called Usi back. "Then you will learn."

First Saka cooled the area to make the pela less active. "When I cut, you will need to separate and grab. Use magic to draw it out. I don't want to have to cut deeper and risk cutting the pela."

That could get really dangerous. The pela larvae had a toxin that paralyzed muscle.

Wek nodded, and doubts tumbled in Saka's belly. He drew in a breath, located the pela, and made the cut deep but not too close. He pushed more cool magic into the area to still the larva, and blood poured from the wound.

Wek didn't flinch. She spread the edges. The pela realized something was wrong and tried to wake up enough to flee. Its fat body twitched, yellow and glistening compared to the tissue and blood. Could it taste the air on its skin?

"Now, Wek, before it moves."

"I see it." She used her long delicate claws and a touch of magic to grasp the end of the larva. The head remained buried, latched on to the muscle. As long as a handspan, its pale yellow body glimmered. Wek's white fingers were stained red with the blood that had slowed due to the magic Saka used.

"That's disgusting." Lizzie made a gagging sound.

"Breathe. If you cannot stomach this, you will never be able to heal." There was no kindness in Saka's voice. "Wek, keep it cold." It wouldn't take much for the pela to wake, slip free, and dive deeper into Angus.

"I am." Wek's put her fingers back into Angus's arm and freed the head.

Wek dropped the larva into a bowl. It thrashed around as though it suddenly realized its meal and ride had been taken away.

Saka started the healing process and gave Angus's tissues a boost to speed up the process. Then he healed the cut and left shiny new skin. There would be a scar. Another one. But they were lessons that Angus needed to remember. One day Angus would be able to heal the scars himself, when he was ready to move on from what had caused them.

But the scar on Saka's chest was hidden under his shirt. He wasn't ready to move on from Guda's death.

CHAPTER 18

THERE HAD been no rain at all. The trees around the blue pool were dying, and Angus was sure the water level got lower with every passing day. He'd have to go back soon. Would there be any water in the pool when he came back?

Would the tribe still be there or would they have moved on?

It all depended on the whim of Miniti. Angus was sure there was more to it than that, but he wasn't about to ask her. While she treated him with a level of respect, it was clear it was only because he was an apprentice mage. If he'd been any other human, she'd have been happy to eat his soul and be done with the whole thing.

The tribe was planting seeds to grow much-needed crops. Surely they'd be there for a while so they could harvest them? Like everyone else, he'd been given an area to plant. Sticking seeds into a hole was backbreaking work. The ground was dry beneath his fingers. He didn't like the seeds' chance of survival, but he kept his mouth closed. The demons had done it many times before, so they knew what they were doing. He also kept an eye out for beetles that might bite him, but there were none in the sand.

Saka had forced him to put the revolting yellow larva in the ground away from the tents after Norah had finished examining it. The scar was bright pink and ran up the outside of his forearm. He was glad he'd been asleep for the removal. Lizzie had told him every gruesome detail, and he wished she hadn't.

That night Saka had held him close, but nothing had happened. The need was killing Angus. It wasn't just lust crawling through his veins. It was as though the magic he carried from Humanside wanted to escape. He realized how much he drew from himself, even though he tried not to. He had to be careful.

A horned shadow fell across his work area. "Are you almost done?"

"Yeah." He couldn't look up at Saka. Saka had confessed to liking him but also to being jealous of Terrance, and they hadn't touched at all during this visit. He didn't understand Saka's reluctance—unless Saka was trying to be a proper mage and erase what he felt. The thought stung.

Angus wanted it to go back to the way it had been when they used to rebalance or even when Angus had summoned Saka and they met in Humanside. They could have sex there without any side effects. But under the watchful gaze of the underground there would be no summoning.

He could keep the magic locked inside of him while he was in Demonside, but he wanted to at least be able to test his limits. He could wait a little longer. He wasn't ready or desperate enough to ask... yet.

Angus opened his palm. There were six seeds left. He planted them in a hurry and went to stand, but his back protested. Saka offered a hand and Angus took it to steady himself. It was an innocent gesture, but it was the closest contact they'd had. He missed Saka's touch, his rougher, warmer skin. He even missed the demands of rebalancing.

For a moment they stood toe-to-toe. Angus was tempted to lean in and kiss him, and why shouldn't he? What was stopping him? Demons showed affection freely. No one there would judge him the way they did at home. *Skitun.* He hesitated for heartbeat longer.

It was one thing to know that he was looked down upon, but it was another to be outed—outed because a warlock had dug into his mind. And it would happen again. Before he went back, he would make sure that his memories were protected, that they could look, but would see only what he allowed. He could stop them from erasing his memories, and there had to be a way for him to hide them.

Saka held his gaze as though he sensed the private battle.

Angus wouldn't let the underground take Saka away from him the way they'd taken Terrance. And he'd get Terrance back too. He just didn't know how.

He slid his free hand around Saka's neck and kissed him. He'd intended it to be just a brush of his lips to remind Saka of what he was missing, but the spark woke his hunger, and he couldn't stop. The magic within him wanted to bubble free. Angus tasted Saka's lips and needed more. He stepped closer, and with every inhale, their bodies almost touched.

Saka's lips parted, and his tongue brushed Angus's. The familiar tingle of magic gathered around them like static in the air. It felt as though Angus had hardly done any magic since his return.

Playing with rocks, while time-consuming, had so far achieved nothing. But he knew it could be everything, so every chance he got, he did everything but pour himself into the rock that would become his telestone. Saka wasn't happy with the progress of any of the humans, yet he wouldn't let Angus draw on the magic within himself to make it better, to make it work. Angus was sure that was all it would take.

Heat thrummed through his body, and lust tightened his belly and sank into his balls. He had woken up hard every morning but done nothing, and he was tired of waiting. He didn't care if all they had was sex and magic. It was enough. His dick hardened, and he was tempted to press against Saka to see if he was as affected.

Angus raked his teeth over Saka's lip, and Saka pressed his clawed fingertips into Angus's hip. For a moment Angus thought Saka would be the one to pull him close, but he didn't. Instead Saka stepped back. It was a punch to the gut.

Saka rested his forehead on Angus's. "We should wait until tonight."

"What happens tonight?" He didn't bother to hide his frustration. His body was anticipating, ready. Lust tightened its grip and twisted.

"Magic must be raised to feed the seeds. How did you think they were going to grow without rain?" A faint smile curved Saka's lips.

Angus had wondered. "We're going to make it rain?" It had stopped raining while he was across the void, and everything was drying up. Leaves were falling from the trees, and the rivers had started to sink.

"No. Too much rebalancing is needed for rain. However, raising magic to make the crops grow it doable. It is how we grow food."

"I thought you planted for the next tribe."

"If it is a major point and we know another tribe will be there soon, and with water near the surface, we do. We will replant and leave a marker when we leave here. For the moment, though, we need the ynns."

Ynns were the staple diet of demons, along with whatever they caught. While the leaves could be eaten, it was the root that was prized.

"So how do we make the crop grow?" If it didn't involve sex, he was going to blow off the afternoon's lessons for some much-needed alone time.

"Carefully." Saka brushed his fingers across Angus's cheek. "I don't want to see the blue fade from your eyes again."

"I'll be careful. I *have* been careful. *We* have been careful." The raw hunger gave an edge to his voice. "You loved to rebalance with me when I first came to Demonside."

"Yes. And I still do. I am not holding back because my feelings have changed. I am holding back *because* of what I feel." Saka kissed him with a tenderness that he rarely revealed. It did nothing to dampen the need that kept Angus rigid.

That was probably as close to an "I love you" as Saka was ever going to get. Angus didn't need to hear it—and if he told himself often enough, he might believe that.

"You need to be able to work magic without drawing on yourself."

Angus pulled away from Saka's grip. "And I have been, but it's here." He tapped his heart. "Trying to escape. I need to let some out."

"And you will tonight." Saka glanced away.

141

Angus let his gaze follow Saka's to where Usi stood watching them. She was paying a lot of interest to the trainees, given that she didn't trust or like humans. "She's watching and reporting everything, isn't she?"

"Yes. But I cannot focus on her. There are other things to do." Saka squeezed his hand. "Why don't you go and work on your telestone? I will get you at sunset."

Angus bit back a groan. He knew he had to get it to work, but it was tedious. "How will I know that it's done?"

Saka tapped his head. "You will feel it in here."

ANGUS CHEATED. He wasn't supposed to draw on himself, but if the telestone was meant to be personal, it needed to be part of him. As he sat and stared at it so he knew every gold flake on its blue surface, he let the magic out. It spilled forth in a glorious rush that made his skin tingle. There was a click, as something in his mind finally unlocked. Was that it?

He pulled back on the magic. It was slippery, and for a few panicked heartbeats, he didn't think he'd get it locked away. But he did. The ease with which it wanted to spill was troubling, as was the difficulty in halting the flow. He needed to practice.

When he looked at the stone, he felt a connection or a hum. Angus didn't just see the stone—he knew it. He grinned and turned it over in his hands, finally able to claim success.

Next he needed to do something with it. Saka used telestones to communicate with other mages in different tribes. But Angus didn't know how to make a call. And who would he call?

Angus knew some of Saka's friends—mages he trusted, like Becha and Lox. They also had human trainees, so they wouldn't mind getting a call from him. He held the rock and thought about Becha. When nothing happened, he let a bit more magic from within him slip free and into the connection. The door in his mind opened.

He could almost feel something brush the edges of his consciousness, and he reached to grab it. Something wet touched his lip, and then red splashed onto the rock in his hand. His focus wavered, and the door slammed shut.

Another drop fell and trickled down the side.

Blood.

He touched his nose, and his fingers came away red. The rock tumbled out of his hand, and he pinched the bridge of his nose. Trying not to drip everywhere, he searched for one of the cloths Saka kept for blood magic and used it to wipe his face. His nose was still bleeding.

There was no way he was leaving the tent to find Saka.

Saka would know immediately that he'd drawn on the magic within himself. Angus needed a mirror—had his eyes lost color? He bit his lip and willed his nose to stop bleeding. He wasn't brave enough to try self-healing—he might make it worse or give himself a growth on his face.

Saka swept aside the tent flap and stopped as soon as he set foot inside.

There was no hiding that Angus had used magic. Saka would be able to feel it and taste it. Magic was a tangible presence, not something mysterious like it was across the void.

"Umm." Angus's voice sounded off because of the blood coming from his nose.

Saka shook his head. "Got it working and tried to make contact with someone?"

He crossed the floor, knelt in front of Angus, and took away the cloth. He put his fingers on Angus's nose, and the flow of blood stopped immediately. But it wasn't Angus's nose that Saka studied. It was his eyes.

Angus hoped they hadn't changed. Should he say something? Better to be honest. "The stone works, but only because I drew from myself."

The magic had rushed forward. It had been glorious to feel it spill.

"So you got it working, but that wasn't the test for you. I knew you would get it as soon as you took the easy way." Saka shrugged. "What have you learned?"

Angus was silent for a moment. He thought Saka would be glad he got the stone working. Instead he was disappointed. The joy of his success broke apart, and he wished he hadn't been so intent on making the stupid stone work. "Nothing." That was the wrong answer. He could tell from the way Saka's eyes narrowed a little. "That contacting people is hard?"

"Yes, it is. Why do think only mages can do it? When you have made a new stone, we will practice with small distances. Pick a new stone and start again. This time use only the magic around you."

"Can I draw it up?"

Saka smiled. "Of course. I'm surprised it took you this long to think of that."

"Maybe because I didn't want to do it in front of the other trainees." Which was a lie. It hadn't occurred to him that he could do his own little ritual to draw up the magic that was around him. All that time spent with Saka, learning about sex and blood magic, either for rebalancing or healing or whatever Saka needed it for, and Angus could've done it for himself.

"They will be in the field tonight, helping to raise the magic. Are you going to be trainee or apprentice? You cannot be both." Saka stood in one smooth motion.

That was the reprimand. He either acted like he was an apprentice and didn't worry about the trainees, or he did only what they did. And they weren't learning anything fun.

Norah was disgusted by the idea of sex magic, though she was interested in blood magic. Lizzie was curious about both. She liked magic and power and understood that, to bring down the college, wizards needed to be powerful. They needed to prove that magic didn't require demons. She asked far too many questions about what Angus had learned.

"Wash and get ready for the rite."

His heart gave a hard thump as he got up. If everyone was going to be there, what kind of power raising would it be? "How did you know I tried to contact someone?"

"I felt you reaching out. Plus, I do not think there is a mage who did not get their telestone working and try to use it straightaway. One or two killed themselves trying. Magic is dangerous, and you know enough now to do damage to yourself and others if you do not remain in control."

"I'm sorry. I didn't realize it was dangerous to use the stone." He wanted to know how the others had died, but wasn't brave enough to ask. He was already having thoughts of brain ruptures and dying in a pool of his own blood. He would never cheat again.

"You have not harmed me. Only yourself. It is a lesson we all must learn." Saka pulled down some of the orbs that were strung from the roof. "You'd better hurry as sunset is approaching."

If Angus concentrated, he could feel the change in the air. He wasn't going to disappoint Saka again by being late to the crop growing.

THE WHOLE tribe gathered and formed a loose circle around the area they'd planted. The mages were evenly spaced along the perimeter, with their trainees next to them. Lizzie seemed to be excited, while Norah was more wary. She seemed to fear magic as much as she was fascinated by it.

Angus glanced at Saka. Already there was a level of excitement, a slight vibration. It was nothing as sharp as an approaching storm, but something close. Maybe it was his own anticipation.

Saka was watching Miniti, who stood in the middle of the circle. She made a full turn and took in her whole tribe, one at a time. Was she looking to see who was absent? Then she completed the turn and faced Saka. With each step she clapped. Saka responded by clapping his hands.

After a few more steps, the other mages joined in.

Another couple and the rest of the tribe started to clap. Someone played the drums that Angus often heard around the village. Then he also clapped in rhythm as Miniti made her way over.

If Angus didn't know better, he'd have thought that Miniti and Saka were going to need a room by the end of the night. But Miniti didn't participate in rituals like that. She was the leader and was there because it was clearly a whole-tribe event.

Everyone needed to eat.

Everyone knew what to do because they'd done it so many times before—except the three humans. Maybe Lizzie and Norah knew what to expect, but Saka liked to let Angus stumble around and find out on his own.

Miniti took her place on the other side of Saka.

The music became louder, no longer just drums.

Any riverwyrm that had been close would swim away before it got a migraine. As one, the tribe moved and made the circle around the crops come to life. Saka hadn't stopped clapping, but it was clear that his focus was not on his hands. It was on the circle. As everyone danced, lights blossomed in the field. The orbs that Saka had brought began to gather up the magic.

While it was nothing like the ritual that Angus had been part of on top of Lifeblood, there was magic drawn up in every step. When someone started to sing, others joined in. It was more joyous than what he'd seen mages do in the past. They celebrated as though the crops were already grown, and they sang about feasts and family.

While he didn't know the words, he hummed along.

The magic surged through his blood as though seeking a way out. He wanted to pour magic into what was going on, but he didn't. Instead he reached out into the night, into the ground, and drew the magic to the circle.

Saka took his hand. His gaze met Angus's for just a moment. Then he lifted their joined hands high. Other couples linked hands. But not everyone. The lights in the field burned bright, and the magic tasted like earth—or maybe they had kicked up sand and it had gotten into his mouth.

Saka dropped his hands.

The music stopped and energy crashed down. Angus was sure that the ground rippled beneath his feet. The orbs went out, and his eyes didn't adjust to the darkness fast enough. The circle was gone.

But people were moving into the field. Laughter danced over the air. In the starlight couples kissed and touched. It wasn't just the magic within him that was awake. He glanced at Saka. Their fingers entwined, and Saka pulled him into the field.

The ground was alive beneath his bare feet, as though all the living things in there had suddenly woken. Were there more of those larvae or beetles? He didn't have time to think about it, and Saka didn't seem to care. He drew Angus close, his black horns glinting and his eyes bright.

"It has been too long," Saka murmured against Angus's lips.

Angus didn't use words to respond. He slid his hands under Saka's shirt so he could feel the heat of his skin. As much as he didn't want his eyes to lose their color again, Angus wasn't convinced that was a good enough reason to avoid all sex. "We can work this out."

Saka nodded and drew Angus to the ground.

"What about the seeds? I don't want to damage them."

"You won't." Saka kissed him hard and with a heat that Angus had missed. Saka could make his bones melt with just the tip of his tongue.

He moved over Angus. With his tail he traced up the inside of Angus's leg and over his hardening length. If Angus closed his eyes, he could almost pretend that they were back in the tent. Was it part of the ritual? There was no circle. Saka pulled open Angus's shirt, and his tail found its way into Angus's pants and wrapped around him. His breath caught as he gave in to the caress, and he moaned against Saka's lips. That wasn't exactly what he'd had in mind. They were in the open where everyone could see them.

The worst bit was that the sand beneath Angus's back was definitely moving. He pulled away and gasped for air. "We could go back to the—"

"It's tradition that couples celebrate in the field." Saka glanced up. "This is what you have been waiting for. You can let some of that magic out tonight. Rebalance. But you must be careful. I will be careful." He brushed his lips against the scar on Angus's stomach and went lower. His horns gleamed in the moonlight. "I have been waiting."

"So have I." They could have sex without Angus rebalancing the magic taken from Demonside. He was sure of it. "We could try. I can control it." But he wasn't sure he would be able to when lust took over.

"Not tonight." Saka undid Angus's pants.

The heat of his mouth closed around him, and Angus's hips jerked. Maybe it was the magic in the air or that it had been weeks, but all he wanted in that moment was to grip Saka's horns and keep the demon there until he was done. He settled for cupping Saka's head, thrusting into his mouth, and reveling in the ministrations of Saka's tongue.

They weren't the only people in the field. He could hear the others—the moans and panting—but he could only make out vague shadows. All around them, people did their own bits of magic as they celebrated the planting.

Saka swept his tongue around the head of Angus's cock and drew a shiver of pleasure from him. It would be so easy to let go, but he didn't want it over that fast. He missed the way Saka would torture him and make him wait until lust burned through every cell of his body, until there was no other thought. Their intensity and closeness couldn't be matched by anything else.

Saka drew back onto his knees and tugged Angus's pants off the rest of the way. Angus sat up to help Saka get free of his and Saka's thick cock jutted forward. Saka guided Angus down.

With his ass to the sky, Angus licked along Saka's length and then took only the smooth head into his mouth. Saka had no reservations about getting what he wanted. He thrust deep into Angus's mouth and threaded his claw-tipped fingers into Angus's hair. For a moment it was all Angus could do to breathe and make sure he didn't choke.

The burned-honey taste of Saka's precome coated his tongue. Saka pulled him away and took his breath with a kiss that had nothing to do with magic. It was purely about need.

Angus stroked Saka's cock. His skin wasn't as smooth as a human's, and Angus anticipated the way it would feel inside of him— stretching him. When Saka had told him to wash and get ready, Angus had made sure that he was very ready. He was glad Saka hadn't walked in on him making good use of the oil Saka kept near the bed, although Saka probably would've smiled and approved. Maybe Angus *could* do something right.

Saka tipped back and dragged Angus with him. They ended up in a tangled mess on the sand, with Angus on top. They weren't mage and apprentice. They was something else, something he could get used to. He leaned over Saka, kissed him, and ground his hips against Saka's. His heart hammered against his ribs, and hunger crawled through his veins and scratched at the walls.

"Do we have to wait and raise magic?" he whispered against Saka's lips. He didn't want to wait.

"No." Saka caressed his cheek. "Better you don't resist too much, in case too much is rebalanced."

Angus hadn't forgotten that. He could let go, but not too much. Every time he had sex in Demonside, a little magic slipped free. He needed to learn how to control that flow, but he had no intention of practicing right then. All he wanted was Saka.

The kiss deepened as Saka's tail brushed the inside of Angus's thigh, the underside of his balls, and then along the crease of his ass. For half a moment, he almost expected the tail to probe deeper, but no matter how much he moved, it didn't. The tail continued to tease his tight hole.

It would be easy to keep going like that. The friction was almost just right. Saka's cock was pressed against him, and the heat of his body seeped into Angus. All around them, magic moved through the ground and the air. Even though Angus wasn't trying to raise it and draw it to him, it was happening.

The ground was still alive with magic, and he was part of it—part of a world where everything was possible, where he could be whoever he wanted, and where no one looked down on him for wanting to learn everything about magic, including the bits that were forbidden.

Unable to take the teasing anymore, Angus sat back and guided Saka's thick cock into his ass. Saka gripped Angus's hips, thrust up, and breached him in one smooth motion. A shudder raced through Angus, and lust and magic sought release.

A groan slipped past his lips as he started to move. Saka's claws dug into the skin of his hips, and Angus eased his legs farther apart to deepen each stroke. He moved until Saka's cock rubbed that spot deep within him, and that was all it took. Angus didn't bother to fight or resist. He tipped his head back to the stars as he came. His breath was nothing more than short pants, and every part of him was too sensitive to touch.

Saka thrust into him and drew out the sensation of falling apart. For a few heartbeats, Angus was one of the many stars. But he remembered not to revel for too long in the feeling of letting go. He didn't want the magic to hemorrhage out of him and leave him close to death. With a wrench of will, he dragged himself back to his body, to the feeling of Saka inside of him and the roughness of Saka's skin.

Angus glanced down. Saka's lips were parted, and the stars were reflected in his black eyes. He was lost in the moment, and for once, he was doing nothing but fucking. Saka thrust up hard and growled. The heat of his come filled Angus. Then Saka gave another few strokes and lay back to catch his breath.

His touch gentled, and he smoothed over the indents his claws had made. Then he drew Angus close for a kiss. "Plantings are always pleasurable."

"Yeah." He could see why. But it wasn't the first planting Saka had attended. Angus was tempted to ask who he usually took as a partner, but it didn't matter.

Angus collapsed next to Saka, still in his arms, content to watch the stars and feel the breeze on his skin. Around him, seedlings pushed through the sand.

CHAPTER 19

IT WAS never a good omen when Saka was called to Miniti's tent. If she had questions or concerns, they were covered in a conversation that took place wherever they crossed paths. That she was summoning meant something serious had happened.

Saka walked into the tent and hoped he looked calm, but his insides were knotted. One guard stood by the door. Miniti didn't really need guards as no one would attack a leader they had chosen and who was doing a very good job at managing the tribe and their travels.

A lot of that was because Saka managed the water and liaised with her on a regular basis. His successes were hers. That he had high standing on the council of mages meant that she enjoyed a higher status among other leaders. They were seen as a powerful tribe. People wanted to join them. Tribes fell apart when they got too big, so Miniti allowed only very careful growth, unlike some other leaders.

The tribe was bigger than it had ever been. Because of the other two mages, Miniti had allowed other demons to join. Saka was fairly sure the tribe was at capacity. Any more, and it would stop being a whole. It would fracture. Any more, and finding water and growing crops for all would become a problem.

Usi sat on the floor of Miniti's tent. The knots in Saka's stomach drew tighter, and his heartbeat quickened. Usi had arrived first and spent time alone with Miniti. That was a bad sign.

Miniti rested on a couple of cushions. She gestured for Saka to sit. Like Usi, he was given no cushion. Miniti was treating them as equals. His worry doubled in size. This was no ordinary meeting.

Miniti leaned forward and glanced at both of her mages. It wasn't a general meeting of mages, or Tapo and Wek would be there too. "Head Mage Saka, you are being accused of putting your human above your duty."

What had Usi been saying about him? When it came to politics, Usi and Miniti were close. Saka's position was always more dependent on his success. Usi didn't want trainees. Like some of the other mages, she wanted blood. Those mages wanted to snatch humans and animals from Humanside to rebalance with blood and souls.

But the void couldn't be opened from their side, so they were at the humans' mercy. The unwritten rules had come out of the last war between humans and demons.

Humans couldn't kill demons for magic. Demons couldn't kill humans in Humanside, only in Demonside, and only after they had waited a day and a night to see if the humans would be retrieved. Many weren't retrieved. Only those of value were taken back. Angus was lucky his father had once considered him valuable.

Had he put Angus ahead of his duty to the tribe? He didn't think so. Had he disobeyed Miniti in looking for ways to contact other demons? Yes, but she didn't seem to know about that. His tension eased a little, but he wasn't naive enough to think he was out of dangerous waters.

"My human is my apprentice, and I have been treating him as such." He was glad Angus wasn't in Demonside at the moment. If anything happened to Saka, it wouldn't go well for him or the other humans. Usi would make sure their blood was spilled.

"Explain why the humans need to learn about telestones," Miniti said.

"Communication is an important job of a mage."

"They aren't mages," Usi interjected.

Saka glanced her way. She lacked the composure a mage should have, but that wasn't the time to point it out. If she challenged him directly, there would be a reckoning for whoever lost. One of them would lose status and bleed. If he were still head mage after, he might actually take pleasure in seeing Usi in pain. No, he wouldn't. That wasn't the kind of mage he was. But he would give her no pleasure either, and she would give him none. He'd tasted her blade enough times to know what she was like.

He did not want to lose his position.

"Are we discussing Angus or the trainees?" He looked at Miniti. "Angus is being trained as a mage, as was agreed by the council of mages." Miniti didn't have the power to override that decision, but she could make things extremely difficult.

"Angus. For the moment." Usi received a sharp glare from Miniti.

They would get to the other two humans later. Usi had been watching—not because she was interested, but because she was looking for ways to undermine him. Some people would rather pull down others than lift themselves up. It was a sorry situation when a mage sank to those levels. He would make his own report to the council, regardless of the outcome.

"Angus, like all apprentices, has been learning to make a telestone. I wasn't sure if the human mind was even capable. He has been successful. The other two have not, as yet, but I believe they will be successful."

"And you have been rebalancing?" Miniti watched him closely.

"I'm sure Usi has told you that I have shown him blood magic. She even helped with his training in that area." Saka kept all concern off his face, but he didn't like the focus on what he was teaching Angus.

"But are you rebalancing while he is here? Your tent has been quiet of late."

Saka was silent for a moment. He couldn't lie. Wouldn't. "Not as much as before because I have learned something interesting."

"And what could be more interesting than returning stolen magic to Arlyxia?" Miniti smiled, but her too-wide mouth made the innocent gesture sinister.

Saka could hear the excitement in Usi's breathing. It hummed around her. She thought she was going to walk away as head mage.

"That when humans come here frequently to rebalance, the magic wants to leave their bodies. They come to want, even crave the release, but now I must be cautious with Angus until he learns to control the flow, or he will unwittingly surrender his soul to Demonside." Usi opened her mouth, but Saka held up his hand. "If he is dead, he is no use at all." He didn't want to think about a world where Angus was dead. No amount of magic would heal that wound. It would leave a scar he'd wear for life. "If he can control how much he gives, he is useful. He and the other trainees return with fresh magic and information about the happenings in their world. Coupled with what we learn from the few who are connected to other warlocks, be they underground or college, it gives us a better idea about ways to defend ourselves."

Miniti leaned back. "He joined in after the planting."

"Yes. He likes to be part of the tribe."

"Yet he is not, nor is he demon."

"I know. We both know."

It was clear that Miniti wasn't happy with the answers he'd given. Did she want him displaced? "Your affection for him makes you blind to his flaws."

"And aside from being human, what are they? That he willingly returns to rebalance and learn our ways? That he is actively trying to bring down the Warlock College that seeks to destroy all demons? Who here has no flaws? Mages are supposed to see them and work to fix them. Yes, I am close to him. I was close to my mentor too. There is a bond—"

"He is a warlock," Miniti said. "He controls you."

"And I have the same amount of control over him. Perhaps if more mages volunteered to make the connection with a warlock, we might have been able to stop the drying before it started. Instead we turned away. We have to accept that responsibility." Many claimed that teaching humans wasn't part of being a mage. But teaching was their responsibility. It didn't matter who they taught.

"Now we have trainees instead. People who have no loyalty or ties to Demonside," Miniti said.

"They chose to be here. They trust us." The trainees could be rounded up and killed to rebalance, but if the demons did that, there would be no working with the humans at all. "If we don't work with the humans, then we will be at war with them. Few remember the war, but from the stories told, I do not think a repeat would serve us well. We need rebalancers."

As he said it, he realized the weight of the words. There might be people who had no interest in magic, but who would be willing to rebalance. They could come to Demonside to experience the demon way of life, and magic would drain from them. If a human couple had sex in Demonside, would they both rebalance? It was an idea worth discussing with other mages.

"Then why are the trainees not rebalancing?" Miniti tilted her head.

"I do not follow every part of their training. It could be that they are learning." He paused for a moment. "How would you choose to rebalance if you had to? Soul is out. They did not come here to die. That leaves sex or blood. They are raised with different values."

Miniti considered him for a moment. "It did not take Angus long to decide."

"I did not give him long to decide." Saka had pushed Angus because he wanted to know what the warlocks' limits were. His life and usefulness were at risk.

No one spoke. Usi fidgeted. Saka tried to project calm and remain motionless. He would not let it get under his skin.

"I cannot deny that you have been a good head mage. You have never flinched from your duties." Yet there was doubt in Miniti's voice. "But some of your ideas of late? I question if you are thinking of the tribe or of your own status."

Saka almost laughed. "I never sought to become head mage. I have always put the tribe first—the greater tribe, meaning the whole of Demonside."

And he meant even those demons he'd never heard of before Angus mentioned them—the feathered ones and the others that must live out across the sands. Arlyxia was far greater than he ever thought. If he focused on one small fraction of the tribe, he would limit ideas and possible solutions. What were other mages working on? Was the rest of Demonside so ill? And if it wasn't, could they walk until they found a place that offered a better life?

He'd been making telestones and leaving them when they moved on. Lox and Becha were doing the same, as were a couple of the others he trusted. Maybe a network of stones would have a greater reach. He hadn't yet tried to make contact because his fear held him back. It was a flaw he needed to address.

Miniti looked at Usi. "You raised this grievance. I find nothing to act on."

Saka released a small, silent sigh of relief. Miniti was unwilling to oust him. That didn't mean Usi couldn't directly challenge him. But would she? He regretted ever inviting her into his tent to show Angus the use of pain and magic.

Usi's face hardened. Her annoyance shimmered off her, and she turned to face him. "I challenge you for the right to be head mage."

Saka held her gaze. "Be sure that is what you want. If you lose, you will lose status. You are challenging me without the backing of our leader and creating unnecessary friction within the tribe." Yet it was Usi who had accused him of acting improperly by not putting the tribe first.

Usi nodded. "I am not an apprentice who needs reminding."

She was acting like one.

"Very well. I accept." He could've refused, but Usi would have held that over him, and he couldn't be seen as weak.

"If you lose, Mage Saka, you will become Usi's for three days and nights, as is traditional, but Saka will be the second mage. Usi, if you lose, you will be Saka's for the same period, and you will no longer be his second. That honor will fall to Tapo or Wek. Do you still wish to proceed?" Miniti's words were formal. A challenge was not undertaken lightly.

Saka watched Usi as she hesitated for just a moment. "Saka led the way for the trainees to come. He shies away from conflict, and without his human, he is weak."

"The death of demons in a war will only strengthen the warlocks and do more damage to us. You voted to give this a chance, and the year is not yet up. Take my place as head mage if this trial fails. But give this way a chance. Let us fight smart." He touched the scar on his chest. "Let us not rush in again."

But Usi had challenged him and discussed everything with Miniti. Saka didn't know if he could work with her, and he certainly couldn't trust her. He wanted to fight her, to see her humiliated, and to show everyone that she wasn't worthy of being a mage.

The tribe wouldn't see the battle. That would be done in private. But they would see the result. If he won, he wouldn't want her servitude for the three days and nights.

Usi looked at him with naked hate. She couldn't work with him either. While their relationship had been tense at times, he'd thought they at least had a common goal. But he was wrong. He'd misjudged her ambition.

"Saving Arlyxia doesn't involve saving humans. Or are you scared to fight without yours by your side?"

Usi was dangerously close to revealing what had happened the night Guda was killed. Had she already told? Surely she wouldn't break her oaths.

"I am not afraid to fight you."

But if he lost, he wasn't sure he could stay with his tribe and be her second.

CHAPTER 20

SNOW WAS two feet thick on the ground. The tiny snowdemon Angus had made with Terrance was buried up to its neck, and its twig horns had fallen off while he was away. He felt much the same way. Soon he'd be buried beneath the expectations of the underground and the mages of Demonside. He wasn't moving fast enough to help anyone.

Least of all himself.

If he couldn't save himself, how could he save Terrance? He had no idea how to solve that problem, but he had brought Terrance a present—not that he was allowed to see him until after whatever the underground had planned.

For the first time, Norah, Lizzie, and he were to join an underground mission. Apparently the other trainees were also involved. He hadn't seen them since they'd been split up. Part of him wished they'd all been able to stay at Lifeblood. But he loved seeing different parts of Demonside, even if he did hate the walking, and he wouldn't change his memories of the crop growing for anything. He'd woken up in Saka's arms in the dappled light of ynn shrubs. Their narrow leaves had formed a canopy that took the sting out of the sun's heat. All that growth in one night and from one ritual…. It was amazing.

"We leave in ten minutes." The warlock—or was he a wizard?—called out.

It would be a relief to get out of the house. The dampeners were like too-tight bandages, and all he could think about was the pressure on his skin. Lizzie and Norah hadn't noticed it, though they had realized they couldn't perform magic in the house. But magic could still be gathered. It just couldn't be transformed into something else.

159

He was ready and itching to leave. They were all dressed in dark colors, and they had been warned to stay with their underground leader, Syg. But they didn't know the plan.

Even when they got in the car, they weren't told where they were going. Nervous energy bounced off all of them. Could that be used the way pain and lust were? Angus didn't know, and it wasn't the time to try, but he made sure to gather. In Demonside his skin would take on a faint glow. There would be static in the air. In Humanside he used the mark Saka had carved on his chest to bind the magic to him.

The college had told them that magic couldn't be stored. But that was a lie. Saka could store it in the orbs until he was ready to release it, and, according to his father, the college had been storing magic to weaponize it.

He could hold on to more magic and for longer if he let the scar on his chest heat.

The scar was burning and uncomfortable, but he'd rather have the pain than be unprepared for what would happen next. His trust in the underground had been shattered the moment they took Terrance. They could be leading the trainees to their death, but Angus had to act as though he were loyal and obedient. If he didn't, Terrance would suffer.

The car pulled into the parking lot of a suburban mall. He'd paid close attention to the drive so he would know where he was staying. The underground didn't feel it necessary to tell them where they were living. They'd have everything they needed while they were there—except their freedom.

"Are we going to do some early Solstice shopping?" Norah asked with only the faintest touch of sarcasm.

Syg turned to look at her. "No. A demon is being brought here by the college."

It took Angus a moment to realize what that meant. Everyone in the car knew that the demons couldn't open the void from their side. Screw being polite and obedient. "The college is going to open the void. Here?"

Syg gave him a look that said the other guard had talked too much, and now everyone knew what kind of warlock Angus was. Angus had heard tales of magic users who could turn their foes into rats or fish. Was that possible? The tips of his fingers tingled with the temptation to try.

He could transform Syg, take the car, and flee.

But there was nowhere to go. The college wanted him, and the underground had said all known wizards were being watched, or worse, arrested by the college. He could drive until they reached the border, but they wouldn't make it across no man's land to the Nations. And people who fled into the Mayan Empire were used as temple fodder, sacrificed to the demons, apparently. Or was that misinformation too?

"We are to capture the demon so the college can't kill it for its magic," Syg said without answering Angus's question.

"Capture how?" Lizzie asked.

"You don't need to worry. You just have to help herd it. Any more questions? We're on a time limit."

"Why not just open the void and send it home?" Angus said, determined not to let Syg dodge him so easily. That was the most obvious course of action. It was what should be done.

Syg's smile was cold and calculating. "You open the void, and your friend loses his fingers. His rugby career will be over before it starts. That would be a real shame."

Angus's gut squeezed tight. That wasn't a warning. That was a threat.

Syg got out of the car, and they all followed like obedient sheep, ready for the abattoir. Lizzie gave his arm a squeeze, but didn't say anything.

Across the parking lot, Jim and three other trainees moved closer to the entrance. Where was the other group? Where were the underground warlocks or wizards, the people who knew what they were doing and who'd had years of training?

The tension crawled up his spine and lodged at the base of his skull in a knot of headache-inducing worry. "Where are we herding the demon to?"

Syg gave a small nod to his left, but there was no clear destination.

Lizzie slowed. "I'm not sure about this." Her voice was so soft Angus almost didn't catch her words.

Angus nodded and said louder, "And how do we herd it?"

It wasn't going to be something small. When the college arranged a demon breakthrough as proof that demons were dangerous and needed to be controlled, they always got something big. He'd seen some of the big animals in Demonside, but never up close.

"I'm sure you've learned something while across the void and not just how to suck the magic out of your demon's di—"

The void tore open, snatching away his words and flipping over several vehicles. The power that rippled from the tear was more than Angus had ever seen or felt. The breach rippled over his skin in a cold wash, and the goose flesh on his skin was almost painful.

Norah swore and stepped back.

"If you run, the college will hunt you down. You'll be locked up and forgotten about," Syg warned.

And if they fled to Demonside, no one would ever open the void to bring them home.

It wasn't one demon that came through, but four brilliant, shimmery blue scarlips. They weren't big, but they weren't happy or semitamed with blood the way Terrance's demon had been. They were wild and angry. Their venom-filled tails arched over their heads, ready to strike. They prowled forward and made an odd grating sound as they communicated to each other.

They weren't nearly far enough away. A few yards and a half dozen cars were all that separated them from the scarlips. Terrance would know what to do. Somehow he'd convinced Aqua not to kill him.

The void closed, the scarlips fanned out, and humans who were just out shopping started to scream. Someone yelled that the underground had done it.

Angus didn't know enough about scarlips. He'd been so busy studying magic that he hadn't learned about the creatures that lived in Demonside.

One scarlips attacked the nearest person to it. Screams and the scent of blood filled the air. They had to do something before the college showed up, before the underground called the mission a failure and left them to vanish into the prisons of Vinland. Panic made his heart beat fast and his mind work more slowly.

If the scarlips spread out, they would kill until they were captured. Then they would be sacrificed in a ritual for their magic. Angus was able to appreciate their lethal beauty, having seen Terrance's demon up close, but he couldn't leave them to kill innocent bystanders.

Jim and his group ran toward the scarlips and shouted as though they hoped to scare them. The scarlips just looked annoyed, tails high and that grating noise getting louder.

"I'm going to draw them that way." Angus pointed to the left, where they'd been told to herd them.

"How?" Lizzie frowned.

Terrance had used his blood. All Angus had to do was run and hope the scarlips followed him… and didn't catch him. Angus produced a small knife. He never went anywhere without it anymore. Fear would give his blood a spike.

Lizzie grabbed his coat as though she could stop him. "They'll kill you."

He shrugged out of his coat and kicked off his shoes. He didn't need the extra weight, and he was used to being barefoot in Demonside. The cold bit into his feet, his socks getting soggy immediately.

"I'll open the void before that happens." He hoped he sounded confident, but he didn't know if he could outrun a scarlips while he was bleeding.

"What do you want me to do?" Lizzie dropped his coat.

"Make a magical wall or something to keep them on track. Norah?"

Norah's face was pale—she was a scholar, not a fighter—but she nodded.

Angus ran. He felt Lizzie's wall go up, and wished he could see it, so when he thought he had enough of a lead, he turned and jogged backward. The scarlips were watching him, ears forward and tails vibrating.

He swallowed hard. He'd only get one chance to get it right or screw it up. "Come and get me!"

He sliced down his arm and lifted it high. The cut was just the right depth to bleed freely but do no damage. Usi would be so pleased that her lesson was saving human lives.

He knew the moment they scented his blood. They lifted their muzzles, and the noise increased. Crimson stained the mouth of one, but it left the body it had been feeding on to watch him. Angus had delicious magical blood, which was no doubt infinitely tastier than regular old blood. He hoped so anyway.

Some of the other trainees realized what Lizzie and Norah were doing, and added their magic to herd the scarlips.

The lead scarlips moved toward him at something faster than a walk—faster than Angus was comfortable with. He turned and ran.

The gravel bit into his socked feet, but they were tough after the walking he did in Demonside. The cold cut his lungs with every breath, but he ran anyway. He used the fear to draw more magic to him. When he wasn't surrounded by dampeners, it rolled in like fog and gathered close. He used it to make his stride lighter, faster. He could sense the scarlips gaining now, and someone else joined him in running, but they wouldn't be fast enough without magic. Angus risked a glance to the side and back.

It was Jim.

A scarlips pounced. Angus had time to duck and throw up what he hoped was an effective shield, and the animal went over his head. "Run faster or shield yourself!"

Jim hesitated. That was all it took. One scarlips sensed an easy target and peeled away. Angus dropped his shield and lashed out. The scarlips stumbled, but Angus was too late. It already had Jim, and there was too much blood.

The scarlips prowled closer and circled their prey.

Where were Syg and the other underground members? Had the trainees been left to die or be captured by the college like the scarlips?

Angus's breath came in hard pants as he glanced around. He couldn't fight off all the scarlips alone.

People stood around watching, recording with their phones. Some stood on car roofs as though that would keep them safe.

"This was the work of the college. They bring creatures through to sacrifice them for their magic. That's what's causing the cold."

"Look out," a woman shouted.

Angus glanced to the side as a scarlips leaped for him. He barely protected himself in time. The demon animal didn't want Jim, who was already down and bleeding. Had he been struck with poison? Is that why the scarlips were ignoring Jim and concentrating on him?

The last group of trainees arrived, and they had something with them.

While he tried to get to Jim, Lizzie and Norah's wall drew closer and funneled the scarlips pack toward the last group.

Angus was caught in the open. If he didn't move soon, the wall would reach him and he'd be stuck with the creatures. The animals hit his shield, knocked him over, and circled him. They would wait for him to weaken.

As abruptly as they'd started, they veered off toward a magical cage. Angus could see it but it was partially camouflaged.

Suddenly the scarlips vanished.

His heart beat as though it hoped to break free.

He wanted to be sick, but he got up off the ground. The chill on his skin moved deeper, and the cut on his arm hurt. Angus made his way to Jim, and hoped he knew enough to heal him.

He dropped to his knees. He hated that Jim had taken his father's money, but he couldn't hate Jim. First love was hard to forget, and they'd had good times.

The scarlips had slashed across Jim's chest, and his coat was soaked with blood. Angus put his hands over the wound. It was deep, but he would try to fix it.

Jim put his hand over Angus's. "Don't waste your time."

"Don't be stupid. I can do this. And you'll be up in no time." He tried to sound positive. He started to gather the magic to him.

"It stung me."

It was then Angus realized that Jim's breath was short and labored—not from the wound but from the venom. "I'm sure there's a treatment."

Why was no one coming to help?

"I'm sorry for taking the money. You never knew what it was like to have nothing."

"It doesn't matter." The blood flow wouldn't stop. Jim's blood wouldn't clot, and Angus couldn't stem the flow.

"Let me go to Demonside. My death can balance what I've done."

"What do you mean? I don't care about the money my father gave you." He pressed harder on the wound, but blood oozed between his fingers.

"You should never have trusted me. I knew how corrupt the underground had become. They wanted me to bring you in. It's the college with a new name. They only care about power." His grip on Angus's hand tightened. "They're using you. When the time comes, you're going to be set up."

"Like today." The underground had expected trainees to die, perhaps even wanted that result.

"Worse." He coughed, and red stained his lips. "Please, open the void for me. I know you're trying to contact other demons. People are worried you'll defect."

"To where?"

"To anywhere." Jim choked and coughed again.

"The demons can heal you." Angus looked up. "Someone help him." He shouted, but no one came closer. The bystanders watched and recorded the scene with their phones as the sirens drew closer. If Angus didn't get away, he'd be caught. He doubted the underground would break him out of prison.

"What are they going to do with the captured demons?" Angus opened the void.

"What warlocks do." Jim glanced at the cold, black void, and a warm breeze drifted across with the familiar scents of Demonside. "Except you. You get it."

"If you cross, there will be punishment," a familiar voice said near him. Syg had finally shown up.

"Heal him," Angus demanded.

"He's nothing. An untrained wizard isn't worth the waste of magic it would take." The man stepped closer.

Jim wasn't nothing. He was Angus's ex, a traitor who'd sold his life to the highest bidder. But he had plans and ideals once, dreams of fixing everything. Angus squeezed his eyes shut. He was supposed to be able to hate Jim for what he'd done. He shouldn't have to mourn the loss of his life.

Angus leaned close and kissed Jim's cheek. "Why did you run when you knew the scarlips would chase?"

"Because I didn't want them to get you. You can do what I never could. You can fix this," Jim murmured. Then he released Angus's hand.

Angus used what was left of his magic to push Jim through the void. It wasn't elegantly done, and he had no idea if the demons would heal him or not. But Jim would arrive somewhere near Saka's tribe.

Angus mended the tear in the void and stood.

The man looked at him with disgust. "You shouldn't have done that."

"He asked me to. Final wishes should be respected." Lizzie waited in a nearby car, and Syg shoved Angus toward it. "What will happen to the scarlips?"

"We need the power to fight the college," the man said.

Angus got into the car. He'd have rather gone to Demonside, and there was nowhere else for him to go at the moment. Nowhere was safe. Jim had mentioned defecting... to another country? Would he be safe somewhere else? How would he get to Saka from somewhere else? Until that moment he'd never thought of calling anywhere but Vinland home.

"So use wizard magic, something that doesn't make the snow deeper. You can't fight warlocks with the same tactics. You'll destroy both worlds." How could the underground be so blind? Maybe Jim was right, and the underground was just another faction of the college.

"You don't know the first thing about fighting a war." The man slammed the car door.

It wasn't true. Angus was already fighting, and had been from the day he was first taken to Demonside. He just hadn't realized.

THE ATMOSPHERE in the house was grim. Lizzie hadn't said a word. She seemed to have turned to stone. If she'd cried or been angry, that would've been something, but she pushed Norah and Angus aside and shut herself in her room. Norah sat on the sofa and stared at the blank screen of the TV. Neither of them wanted to turn it on.

Their faces would be there. The trainees would be labeled rogues like him, even though they weren't really. Their greatest crime was using magic without the college's approval, but the college only approved of demon-based magic, not natural magic, the kind wizards used. Wizards didn't need a demon, and Angus was sure that, with training, they could be as strong as warlocks and a threat to the college.

The college wasn't about magical studies at all. If it were, they'd encourage the use of natural magic, even for warlocks. It was about control of magic and power. Those that disobeyed got trampled. The only thing stopping that foot from crushing them was the underground.

It was clear the underground had become just a rival college. Their original purpose of training wizards had been erased. Maybe it would all work out if the underground took over, but maybe the underground would see those trained wizards as a threat and be no different from the college. There was nothing weak about a wizard.

The pressure of the dampeners wrapped tightly around him, like a too-warm coat that he couldn't pull off. He wanted to ask Norah if she felt it, but she wouldn't make eye contact. So they sat in silence as the room got darker. The heater hummed in the background.

"Is he dead?" Norah's voice was rough.

"I tried to heal him, but... he wanted to go." Did Jim's soul balance the betrayals? Had Jim enjoyed his father's money while he was alive or was it always tainted?

If Angus had never contacted Jim, never asked about the underground, he'd probably have died in Demonside. No one would have opened the void for him to get home.

"They expected us to die today," she whispered. They all knew about the microphones.

Angus nodded. "It was a setup. We can never walk free."

They were reliant on the underground for every breath they took, and Angus didn't like it at all. He should get up and bandage his arm properly since he couldn't go outside and attempt self-healing—Saka had warned him that it would be harder to heal himself than to heal others, and here he couldn't see the magic.

Angus tipped his head back against the sofa and closed his eyes. He needed to find a way out of Vinland.

THE DAY before Angus was due to go back to Demonside, Terrance finally visited. Angus had given up asking to see him just as he'd pretty much given up asking for anything. They were under house arrest. He'd resigned himself to taking the rock back to Demonside. He wouldn't leave it in Vinland to be found.

When Terrance walked in, Angus couldn't hide his excitement. "I didn't think they were going to let you come." He glanced at Terrance's hands and was relieved to see he had all of his fingers.

"I was at a training camp." He hugged Angus. "You've been all over the news. I didn't know if you were going to be here."

"I'm not easy to get rid of." But he was. It would be all too easy for Angus to vanish. He needed somewhere to go. If he could get to another country via Demonside, it would be easier than trying to flee Vinland. But Saka didn't know where to find the other demons. He leaned into Terrance.

Neither of them moved, but Angus didn't know how long they had, and he wanted to give Terrance the telestone he'd made him and explain how to use it.

"Come on." He took Terrance's hand and led him toward his bedroom.

Terrance didn't resist or ask why, but there was a question in the lift of his eyebrow. Angus hoped there weren't any cameras in the bedroom—not because he was going to strip off, although he wanted to do more than hold hands with Terrance. He and Terrance had more than magic, though it was magic that had brought them together.

Angus shut the door and leaned against it. "I brought you something."

"It's not my birthday, and it's too early for Solstice."

"When is your birthday?" Angus should know that.

"Spring, so I may never get another birthday." Terrance's lips twisted into a bitter smile at his poor joke.

"You'll get another birthday." Angus rummaged through his bag until he pulled out the blue sparkly rock.

"A rock? It's pretty and all that...." His eyebrows drew together.

Angus put it into Terrance's hand, moved close, and kept his voice soft. "It's called a telestone. The demons use it to communicate telepathically across vast distances. This is the first one I made, but I don't know if it will work here."

Terrance pulled up his sleeve to reveal the dampener. "And even if it does, I won't be able to use it."

"You don't need to use magic to use it." He still had his hand over the stone. "The magic is in the stone. I spent days making it. I brought mine too. I thought that we could try."

"And if it does work, then we aren't relying on the underground to bring us together." Terrance's eyes widened, and he grinned. "That's the most thoughtful gift I've ever been given. Thank you." His kiss was slow and deliberate, as though he didn't want it to end.

Angus was quite happy for the moment to last. It lightened the weight that had filled his soul, but at the same time he didn't want to test the stones and find that they didn't work on the human side of the void. If they didn't, he'd given Terrance the pretty rock that had given him a bloody nose.

Heat coiled through Angus's body. It would be easy to forget about the stones. He hadn't been with Terrance since that one quick fumble, and their relationship was moving slower than the glaciers creeping down from the north. But part of him liked that they weren't rushing. The rest of his life was rushed as he pushed himself to learn more and learn faster so he could bring down the college. Their relationship was comfortable and safe.

"Did you want to try before they take me away?" Terrance's words were punctuated by kisses.

Angus wasn't sure if Terrance was talking about the stones or something else. And from the way Terrance's body was pressed against his, it was clear that something else was on his mind.

"How long do we have?"

"They never tell me. I don't think they'll come barging in here."

Angus lifted one eyebrow. He didn't have that much faith in the good manners of the underground. He'd searched his room for a camera or listening device and had come up empty, but there were some in the kitchen and living room, which made sense. The

171

underground wanted the trainees to chat about what had happened in Demonside.

"All right. Maybe they will. They won't let me stay the night." Terrance sighed. "I'd like to."

"At least they let you come."

Terrance nodded and stepped back. "So how do we do this before I get completely distracted and we end up naked?"

Heat rushed up Angus's throat and settled on his cheeks. He knew Terrance was only partially joking. Where he'd once doubted that a man like Terrance could be interested in him—sportsmen could take their pick, and Angus had never thought of himself as anyone's first choice—they clicked in a way that wasn't just about magic.

It would be nice to get naked, to feel Terrance's touch, and have sex with no magical consequences. There would be other consequences, though. Of that he was sure, but he pushed aside those thoughts. There'd be time later, when Terrance was free.

"Let's sit on opposites sides of the room." He wasn't going to aim for a big distance, not yet.

"And then what?" Terrance asked as he sat.

"Then I'll try to reach you."

"And how will I know?"

"You'll think of me and feel a pull."

Terrance smiled at him. "I didn't need a stone for that."

Angus's lips twitched. He'd forgotten what it was like to smile for no good reason. Demons didn't have lame come-on lines. They were much more up-front. "Close your eyes and relax."

When Terrance shut his eyes, Angus reached out. He hoped the stone would cut through the dampeners because he wasn't working magic—it was stored in the stone.

He picked up his much plainer black-and-blue rock, which he had also filled with magic so it would act as a focus. Saka said they would eventually need to be refreshed, but only after years of use. That was true in Demonside, but Angus had no idea how long they'd last in Vinland.

But if he could put magic into a rock, it was possible the college was doing something similar to store their stolen magic.

Would he be able to use his telestone to find out where it was stored?

Angus's heart kicked over at the idea.

"Nothing's happening."

Angus glanced at Terrance. He had to prove the stone worked on the human side of the void first, so he let his consciousness seep into the stone and thought of Terrance. The door was much easier to nudge open this time. He pushed through, but he immediately hit another door—one not of his making.

He'd reached the door to Terrance's mind. That was the furthest he'd ever gotten in making a connection. "How about now?"

"I'm getting a headache. Is that meant to happen?"

"You need to let me in. I can feel you."

Terrance chuckled. "If you want to do it that way."

Angus bit back his own laugh and retreated away from Terrance's mind, even though he wanted Terrance to throw open the door. "Next is a bloody nose. I was warned that doing too much can rupture blood vessels in your brain."

Terrance opened his eyes. "You tell me this after we start?"

"I didn't say it was safe." He was as bad as any demon for not explaining all the risks.

"Do it again." Terrance closed his eyes.

"Are you sure?"

Terrance nodded. "I know what it feels like. I just can't grab it."

"I see it as a door to be opened. That might help." Did Saka feel it differently?

"It's like a hand or a rope in the darkness, I need to grab it and then... and then I guess that's how I answer your call." Terrance picked up the rock. "This is just a focus. We should be able to do it without."

"But then we'd need to draw magic to us." He glanced at his own stone. "They might drain faster here."

"I'll keep it in the places where magic naturally gathers. I can still sense it, even if I can't use it."

"Does the dampener bother you?"

"No. We have to wear them when we play rugby anyway, to make sure no one is cheating."

It was just Angus who felt the pressure on his skin and the itch in his veins that made him long for the freedom of Demonside.

CHAPTER 21

SAKA COULDN'T walk through the village without people watching his every step. Usi's poison had worked, even though she hadn't won, and the trust people had in him was shaken. There was no magic he could work to counteract that.

Angus walked with him, but was wise enough not to speak about the shift in mood where they could so easily be overheard. That Saka even had Angus at his side and in his tent was cause for grumbling.

The tribe wondered if he was weak, or if he favored the human the way Usi claimed. Humans *had* caused the damage to their home, and *maybe* it was time for blood. He heard the whispers even though he'd tried not to listen.

Wek, and Tapo, the new second mage, had been told that their trainees must do some public rebalancing, some part of their training that could be observed without it being a formal ritual. They needed to be united against the violence that Usi wanted to see. If the opinion of the tribe swayed too much, Miniti would remove him without a second thought. She wasn't rash, but she was smart, and she didn't want to see her tribe divide into hostile factions over how humans should be treated. Neither did he.

They made it back to Saka's tent, and Saka made a circle so they could speak.

"Your talk with Miniti?" Every time Angus arrived in Demonside, he had to see Miniti first, alone.

"Went okay." Angus frowned. "The college brought a small pack of scarlips across, and the underground went to intercept. But not to return them. They kept them." Angus closed his eyes and drew in a breath. "Jim's dead. I couldn't save him."

175

Saka put his arms around Angus. "Healing is not easy. Harder when it is not wanted. We laid him out like a mage. He didn't die alone." Saka was surprised to feel the opening in the void and then shocked to see Jim tumble through, bleeding and partially paralyzed from the scarlips' sting. All he and Wek had been able to do was hold his hand and ease his suffering until he gave his soul to Demonside.

They had a short debate about whether he should get a cairn or be laid out like a mage. In the end they decided to make a big deal about a trainee choosing to die there and rebalance. Thus he was laid out on the sand, away from the tents, so the animals of Demonside could use his body.

"I should've been able to save him." Angus's body didn't melt toward his. It remained rigid, filled with anger and hurt. "I was a fool to trust the underground. There has to be another way."

"I am looking for those other demons—Becha, Lox, and a few others I can trust—we are making a network of telestones, and I reach out every evening and go farther across the sand than I ever thought possible."

"But not far enough."

Saka shook his head. Maybe the other demons were so far away that they couldn't be reached. But he had started the process, and he had to keep going. He wasn't ready to give up on something so important. "For the moment the underground is all we have."

"No. They just want to take the college's power for themselves."

"They don't need to destroy two worlds to have power. Helping them tear down the college is still our best option."

Angus grimaced and broke Saka's embrace. He took a few steps away and kept his gaze on the floor. "You should know I took the two telestones I made with me. I gave one to Terrance."

Saka pressed his lips together. He didn't go through Angus's things while he was away, so he hadn't noticed the stones were gone. Miniti would be furious if she found out what Angus had done. He should've asked first, though Saka would've said no. Not because he was jealous, but because he didn't want to accidentally hand demon technology to the enemy. "Those stones shouldn't have crossed the void."

Angus went on as though Saka hadn't spoken. "We got them to work in my room, despite the magical dampeners. No nosebleeds." He smiled, but it didn't reach his eyes. "What if the college has made a giant telestone to store the magic stolen from here?"

"You can't store magic over there."

Angus touched the scar that Saka had carved into his chest. One day Angus would have enough control over magic to erase Saka's name and his claim on him. "It can be stored, just not for long. It needs an anchor to keep it from dissipating. I know that because I can gather and hold on to magic by using this scar. The telestone will probably empty faster over there, but we're going to put them in areas where magic naturally gathers, to see if that will help keep them charged. We'll keep them safe and hidden too. But what if the reason the college keeps bringing the demons through is to top up their magical battery? They must be constantly trying to stop the magic from leaching out. The minute they use it as a weapon, the magic will be available for everyone to use again."

Saka rocked back on his heels. His tail curled around his thigh as he considered what Angus had suggested. That he and Terrance had gotten the telestones to work across the void was amazing. That the college was using something similar to lock up all magic was something he hadn't thought possible. "What they see as power is a weakness they are trying to hide. They cannot keep it charged no matter how many demons they kill."

"And if it doesn't exist? Maybe the idea of it has power. After all they don't need all magic. They just need most. Enough that other countries will bow to them because they want the cold to end."

And then Vinland would dole out just enough magic to keep everyone happy but not enough that they could ever rise up. In the meantime Demonside would be destroyed. "When they run out of demons, they will all be wizards."

"I don't think they even care about that. Demons are a means to an end. It's not yet Solstice and the snow is knee-deep. There'll be no crops this year. People are going to die. They already are dying because of the cold. Other countries won't trade with Vinland and countries that don't use magic are talking about military strikes. There's going to be a war. If they targeted the college's magical store, that would actually be a good thing. Then the magic would be free to be rebalanced."

It was a wild idea, possibly with deadly consequences. As much as Saka wanted the magic rebalanced, destroying a device used to store magic was not the way to do it. "Bring your telestone. Let me show you what happens when one is destroyed."

Angus paled, and his freckles looked dark against his skin. "This is not going to be good."

"No it is not. You best hope Terrance is careful with the telestone you gave him." It wasn't that Angus had given Terrance a stone, it was that he'd gone behind Saka's back to do it that hurt.

"You didn't warn me that telestones were dangerous."

"I didn't think you would sneak one across the void. I thought you would speak to me first. Tell me about your planned experiment." Angus hadn't trusted him. So few did. Perhaps it was him at fault.

"I thought you'd be weird because it was Terrance. And I thought you'd say no." Angus glanced at his toes. "The underground is keeping us apart, and I wanted to be able to talk to him."

He would've said no, but he could understand Angus's reasons. "And if the stone fell into the wrong hands? If you had been discovered? You want to keep him safe?"

Angus looked up, his face hard and unreadable. "Of course I want him to be safe. But I need to be able to talk with him freely, not with the underground determining when and where. He wants to be free of all of this. He no longer wants to play rugby, which was the whole reason he was at college on a scholarship. He never wanted to be a warlock."

"Sounds like someone else I know."

Angus blinked as though he realized the truth in that statement for the first time. "And yet we both are."

"Being a warlock doesn't have to be a bad thing. Demons and humans have worked magic together for eons. It is only because of the college you see it as a bad thing. But even then, not all college warlocks are bad people."

"They let this happen without saying a word. They had a choice."

Saka's lips turned up at the corners, but it wasn't really a smile. "We all have choices. Sometimes doing nothing is all that can be done." He paused. "Usi is no longer my second. You will hear talk about what happened. How I am weak for not keeping her for three days as punishment."

He hadn't wanted her anywhere near his tent. Tapo had fulfilled that part of the tradition. His first job as second.

"This experiment won't last the year." Angus's words were soft.

"No." There was nothing else to be said. They were fighting a losing battle, and their allies had turned their backs.

THEY ATE with other demons and acted as though everything was fine despite the tension. If Miniti didn't do something to heal the fractures, soon the tribe would splinter—though the blame for the damage lay with Usi and her ambition. She'd voted for the human trial, but changed her mind before it had enough time to work.

Saka had shared with no one the turmoil within the underground.

Usi also ate with the tribe. She wasn't hiding or healing the scars, and she acted as though she didn't care about the loss of status. No one spoke about it. Maybe they didn't want a human to overhear demon problems.

The other two human trainees were absent. Saka could only hope that Tapo and Wek would take their responsibilities seriously. He had no idea how close they were to Usi or how easily they would be swayed by her talk. For all Saka knew, she was rallying support among the other mages who wanted immediate action.

As pleasant as it was to sit under the stars after a good meal, they had already watched the sun set and the moon rise. The sky was dark, and he had work to do.

Saka put his hand on Angus's thigh.

Angus glanced at him and nodded. While no one had treated him any differently, attitudes had changed. Did they all think Angus was a college spy?

Saka stood and gave his thanks for the meal. He didn't wait, but he hadn't gone far before Angus caught up with him. "Miniti will be expecting to see some rebalancing tonight."

"The void won't be opened for another nine days." Once there would've been fear in Angus's voice. Now it held an edge.

"I know." Saka was well aware that there were nine days to go and that, if Angus let too much of the magic out, his eyes would go pale again. How long until he was drained completely after that happened? He needed to teach Angus how to survive. He wanted to be able to lie with Angus without worrying about killing him with each caress. "You need to work on holding back and controlling the flow of magic."

A groan slipped past Angus's lips.

Saka smiled. Angus groaned now, but later they would be sounds of pleasure. "It could save your life."

Self-healing was something else Angus would need to learn to survive. And water raising. He had to be able to use the magic around him, not what was within him. Demonside would suck him dry long before lack of water and injury could claim him.

Saka held open the flap of his tent, and Angus followed him in. Angus went around and lowered the other flaps, cutting off the breeze, but giving them privacy.

There were some who had watched them in the field before they took their pleasure alone. While Saka didn't begrudge them their curiosity, he didn't need to satisfy their every desire.

Had that night in the field pushed Usi to the edge? She hated that Saka was happy and teaching and head mage. And in love. She must have seen Angus and him. While Angus was away, Saka had thought a lot about what Guda had said. Love didn't have to be a weakness. He still valued her words above others. But he didn't know how to put those words into actions that wouldn't appear that he was betraying his tribe.

Angus pulled off his shirt. He was still pale, but not like he had been. Demonside had dusted him in gold and copper freckles. It had carved muscles in his limbs and chest.

"Shall I continue?" Angus had one hand on the fastening of his pants.

"No." Was Angus ready? Saka had to push. If he didn't, Angus would never survive what was coming. "You are in charge tonight. You control the magic, your rebalancing."

Angus swallowed, and his eyes widened. "I don't know. What if I screw it up?"

"Then we try again another time. I do not expect you to wait until the stars have spun across the sky. Just try. Maybe it will help you gain control of how much you release if you are the one who has to think about what is happening."

"And you're just going to go along with it?"

"I have rediscovered the joy of not being in control." Saka drew back the bedsheet. "Although I will ask that you do not let the magic dissipate."

"Right. So I need to think about directing the magic into the orbs at the same time as doing the rest." Angus's forehead furrowed as he thought about what he needed to do.

"And holding the circle." Saka wasn't going to help him. "You have done it before on your own."

"But I also have to control how much magic leaks out of me and think about you."

"Yes." Saka nodded. "I never said it was simple."

"You made it look easy." His teeth raked over his lip in a way that was most tempting. Angus's lips were soft, the lower lip plump for biting.

Saka clasped Angus's hand. "It is not. It takes time to learn and longer to do well. You need to start. Sex magic is your strength."

The frown hadn't left his forehead.

"I will go and make myself ready." Saka gestured to the bed. "You can gather your thoughts."

"I don't think that's going to help."

"You know what to do." Saka placed his hand over Angus's heart. It beat fast beneath his palm. While Angus thought about what needed to happen, Saka was already anticipating it. It had been a long time since someone else had been in charge. Mages looked to him and while there was satisfaction in pushing someone to their limit and watching the magic build, there was a different pleasure in being the one who was pushed. Lust swam through his blood like a dangerous creature looking to feed.

Angus kissed him and swept his tongue across Saka's lip. But when Saka opened his mouth, Angus drew back. There was a glint in his eyes, and Saka realized it had begun.

CHAPTER 22

SAKA WALKED away and let the delicate cloth unravel to block the bed from view. Angus released a sigh but knew he didn't have long to get himself together. He had no idea how do to this. He liked it when Saka was in control. Heat raced through him at the memories, but he was never going to be able to pull off anything like what Saka did.

But just thinking about having Saka at his mercy made him hard.

He'd failed horribly the first time he ever tried sex magic with Jim. He winced as he remembered again that Jim was dead. But that was a scab he could pick at later. He needed to think about what Saka did to him and why it worked.

The first time Angus had been with Saka, Saka hadn't even come, and he'd been fully dressed. The whole aim had been to make Angus come and rebalance. That was still going to have to happen, but he needed to control how much. There were so many things to think about, but that was a good thing. They were distractions from what his body would want the moment he got naked.

So he wouldn't take his pants off.

The tension eased a little. And while it wasn't a plan, it was a start, and that was better than nothing. But he hadn't asked what Saka planned to do with the magic stored in the orbs. Maybe nothing.

Was there anything he wanted to do with the magic once it was gathered and controllable? He ran his hand over his stomach. His scar was still visible—a jagged line that hinted at how close he'd come to losing his life at his father's hand. Removing that would be a fitting use for the gathered magic.

He rolled his shoulders and crossed the floor of the tent. Then he paused for a moment before he swept aside the cloth.

Saka lay on the bed, naked and looking perfectly relaxed. He must have done it so many times that it meant nothing. It was all about the magic. Angus would have to separate lust from magic when he was with Saka.

A small smile formed as Angus looked at Saka. The lines were blurred. They weren't just warlock and mage, bound together by magic. But Angus needed to make this about magic, not love or lust.

Saka watched him and slid his tail over the bed as though inviting Angus to join him.

Angus brought up the circle. It shimmered brightly and blue. That was the easy part. He glanced up at the orbs strung from the ceiling. If he could get them to glow even slightly, he'd call his attempt a success.

How did he start? When he'd been alone, it hadn't mattered if he failed. Now Saka would judge his every move.

Angus swallowed his nerves. He needed to move and not make it awkward. With measured steps Angus walked to the bed and knelt on the edge. It would be so much easier if Saka weren't watching him. He glanced around and saw the oil and a clean cloth near the bed. Saka had gotten organized while Angus was wondering what to do.

Angus reached out, snagged the cloth with his fingertips, and turned it into a blindfold. Saka's lips twitched into something resembling a small smile, and he lifted his head without being asked. While there wasn't enough cloth to tie it closed, when Saka rested his head again, the blindfold was in place.

Angus was free to do what he wanted.

He ran his fingertips up Saka's chest, over the scar he'd made after Guda's death, and up his throat to end on his lips. Then he kissed him slowly. And as much as he wanted to sink into the kiss, he held back and then broke away. He thought he heard Saka's breath catch as though he wanted more.

Angus swung his leg over and straddled Saka. There was no doubting Saka's desire. He was thick and hard, and Angus took a moment to rub against him, which did nothing to calm the heat in his blood.

Keep my pants on.

It was a reminder and nothing more, because he wouldn't need to take his pants off if he was creative.

He kissed and used his nails on Saka's skin, and he monitored the feel of the magic, the way it moved and swelled and the way Saka responded to each touch. He liked gentle scratches—what would've left a mark on Angus's body left no trace on Saka's much tougher skin. He also liked the little bites.

And as Angus worked his way lower, the magic took on a different vibration. While the orbs glowed faintly, the rest of the magic eddied around the room like a building storm. It lifted his hair and made the cloth walls ripple. The gold sigils on the cloth glimmered as though lit from within.

Last time he hadn't worried about directing the magic, but there hadn't been as much.

He glanced down at Saka to be sure he wasn't watching. Then he lifted his hands to flick the magic to the orbs… and it worked. The magic circled the ceiling, caught in the orbs, and intensified the glow. Magic burned beneath his skin as though seeking a way out.

Angus took a couple of slow, even breaths.

This is ritual. Nothing more. I've done this before.

But always from the other side, from Saka's position.

He ran his hand over Saka's cock, which was darker than the rest of his skin but just as rough. His own twitched in response. Saka drew in a breath as Angus grazed the sensitive head with his fingers. He nudged Saka's legs apart so he could pay some serious attention to the thick, hard length in his hand.

A quick lick and a stroke. Then just a taste of the head. He loved the rough texture of Saka's skin on his lips and tongue, but he couldn't get carried away. The idea was to keep Saka on the edge.

His own dick throbbed with the need for attention, but Angus was determined to ignore it for as long as possible. He took a little more in his mouth as Saka lifted his hips, and Angus continued to tease and indulge himself, knowing that he controlled when it would end. That alone was heady. The power of the ritual—the magic and lust— tumbled through him.

He became lost as he focused only on breathing and sucking and making Saka squirm with need. Angus would continue until he got a taste. He wanted Saka to lose his careful restraint. But the temptation to put his hands down his pants became stronger with each beat of his heart. He swept his tongue over the head and tasted the burned honey of Saka's come. Just a drop. Angus groaned around the mouthful of cock.

He released Saka and struggled with his own desire for several breaths. He welcomed the distraction of the building magic as lust lit the room so he could regather his fragile composure. The orbs were bright. If nothing else, he'd gathered some magic and captured it for later use.

Angus slowly moved his hand up and down the length of Saka's cock. Saka clawed his nails into the bedsheets, and his chest lifted with each quick breath, but he managed to retain control.

He was never going to get Saka to beg for release, but it wasn't about begging. It was about magic—building that edge of excitement and maintaining it. Saka couldn't fight the lust in his blood, but he had learned to control its release. Angus was fairly sure it wouldn't matter what he did. Saka would be able to hold out. Even the friction of Angus's pants on his skin was torture on his aching cock. He needed to finish while he was still in control.

Angus grazed Saka's balls and then slid lower to the tight pucker of his ass, and Saka sucked in a breath. Angus pressed one finger in and felt the slickness of the oil Saka used to prepare. If he hadn't been watching for every reaction, he would've missed the slight arching of Saka's back and the quivering tip of his tail.

He added a second finger and left his other hand on Saka's dick.

Saka bent his knees and lifted his hips as though he wanted more, but he didn't say a word. Angus's breathing was fast, and the knot of lust in his belly was tight. The magical light made the sweat on his skin gleam. He hadn't released any magic yet, but it bubbled in his blood, and it would be too easy to let it all wash out of him in one massive tide of ecstasy. If he did, he'd never survive the nine remaining days.

He released Saka's cock and fumbled with the tie of his pants until he felt warm air on his sensitive skin. He'd never fucked another man, but that was all he wanted to do. He pressed his cock to Saka's ass and hesitated for just a moment, in case Saka didn't want it. But Saka spread his legs a little farther and offered himself up. Angus pushed in and stretched the tight ring of muscle.

It was different to being in a mouth—hotter, tighter. He groaned and almost forgot about the magic. But he rocked back and thrust in deeper.

Never once had he thought he'd have Saka blindfolded and spread before him, but it was a sight he'd never forget. His balls tightened. He wouldn't last much longer, and he still had to hold back the magic but not his climax.

He gripped Saka's hips. "This is it."

Giving in felt good.

Saka used his tail to flick the blindfold away. He held Angus's gaze. "Touch me."

Angus wrapped his hand around Saka's cock, and it only took a few quick strokes. Saka's come spilled onto his belly in thick ribbons as he gasped for breath.

Angus, having outlasted Saka, shuddered and came. He drew out the sensation with each thrust, and it took everything he had not to let all the magic rush out of him. He let a few drops out, like a tap that hadn't been fully turned off. Then he tightened his grip and stopped even that small release. His blood still fizzed, and his skin tingled. For a few breaths, it felt as though he wasn't done. But the sensation faded as his body recognized that the lust had been sated.

Neither of them moved. The room was bathed in light from the captured magic. Saka gave a small nod. "Now to use the magic."

Angus glanced down. "I want to know how to heal myself."

WHERE THE river had been, there was just a dry gulch. When Angus dug his fingers in to feel for wet sand, he had to dig down a forearm's length. He brought up a handful and showed it to Saka. "It's not that deep."

"Not yet, so it shouldn't be too hard for you to raise it." Saka sat back and watched while he made another telestone to leave there when the tribe moved on. Miniti knew nothing about the web of telestones he had laid across Demonside. No one knew, except for the mages who also left stones.

The sun struck Angus's back hard. Even through his shirt, he felt as though he were burning, cooking from the outside in. Saka had told Angus not to bring water. And while the tents weren't that far away—maybe one hundred paces—there was still an expanse of shimmery red sand to cross. In the middle of the day, one hundred paces might as well be one hundred miles.

His throat and tongue were dry, and they hadn't been out there long.

No, he wasn't cooking. He was desiccating—drying into a piece of human-shaped jerky. If he failed, he'd die. Angus tried to swallow, but there was no moisture in his mouth.

He brought up a circle and drew magical energy to him. Then he tried to drag the water up through the hole he'd made. His fingertips brushed water and he was able to scoop out a small handful of gritty liquid. He didn't care. He drank and relished the sweetness in his mouth. Then he spit out the sand, and grit clung to his gums.

"You just wasted what you took in. A little sand won't kill you. A lack of water will."

Angus reached his hand down the hole, but the water was gone already. He swore. At least it was cool in the hole. It would be nice if he could climb in. "It's sunk already."

"If water were easy to pull up, everyone would be able to do it. You know enough magic to bring up plenty of water to stop us from dying."

"You're going to make me sit here until I succeed or die?"

"Are you going to sit there and question me until you are too close to death to do anything?" Saka tilted his head. His dark red skin glittered in the sunlight, and his horns gleamed. He was beautiful and as perfectly calm as though it weren't an important lesson.

Angus shivered despite the heat. He was pretty sure Saka didn't use sex magic to draw up water.

Blood magic?

Just the magic that was around?

He could cheat and draw from himself, but if he were in the desert alone, that would only hasten his death. He had to do it without cheating or Saka would know, and he would wear that disappointed expression that Angus couldn't stand.

He pulled one of his sharp little knives—the handles were bone and always felt cold, which in the heat was a relief.

"Given that you can't heal yourself, is that a good idea?" Saka asked. He wouldn't help, but he wouldn't let Angus fail either.

Angus stared at Saka. "Fine. Come and bleed for me."

"And what emotion will you use?"

He was all out of lust, and it was too hot to do anything. His skin was sticky with sweat, and he wasn't even moving. It was clear that fear wouldn't work on Saka, and Angus didn't want to delve into pain.

He shoved the knife away and stuck his hand back into the hole. He was about ready to widen the hole, shove his face in, and suck on the wet sand. He hesitated, but then he did exactly that. With his mouth only an inch from the bottom of the hole, he took a moment to enjoy the damp and shade. Was Saka checking out his ass? He almost pulled his head out to glance at Saka, but he didn't.

His lips twisted into a smile. He'd thought he was out of lust, but maybe he could use it. So he reached out to the magic and to the water that he could feel flowing swiftly beneath the sand and rock. He could also feel the fissures in the rock that would let the water through. He exhaled and imagined the water funneling up toward him.

It splashed him in the face and then eddied around his ears. He drank, but not enough to make himself sick, and he swallowed the grit. When he pulled his head out of the sand, he flicked back his wet hair and put his sun hat back on.

"Water is ready."

Saka got up and had a look. He took a small drink and nodded. "Now how will you do that when the river is deeper than you are tall? Will you waste your last few hours digging down? You need to bring it to the surface."

Angus followed Saka a dozen paces away.

"Draw up water." Saka sat down to continue his work.

Angus's hair was already dry. He was hot and longed for the shade of a tent. "If I can't bleed, then how? Why insist on me bringing the knives?" But even as he spoke, he realized it wasn't Saka or he who should bleed. He needed a sacrifice, but there was nothing but sand and a few trees desperately clinging to life on the other side of the dry riverbed.

If there were trees, then there was life.

He turned to Saka. "And what happens when there are no more trees and nothing left to kill?"

"There is always life. You just aren't seeing it. Creatures hibernate through the dry."

"Is that what you do, kill to raise the water?"

"No, I can do it without. But few can. You should be able to, eventually."

"So I have to hunt before I can drink? Won't that eat into the last few hours I have before I die of thirst?" Although he was hungry. Could he kill something and then eat it? His stomach rolled, and it wasn't from the gritty water he'd drunk. He'd never killed anything or had to prepare it for eating. But if he were to survive, he needed to learn. "This would've been done already with sex magic."

"Yes, but what is the point of proving something we both know you can do. You need to learn the harder ways. You need to be able to draw on many skills, not one. Your life—"

"I know." He pulled off his hat and wiped sweat off his face. "I also know that I wouldn't be sitting out here in the noon sun doing this. I'd be fine if I could rest somewhere until dusk."

"I thought you'd need the motivation."

Angus scowled. His mouth was gritty, and sand scoured his throat every time he swallowed. He glanced back at the hole and wished he could stick his head back in to take another drink.

Find something to kill. What kind of person was he becoming where that even seemed like a reasonable thing to do?

Saka turned the rock over in his hand. "We aren't leaving here until there is surface water."

"That means you go hungry and thirsty too."

Saka shrugged. "I was an apprentice before I was a mage. Guda was far less gentle than I am being with you."

Angus couldn't imagine Guda pushing Saka to his breaking point. If she had, it was all forgiven a long time ago. Saka missed her, and he still wore the scar.

Instead of reaching out for water, Angus searched for life buried in the sand. His magic touched something big in the river below, but it swam away. He had reached too deep. He wanted to close his eyes to concentrate, but Saka was trying to break him of that habit too. Angus needed to be able to see what he was doing and the magic he was using. He probed the sand, and ribbons of yellow magic darted across the surface.

Then he felt it—a stirring of life. Was it one of those eel things curled up in a burrow? If it was, it would do. And they could

191

eat it. The eels were greasy and delicious when cooked over an open fire.

He walked over to where he was, sensed it, and began to dig close by. When his fingers brushed its hardened cocoon, he pulled it out and dropped it into his hat. It did not look as appetizing as the eels did when they were swimming, or even cooked.

Without his hat, the sun struck the top of his head as though it were trying to bake his brain. The sooner he got water up to the surface, the sooner it would be over. Angus walked back to where he'd been standing and knelt down. He had to do it right, so he made a circle, drew up everything he could without tapping into himself, and then he laid the eel on the ground. He kept a hold of it with one hand, in case it woke up and escaped, and then he took its head off with one of his knives. Its dark, greenish blood spilled on the sand, and Angus let the rest of the magic go too and used it all to bring the water to the surface.

He expected a gush, but it was more of a trickle. His knees grew damp, and then the water bubbled up around him and made a very shallow small lake. Still holding the eel in one hand and the knife in the other, Angus lay down in it and relished the cool on his skin.

"Water." It was the most wonderful thing ever.

A shadow loomed over him. "Good. Now you can cook the eel, and we can eat."

The sun behind Saka's head blinded Angus, and he blinked. "I'll gather some wood in a moment."

"No, you will cook it with magical fire. Wood or dung is not always available."

Angus let his head tip back. Water swirled around his ears and blocked whatever Saka said next. Would the day's lesson never end?

IT WAS dusk by the time Angus got to have a proper meal—eel wasn't as tasty when he had to clean it and cook it, but as Saka had said, it was better to eat it than waste it, and he needed to know how to find and prepare food—and a shower. He'd never appreciated the water in the wash tent so much.

It was terrifyingly clear that Saka was preparing him for a time when the underground wouldn't open the void. That was a possibility that he tried not to think about every time he stepped across to Demonside. The tribe would be there... wouldn't it?

Or did Saka expect more trouble?

Lizzie walked into the wash tent. Angus had to either talk to her or politely ignore her. That seemed to be the only two ways of dealing with other people in the communal showers. Many people came with their friends. Angus wanted to be by himself. He was exhausted and just wanted to shower and sleep, so he opted to politely ignore Lizzie and focus on washing.

She had other ideas. "We need to talk."

She hadn't spoken to him since Jim's death. And given that he had no idea what to say to her, that was fine. He turned to face her, but she hadn't taken her clothes off to wash. There was a shoulder-high fabric screen between them, and his towel was with his clothes. Usually he wouldn't be bothered about the naked walk to retrieve the towel, but he didn't want to step past the screen. "About what?"

"About everything."

The water ran out. His time was up. After seeing how hard it was to raise water, he wasn't about to sneak a second shower the way he once had.

"Can you pass me my towel?" Couldn't it have waited until morning... or never?

She looked at him for a moment and then crossed to his pile of clothes and tossed the towel to him.

He caught the cloth, wrapped it around himself, and stepped away from the shower. "I'm sorry about Jim. I tried. I really did."

He'd spent a lot of time trying to block out the hot, sticky feel of Jim's blood, the way he could feel Jim dying with every beat of his heart, and the panic and the realization that no one was coming to help. Jim had known the underground was being poisoned from the

193

inside, and Angus suspected that the underground knew Jim could be bought by the highest bidder and had decided it would be better to let him die.

"I know. I don't blame you. I blame them." There was no sadness in her eyes. Her expression was hard, her mouth set in a grim line. "It's them I want to talk about… in part." She tilted her head.

Angus frowned. Then he realized she also wanted to talk about what was going on around them. "There's been a few changes," he said carefully.

"Yes…." She moved closer. "We need to be careful. There is very little stopping them from sacrificing us. Tapo has been teaching me how to rebalance in blood to prove my usefulness to Demonside."

"Too much, and Demonside will suck you dry." Angus stepped closer and lowered his voice. "You need to control how much you let out."

"We need a plan. If Saka's toppled, we're dead."

"He's not going to be toppled. Usi has been demoted."

"She still has supporters who'd like to see us bleed out. If the underground fails to open the void, that may happen. Saka and others threw in with the underground, but if they're no longer seen to be supporting us, what then?"

Then they were stuck in Demonside until it gradually killed them. That was the future Saka was preparing him for. And where would Saka be in all of that? Did he expect Usi to knife him?

All relaxation and sense of satisfaction from a day of success fled from Angus as worry turned the screws on his delicate future— too tight and his life would fracture. He wasn't ready to give his soul to Demonside. "What do you propose?"

"We can't refuse to come here. If we do, we'll be turned over to the college. They were quite clear in their threats. We need to get across the border."

Angus huffed out a breath. He'd had that thought so many times. "Where to? To the Nations? They don't like demon magic. I'm tainted, but you might be able to convince them you're clean.

The Mayan Empire kills those who cross their borders." Yet they understood demon magic and rebalancing.

"There are other counties. We could get a boat and get to international waters."

"Vinland would kill us before it let us go. We'd never reach the ocean, much less be able to defect. That's what you're talking about. It means giving up on our country and believing that we can't make a difference."

She gave him a sad smile. "You sound like Jim."

Maybe he still believed there was a chance for it all to be put right, but he didn't know how. He didn't want Vinland destroyed, and yet the sanctions and the ice age would do that. The college's propaganda had seeped into the hearts and minds of too many. They wouldn't believe a lone voice that spoke the truth. "Even he sold out in the end."

"No, he gave his soul to Demonside. He did the right thing at the end. You helped him do that. I'm glad you were able to do it before you were stopped." She gripped his arm. "Can you open the void from inside the house?"

"No, but I can in the garden," he said carefully.

"How did you get so fast? You didn't even walk the circle to contain it. I thought only third-year students could open it without a prop."

He was about to say practice, but that wasn't everything. He was becoming more sensitive to magic. He was able to use it better and direct its flow. While he was a long way short of Saka, he was well ahead of Lizzie because Saka was teaching him how to work like a demon, and for demons, magic was always there and ready to be used. Lizzie's mage was teaching her as a human and not sharing the power of sex magic or blood magic.

"You know the answer."

"Skitun," she whispered.

"The worst kind of warlock." He smiled, but it was spoiled by the bitterness he felt at hearing that word. He was a rogue, and he was having sex with his demon.

"You're the only warlock I trust." She held his hand. "If… when this all goes sour, do you have a plan?"

"Not yet." He glanced at her. She was hoping for something… anything. And he had nothing. "But I'll die here before I let the college arrest me and throw away the key."

Lizzie nodded. "Count me in."

CHAPTER 23

SAKA KNEW the moment he woke up that something was amiss. There was a vibration on the air, and a scratching at his brain that meant other mages were trying to contact him. While Angus slept, Saka slipped out of the tent to return their calls. He knew what they were about the moment he reached out to the rest of Demonside. The flow of magic was in turmoil. A sandstorm of massive proportions was coming in fast.

He used the telestone to make contact, and the other mages confirmed what he sensed. Some of the smaller tribes had been hit hard and were requesting assistance. Given that his tribe was about to be hit, he had to apologize and promise to call after the storm passed. He woke Miniti and informed her of the coming danger so she could get everyone to prepare. It was crucial that they store water to last the storm. Saka gathered the mages and their humans to discuss how best to protect the town. He didn't know if Norah and Lizzie would be able to help, but anything they could offer was better than nothing.

Usi stood opposite him with her arms crossed. There was still a rift between them that Saka had no desire to heal. But she was as ready to help as everyone else. He had to keep in mind that she believed she was acting in the best interest of the tribe. While he didn't agree with her assessment, he still respected her position. It was easier to see her point of view when he wasn't being directly threatened. Because she had caused the divide in the tribe, she should work to mend it, and as far as Saka could tell, she wasn't.

197

"This storm will take close to a day to pass. Tribes with only two mages have suffered deaths. We are fortunate we can take it in shifts to defend the town, but it will still be hard."

"What exactly are we going to do?" Angus squinted at the horizon as it darkened with the approaching storm.

"Tapo will make a hard circle." As second mage, Tapo needed to perform those duties. And Saka needed to split up the mages into shifts. He glanced at their expectant faces. Whose magic was strongest, and whose was weakest? "Wek, you will work with me and Angus and Norah. Usi, Tapo, and Lizzie will be the other shift. When you aren't holding the dome, you will eat and rest. Understood?" The humans had the wide-eyed expression that hinted they had no idea but weren't willing to say anything. It was most unhelpful. "Angus?"

"Will we be outside the dome?"

"No. We will be just inside." Being outside the magical dome was a death sentence.

"Pouring magic against a storm that has flattened other tribes?" It wasn't a lack of understanding on his face. It was fear. Angus had never seen a sandstorm.

Saka had never seen one that big. "The only reason the other tribes were damaged is because their mages tired." Saka took a moment to look at each of his mages. "Usi, can you please check on the water depth?"

Water had been known to drop away when a storm approached. They wouldn't be able to stop and raise it again until after the storm passed. If people hadn't gathered enough before the storm hit, there would be some thirsty people waiting until someone was strong enough to raise it—which could be a while if they poured everything into protecting the town.

Usi nodded. "Anything else?"

"Not at the moment. Be ready for the second shift."

When she left, Saka looked at the humans. He didn't bother to be gentle with them. "Be ready to pour that fear out in your blood. We may need it to survive."

STANDING AT the edge of the circle and feeling the wind pick up always filled Saka with nerves. He wouldn't call it fear because it wasn't that developed. He faced the storm. Angus was a quarter of the way around to his left and Wek was to his right. Norah was on the opposite side, where the storm would be weakest.

The hard circle was a line of sand that Tapo hardened into a small ridge of stone no higher than the length of a finger joint. Having a physical focus would make it easier to hold the dome when they started to tire. The sand had already started to build up along the edge. Sand danced across the surface and was flung into the air, stinging his skin. He didn't want to raise the circle to early or too late. So he waited.

He narrowed his eyes to protect them from grit. The sky was dark, and the storm towered over them. They would survive. Miniti had made sure the village was made as small as possible. Tents on the edges had been brought down, and all the livestock had been brought to the center. The tribe wouldn't clean up afterward. They would spend the day packing. By the time the storm passed, they would be ready to move.

And he'd be ready to sleep.

The wind grew stronger, and the sand more furious. Saka exhaled, brought up the circle, and snapped it closed at the top. Angus, Norah, and Wek pushed energy into it.

It wasn't a perfect barrier, but it would break the force of the storm. The sand would fall on them, but not wipe them off the surface of the world. All they had to do was hold the circle while the storm was within touching distance.

He could've sat in the middle of the circle, hiding among the tents, but the magic wouldn't have been as effective. He needed to read the storm and feel its rage so he could adjust the dome. The side that faced the storm was the strongest, the other side weakest. That would change as the storm hit and swallowed them.

Sand and wind hit the dome and pressed against the magic as though the storm wanted to destroy them. The energy of the storm was too wild to draw up and use, but Saka could reach the edges. He could pull from the ground. Sand drifted across the magical barrier and settled. He couldn't hold back every grain. No one could.

Sand had piled against his shins, and his mouth was dry when Usi came to stand beside him. Without a word she took over, and Saka stumbled back. He'd been still for so long that his legs needed to remember how to move. His body ached, but before he could rest, he needed to make sure that Wek, Norah, and Angus had been relieved.

They had been, and the three of them were given a meal in Saka's tent. Angus had three new cuts on his arm. Saka wanted to check his eyes, but Angus stared at his bowl and shoveled down the food without looking up. For the moment, Saka let him be.

Wek put her bowl down. "The center hasn't reached us."

"No. It won't for a while. Do not be fooled by the lull." Saka tapped Angus on the knee.

He nodded without looking up. "Eye of the storm is always quiet. I know."

"Get some rest. I will get you before we need to take over." Saka hoped that Tapo and Usi would be all right. He hoped that Lizzie wouldn't crumble, and that if she did, the mages could fill the weakness. The strongest mage always faced the storm, so that if the others weakened, the village would still be mostly protected.

When Wek left, Saka put his fingers under Angus's chin and tilted his head. Angus didn't resist, and his eyes were still blue—though Saka would swear they weren't as dark as they had been.

"I'm okay." He didn't sound all right.

"If you need to step away, then do it. I do not want you dying out there." The wind screamed, and the sound of sand falling on the tents was a constant rustle. Saka hoped they wouldn't be buried alive.

"I'm going to lie down." Angus got up and lay on the bed. He was asleep almost immediately.

Saka didn't sleep, but he did close off his connection to the magic so he could block it out for a little while. He didn't like being blind to the magic, but sometimes it was a relief, and he needed the rest. Too soon he'd have to stand against the storm.

On Saka's third shift, the storm trailed off. Sand drifts pressed against tent walls, but no one had been swept away, and no animals had been lost. They had survived, but it didn't feel like a victory.

Wek, Angus, and Norah had wavered for much of the shift, and their contribution was uneven. It was a relief to let the dome fall. Saka bent over and rested his hands on his knees and tried to muster the strength to step out of the sand piled against him and then the energy to check on the mages and humans.

There was still the stronger wind to contend with, but none of the mages had more to give, and he couldn't ask them to do more than they had. It was easy to see why so many tribes had succumbed.

Saka ate and drank as he walked. Wek and Lizzie were still at their places, but Angus had already left his place by the time Saka got there. He made his way back to his tent, but Angus wasn't there either.

The wind had almost blown itself out by the time he found Angus. He was standing at the riverbed, stripping off his clothing. The riverbed wasn't dry anymore. Water glistened in the evening sun. How had he raised so much water?

Angus walked into the water and disappeared beneath the surface.

Saka forgot how tired he was and ran over as Angus resurfaced and floated on his back. "You shouldn't be in there."

"I have been fantasizing about a bath since the first ten minutes of the storm. I have sand in places where there should most definitely be no sand."

Didn't everyone? "So use the showers."

"No."

"What did you do to raise the water?" Saka stood at the edge of the very small lake. The edges were made out of the sand deposited by the storm.

"I used the end of the storm. I realized it was fading and that there was magic in it. It's not very deep." He moved, and his head was all that was visible. "I can sit on the bottom."

"You used the storm to draw up water. Do you not realize how dangerous that is?" Not that splashing around in a lake tempting any lurking riverwyrms into taking him was any safer.

"The *end* of the storm. I stood there for hours feeling it, getting to know it. The end of it seemed pretty safe. It lacked the sting of a scarlips' tail." He ran his fingers through his hair and floated up onto his back again. "It took from me, and I took something back."

Angus drifted closer so he could look up at Saka. It was then Saka saw that Angus's eyes were completely white, and the void would not be opened for days.

"You don't have to watch me. I'm not going to drown," Angus said as though nothing were amiss.

Saka squatted down, and the water lapped at his toes. "You should've stepped away instead of drawing on yourself."

"It kind of slipped out. There's still more there. It bubbles in my blood."

"But your eyes...." He brushed Angus's cheek with his fingers.

"I think that's just the first sign."

That made sense. Clearly Angus was still strong enough to work some magic, and he seemed to be aware of when he was rebalancing and how much he had to give. That was progress. "What's the second one?"

"Thirst that can't be quenched."

How long before death followed?

Saka didn't want to watch Angus wallow in a lake of his own making. And Angus should have let people refill their jugs before he waded in.

As head mage, Saka needed to check on the water level near the spike, but he couldn't leave Angus alone out here either. He was too tasty a meal to any predator who had survived, though Saka didn't sense any nearby. "I'll send a hunter to watch."

"You could join me for a swim... well, it's more of a splash."

He could, but all his life he'd been told not to go in the water because of riverwyrms. "I'd rather not get eaten."

Angus reached up to grasp Saka's hand. For a moment he thought Angus was going to pull him in, but he didn't. Angus grinned. "I used the storm to do this. I didn't draw from me. Imagine being able to control a storm like that, to use the magic and redirect it."

"You can't harness a storm." But it was possible to use the tail end or the magic at the edges.

"But if there were more than one mage and you all worked together...." He released Saka's hand and drifted away.

Saka stood. Angus clearly wasn't ready to come back to the tent yet. "What would you do with that magic?"

"I don't know. Send it through the void the next time the college makes a tear and strike them all down?"

"That would just take more magic from us."

"Then I'd learn to control a blizzard... a snowstorm over there. Or I'd harness the people's fear about the ice age." He circled closer. "We will have to make a strike at the college soon, before the underground reveals itself as just another branch of the same toxic tree."

"And if you act too soon, you will pay the price." The demons couldn't win a war against the college. Last time there had *been* no college, only a loose collection of warlocks.

"I'm already paying. I have been since the day you dragged me across the void and showed me that magic is so much more than what they were teaching."

Saka looked away. He *had* dragged Angus in. The demons needed warlocks on the inside, people who could be shown the truth or at least used for information. Saka got more than he expected.

He left Angus to his swimming and sent a hunter to watch over him. Then Saka checked on the water level. Only then did he allow himself to lie down. His ears strained to hear Angus walking into the tent, but sleep overtook him before anyone slept next to him.

The bed was still empty when he was awakened by shouting. Something had happened to Angus. He created a light on his palm, pulled on pants, and went out expecting the worst.

Amid the shouting there was laughter as the demons praised a great hunter. Saka went toward the noise. Laid out in the center of the village was a riverwyrm. It was as long as two demons, and its head was broad enough to swallow a child whole.

Angus was no hunter, but that appeared to be part of the joke, as the real hunter, the winged demon he'd sent out to watch Angus, patted him on the back.

"What happened?" Saka asked the demon next to him.

"Angus makes good bait. He should go hunting more often."

People were already lighting fires to cook the riverwyrm. There would be a feast to celebrate surviving the sandstorm, and tomorrow they would walk to a new location. They should've started that night, but Miniti had seen how drained her mages were.

Angus's cheeks colored as he caught Saka's gaze, and he mouthed something that could've been "You were right."

CHAPTER 24

IT TOOK three days of being back in Vinland for Angus's eyes to return to blue. And he was sure they only changed back because he went outside, away from the magical dampeners. He'd been worried that the blue was never going to come back and that he'd be forever marked.

Angus ran his hand over his stomach. The scar that had been there was completely gone. He'd spent days working to heal that reminder. There was no longer any sign that his father had tried to kill him, just the occasional dream.

Magic couldn't heal everything.

As the Winter Solstice drew closer he wanted to call his mother to find out how she was doing, but he wasn't brave enough to make the request. She would've been told he was dead or believed him to be rogue and responsible for his father's death—and she'd be right about the latter.

The underground hadn't made him a criminal. He'd done that himself, but they were using it to keep him safe and keep him isolated. At first he'd been glad he could come back and be safe. But he'd come to resent it. He and the other trainees were all chafing to get out and do something instead of waiting.

If they had freedom, they wouldn't stay in Vinland. They'd find a way out. The underground must suspect them. Jim had said as much. But how much of what Jim said could he believe?

People did leave Vinland. He was sure that some of the stories about the surrounding lands were just to scare people. But he didn't want to find out if the Mayans really sacrificed those who crossed the border, and he didn't want to cross the no man's land between the

Nations and Vinland because it was said to be patrolled by creatures that weren't human or demon.

The telestone was cool in his hand. He wanted to sit outside and use it, but one of their guards was there, happily smoking a pipe and reading a newspaper. So Angus did another lap of the yard and another, as though he were getting his daily exercise by walking around the space like a rat on a wheel.

He was sick of the propaganda on the TV, but that was all they could get. The hacks into the outside world had been shut down, and he didn't know enough to find any for himself. Eventually he sat at the table with the guard. Sour blue smoke coiled out of the pipe. The man glanced at him, but he didn't seem to hate him like the other guard did.

Angus took it as an invitation to start a conversation. "Any exciting news?"

"Vinland has taken out several Mayan Empire ships that were forming a blockade to stop supplies getting through."

That was the front-page news, but was it the truth or something cooked up to make Vinland look good? "Who fired first?"

The man smiled. "What does it matter? We're at war."

"Who with?"

"Anyone who wants to stop us. They want our magic."

Except it wasn't Vinland's magic. Magic was like air or the oceans. It flowed and circulated. It made its way back and forth across the void. Or it *should* flow and circulate. Holding it stagnant had caused all the damage.

And that amount of magic couldn't be hidden.

The guard seemed to believe that Vinland was entitled to all the magic. Even those countries that banned demon magic and only allowed the use of what was naturally available must understand the flow.

"So what? They're going to bomb us until we give it up?"

The man nodded. "There was bombing over New London while you were away. The college fought back, created a storm that knocked the planes out of the sky."

Until that moment Angus had scanned the front page of the newspaper and tried to guess the words hidden beneath the man's thick fingers. He looked up. "New London was bombed?"

That wasn't the bit he was interested in. The college had made a storm. Had that been what triggered the storm in Demonside?

"Yup." The man flicked through a few pages and showed Angus the photos of the storm and the article that praised the quick work of the college—like the paper was ever going to criticize the college. The editor and writer would find themselves vanished.

"The underground must be concerned that they aren't acting fast enough." They were supposed to stop the college before it got serious.

The man shrugged and put down the paper. "I'm just here to make sure the college doesn't get a hold of you lot." He puffed out a cloud of smoke and then stood. "Have a read. Just remember, not everything in the paper is true. Hasn't been for a long time. Not since I was in college."

The man took his pipe and walked to the other end of the garden.

Angus wanted to read the paper—he hadn't read a good story in a while—but he desperately wanted to talk to Terrance. With the stone in his pocket and clasped in his hand, he stared blankly at the story of the attempted bombing and willed Terrance to answer.

Had the stone gone flat already or were they too far apart? It would be that much harder to charge, given that he couldn't work magic in the house and he was watched when he was outside. He should be grateful they didn't put a dampener on him when he stepped through the door. If they did that, he'd never be able to recharge, and he'd go back to Demonside depleted of magic and die that little bit faster. Maybe they didn't realize that. He wasn't going to tell them if they hadn't made the discovery.

He should've made another to swap it with Terrance and keep his own charged. He was about to give up, but he felt the touch of Terrance against his mind.

Then he was as clear in Angus's mind as though they were together. Angus didn't know if he was actually seeing him or recalling a memory. He'd have to ask Saka.

I really need to see you, Terrance said.

Me too. Angus knew his lips were moving. Hopefully the guard would just think he was sounding out the words. *Are you well?*

Terrance nodded, and a lock of his dark hair fell forward. He flicked it back in a move that Angus knew well. He *was* seeing Terrance, not a memory. He was almost sure of it. Or was he seeing a little of both? The image was what he knew, but it was given life by Terrance's thoughts.

We should ask them if we can get together for Solstice. Have a bonfire here or something. There would be music and dancing and bigger bonfires in the city as people rejoiced on the shortest day because the days would start to get longer until Spring arrived. Was there anything to celebrate this year? The days might lengthen, but winter wouldn't release its grip. *Or do you have plans?*

Terrance had a life. He wasn't trying to live between two worlds. He had a fledgling career and teammates and friends. For a moment Angus was jealous that Terrance was able to put aside everything and have a life, even if rugby was no longer his dream.

My only plan is to be with you.

Angus could hear the smile in his voice. He didn't deserve what Terrance offered. *We can only ask.*

I have already. Terrance paused. *I might have some good news by then. I'm meeting with someone. These bracelets can be tampered with. Not everyone plays rugby without using magic.*

What do you mean?

That some wizard players have found a way around the dampeners.

Angus's chest tightened for a moment. *There's a way around them? Why does no one talk about it? Why isn't the underground eliminating all of them?*

How could he switch off the ones in the house and stop the smothering that happened as soon as he walked through the door? He spent as much time as he could outside, bundled up against the cold, because he felt as though he couldn't breathe in the house. He let the guards assume it was because he was used to being outdoors in Demonside and that he was quite uncivilized. They had no idea how complex demon society was, how essential it was that everyone contributed.

Even him. Even when he was being a selfish idiot and making his own swimming pond. Saka had used him as bait to provide a meal for the tribe, instead of ordering him out of the water, but he had learned the lesson. The moment the riverwyrm made its presence known as it moved through the underground river, Angus had nearly gotten out of his little lake. Or was it a large puddle? Instead he signaled the hunter.

Panic had made his heart race, but he kept silent. The hunter drew her weapons, and a few heartbeats later, it was over. The riverwyrm broke the surface, tunneled through the sand, and burst into the pond. A spear through the head killed it, and his heart almost stopped. He'd been staring into the creature's eyes and could see its teeth. His hand shook so badly that it took him several tries to get dressed. If he hadn't been reaching out and feeling the magic that ran through Demonside, he would've missed it. Did riverwyrms also swim along the magical currents?

Terrance frowned. *Am I seeing bits of Demonside?*

Angus blushed. He hadn't realized Terrance was able to glimpse all of his thoughts. *Yes. That was me playing bait so we could get dinner.*

It looked dangerous.

It was. *I think it's safer over there.*

Terrance gave him a grim smile. *If I can get free of the dampeners....*

They won't know? You won't get into trouble?

I'll be careful. No one wants the college to know they can be gotten around. But I need to do it.

Given the way they've infiltrated the underground, they probably do know. It was the safest assumption to make—that the college knew anything the underground knew. *How worried are you about what's going on?* He'd thought Terrance safe and protected from the fear and hunger that was spreading everywhere. And Angus was sure he could only see a tiny part of the truth.

When I see you for Solstice, I don't want to go back. I need the bracelet disabled.

Angus swallowed. That was so soon—only days away. No one had made any good plans. *There's nowhere to go.*

Didn't you once say you'd rather take your chances in Demonside?

Yeah. That sounded like him. *But it's dangerous.*

But I'd be free and not constantly waiting for the threat to change to violence. I can't keep living like this. I know it's only a matter of time until the underground uses me to get to you... or the college makes me vanish.

Angus's heart lurched. He didn't want to imagine a world where Terrance wasn't around. And Terrance was more worried than he'd ever let on.

Footsteps crunched through the snow, and Angus looked up from the newspaper he was supposed to be reading. He hadn't turned a page, and he had no idea how long he'd been staring at the same one.

I have to go. He wanted to say more, but couldn't make the words, and he didn't know if he should say them even.

You too, Terrance said with a smile, as though he understood perfectly what Angus didn't say. Had Terrance sensed it? He was gone before Angus could ask what he had meant.

The guard drew closer, and Angus turned several pages at once to make it look like he'd been reading, not talking to someone using magic rocks. The telestone was hot in his hand.

New Holland was under attack by its northern neighbors. The paper called it another attack on demon magic by those who wanted to outlaw all magic.

"Time to go in. It's freezing out here." The guard took his paper away and tucked it under his arm. "I'll come out for a smoke after lunch."

Angus looked up at the man. That was an invitation to come out again. Angus could search for the college's telestone—their magical storage facility.

He smiled. "Are there any plans being made for Solstice?"

If Terrance was there and they got together with the other trainees, they might have a chance to flee. But there would be no coming back. He'd learned to not give up his magic. The others would have to learn fast or do no magic. Demonside would suck them dry. And once they got there, what then? They couldn't stay with Saka's tribe. They'd need to find the other demons.

The guard snorted. "You really think there will be a Spring to look forward to?"

The globe would still turn, the days would lengthen, but the world would be frozen for as long as magic was locked up. "I hope the underground will give us a reason to celebrate."

But he wasn't relying on them—not anymore.

He wasn't just a rogue warlock with a price on his head. He would soon be a traitor. But dying in Demonside would be a gentle death compared to what Vinland would give him, Terrance, and the other trainees.

CHAPTER 25

THE TRIBE was settled in their new location and water was assured. It hadn't dropped below the spike that was driven into the sand years before to provide ease of access for traveling tribes. Saka sat in his tent and unwrapped his telestone. A web of them now spread over the sand, but he wasn't sure if they'd be enough.

He didn't even know if the tribe was moving in the right direction. What if the other demons lived across the sea?

Before he tested his web of telestones, he did his job and contacted some of the other mages. He needed to find out how they fared during the storm. The news was troubling.

Demons have gone missing. And not just from this tribe.

During the storm? But Saka already knew what Dayth was suggesting.

No. Some of the demons had warlocks. The people last seen with them also vanished. It seems as though the warlocks are determined to take whatever they can. There is talk that we should do the same.

Usi would know that, and she would agree with those who wanted to take warlocks.

Dayth went on. *I know that we are supposed to wait for the humans to fight their own battle, but will there be any of us left? That storm was unprecedented in my lifetime.*

There is talk that large storms happened during the last war. Saka wasn't ignorant about the past, but he didn't want to relive it either. The war had devastated many tribes. It was said that before the war, there was much less desert. If Demonside hadn't healed from the last war, would it survive another?

Yes. Perhaps the war has already started, and we are refusing to see.

The war started the moment the warlocks broke the unwritten rules and stopped rebalancing.

How could they fight an enemy that controlled when the void would open?

Dayth nodded in agreement. *Some have been fighting back.*
What do you mean?

Not my tribe, but I heard that some have been attacking the warlocks. Demons with warlocks should be armed at all times. If nothing else, they should take their own life before the warlock can use it.

Saka rocked back. He didn't want to tell any of the demons in his tribe to take that precaution. *All demons with warlocks must be taught to open the void so they can escape from Humanside.*

And drag the warlocks through with them? Yes, it's already happening. But the warlocks are no longer summoning alone. They are gathering in groups and hitting hard. The animals are helpless. Warlocks have already grabbed a pack of scarlips. And that's just the one we know about. Your trainees didn't return them.

No. Angus had wanted to, but Saka understood Angus's reluctance to disobey the underground. Terrance would pay the price. Saka was in a similar position. He didn't want to push too hard in case Angus ended up suffering.

He had to put the tribe first, but how did he do that? What would guarantee the tribe's survival? Killing themselves to avoid capture wouldn't help them in the long run. The warlocks would just seek new demons to bond with. Saka doubted that any mages would step up, though they had the best chance to fight back, and that was the only way to win.

He wasn't ready to say that yet, certainly not to a mage he didn't count as a friend and ally. Dayth had supported the trainees because he wanted to know more about the humans, not because he thought it would save them. Saka only wanted the chance to avoid war, but he hadn't realized they were already fighting.

The scarlips didn't end up in the hands of the Warlock College, Saka said. If Angus was right, the underground *was* the college. The loss of Guda and her high-level warlock didn't seem accidental anymore. If the demons didn't fight back, the warlocks would drain Demonside until there was no more magic and no more demons. Nothing.

AT DUSK Saka contacted the half dozen mages he trusted the most. They gathered magic, and Saka pushed his mind through the web of telestones. He fragmented a little with each leap to the next one, until he was spread thin across the sand and stretched like a fiber to the point of breaking.

The other mages pushed their magic into the connection, and he reached to the next stone. In his mind he saw the stones glowing softly like fallen stars on the dark sand. He wasn't touching them all, so he reached a little farther.

The whole time he pushed out a message. *Mage Saka of the Lifeblood Mountain tribes is seeking contact with mages from across the sand.*

He was careful to keep the message open and not focused on any demon he knew. He wanted mages he didn't know.

There was another telestone, and a ripple brushed against the fraying edge of his mind. One of the supporting mages faltered. The stars in the sand wobbled. Then the flow of magic cut off, and all the stars went out.

Wek shook him. "Saka."

There was a herd of tacra stampeding in his head, and his mouth tasted like blood.

Wek touched his cheek. The cool brush of healing magic invaded his nose and head. At first it was pleasant, but it became painful fast. He grunted but didn't have the strength to fend her off.

Why was Wek in his tent?

He tried to form words, but nothing came out. Had he lost part of his mind? Reached too far? For just a moment, he'd felt the answering

214

mind of another mage. He didn't know who they were, but they'd heard him. It was a small victory.

He let Wek work and tried to recall the direction of the contact so he would know which way to focus. It was close to where the sun rose.

When Wek finished, Saka tried to sit up. She helped him and handed him a cup of water.

"Whatever you were doing, I felt it ripple over me. Then Becha called me and said I had to get to your tent." Wek squatted in front of him, concern etched on her face. Saka was head mage, but he wasn't invincible.

Becha had probably saved his life by calling Wek. Saka had warned Angus about the dangers of pushing too far, and then he did exactly that. Saka sipped the water. His mind couldn't be that broken because his thoughts seemed to be clear.

"I am okay. Thank you." Forming the words on his tongue was harder than it should be.

Wek looked skeptical. Saka saw the blood on the floor of his tent. It wasn't a few drops. His brushed his hand over his top lip, and dried blood came away. For how long had he lain bleeding? Had his brain also bled? "Was it bad?"

"You would have been dead by sunrise. Do not do it again without someone here. Becha told me to tell you that. I have to agree, even though I don't know what you are working on."

Saka breathed out and tried to contain the panic that speared his heart. He couldn't die. He had too much to do, and he had reached another mage—someone far away.

He wanted to try again that night, but he wasn't a fool. He'd need to wait—add more stones and increase the web. But there was no time. Every day he wasted was another day the warlocks stole and stored magic.

"Thank Becha for me." Again it took effort to form the words. Was there lasting damage? He didn't have the energy to heal himself.

"I am going to get you something to eat. I will not leave you tonight."

"Not a word to Usi."

"She will not hear it from me."

But if Wek had felt the ripple, how many other mages had?

CHAPTER 26

ANGUS DRESSED without a word. Whatever mission they were being sent on that night was obviously dangerous. Trainees were only sent on dangerous missions. They were never told where they were going or what they were going to be doing, until the last moment.

He never traveled without his bone-handled knives. On both sides of the void, they were always strapped to his wrist. They were the only weapon he could carry without raising questions.

Norah, Lizzie, and Angus got into the van. Three of the other trainees were already there, all dressed in black. He nodded to Dustin, the one trainee who'd offered his condolences and claimed to be a friend of Jim's. Syg was there, along with another man—both of them dressed in black.

No other trainees had been killed since Jim's death. But two had been injured and healed, which added weight to his suspicion that the underground wanted Jim to die. They expected him to turn again for the right price. Maybe they were right. Maybe he would've. The college was sentencing suspected traitors to death on a daily basis. There were no trials. Their lives were given to the college for ritual.

The only TV station still on the air talked about how great Vinland was and how jealous their enemies were. It claimed the Mayan Empire and the Nations were trying to steal their magic, that the World Council of Demonology had created the ice age.

It was all lies. How did everyone not see that?

But the college had been lying for years, pushing the truth a little further away each time. First it was the wizards who were to blame. They were unreliable and dangerous. Then, when the cold

217

became a fixture, they blamed the underground. Finally they turned against anyone who criticized them.

"Where are we going?" Angus tried to be calm.

"To save demons," Syg said. "You should like that." There was a curl to his lip when he spoke. He leaned closer. "Could you not find a human to satisfy you? What does your boyfriend think of that?"

Angus held Syg's gaze without flinching. He didn't say a word.

"He hardly gets to speak to his boyfriend," Norah said in his defense.

Syg leaned back and shot her a glare that would've made most people recoil. Norah didn't even blink. She'd been trying to get her hands on the old texts. Between the three of them they'd decided that she had the best chance. When they were in the house, Angus kept his distance and barely talked to the two women. In Demonside they talked about everything.

"Safer that way. Too many good wizards have been arrested."

The college ran the government—not officially of course, but the president seemed perfectly happy to let the college order him around. Did they have something on him, or had they helped him to power? The Vinland Angus thought he knew was unrecognizable.

The change had been so slow that he'd barely noticed it.

If Saka hadn't taken him to Demonside the day Angus first opened the void, he might still be blind. If Jim had never talked about the underground, he'd still be ignorant. Would he have followed his father's footsteps and helped the college or would he have woken up? He hoped that the latter was true.

The van stopped.

"We believe this is where the college is holding the captured demons. There are magical dampeners to stop the demons from attacking us."

"Then we can't use magic either," Angus said.

"No need to. We're breaking in and getting the demons into a truck that will be here in ten minutes."

No one spoke for several seconds.

"You should've brought thieves on this mission. Our strength is magic," Lizzie said without a smile.

"I am the thief," the other man said. "You're the demon herders. You know all about demons. You might even know some of them. Your job is to get them on the truck."

Dustin leaned forward. "And then where do they go?"

The thief shrugged. "I don't know. This is my part of the job."

"Now we have nine minutes. Try not to get caught unless you want to die before sunrise." Syg stood and opened the door.

A half-moon made the snow and ice gleam. The world was black and white and gray. They moved through the light industrial area and heard nothing but their own footsteps.

Around them magic glided over the snow and whispered in the breeze. Angus gathered it to him, and it heated the sigil Saka had carved into his chest. He was sure his eyes had darkened—no longer blue but closer to black as he held the magic within his body in case he needed it.

His skin tingled as though there were a storm brewing, but it was just because he was too full of magic. Oh, the rebalancing he could do....

He drew in a breath and let the cold fill his lungs. When he flexed his fingers, there was a crackle of static. When they reached the dampeners, it was going to hurt. The dampeners exerted pressure when they encountered magic, and it was worse when he was full.

He glanced at Lizzie, who gave a small nod.

She was gathering too.

They couldn't kill the dampeners with magic, but maybe they could take out the electricity. The thief was well ahead of them, and no one else was supervising them. Syg was staying warm and safe in the van.

Angus could've run. He could've vanished into the night. But for how long could he manage on his own? He wasn't ready to live in Demonside, and he wasn't ready to abandon Terrance. He had no doubt, if he ran, evidence would turn up and Terrance would be charged with treason to the college.

Then there were the other trainees. All their lives were in the hands of the underground. As much as he wanted to think the underground was the answer, he didn't believe it anymore. All they wanted was the power the college had. It had become infected by too many disaffected warlocks.

He'd been one of them once.

The thief opened the door, and no sirens went off. He beckoned them forward. Were there actually demons inside, or was it a trap? Angus wanted to take out the dampeners so they wouldn't be helpless. Powerful warlocks had ways to make sure they weren't affected by dampeners. Maybe they wore antidampener bracelets.

Would it be hard to make an antidampener? He'd look into it later.

Angus glanced up at the cable that connected the building to the electricity grid. No electricity, no dampener. He wasn't close enough for the dampener to dull his magic yet, but he could feel the edge. He'd be walking into a magic-free bubble in less than a dozen steps. In the distance a truck rumbled closer.

The demons couldn't get on that truck. He wouldn't let the underground take demons out of the college to use for their own rituals. The trainees slid along in the shadows of the building, but it was too quiet.

Angus glanced along the line and realized one of the trainees was missing.

Lizzie brushed against him and glanced at the side of the building where a dark shape was climbing. "Dustin's taking out the dampener. Saw you looking. Said good luck."

Angus nodded and hoped that Dustin didn't electrocute himself.

The dampener pressed against his skin. It smothered him and made the air thick like molasses. He was tempted to let go of some of the magic he was holding, but that was the way dampeners worked. They encouraged people to release magic, even if they didn't realize it. Angus refused to comply.

220

The thief was just inside the door. "Get the demons. The truck will be here soon." In his hands were the cables. The thief kept the alarm from going off by using the magic in his body.

Angus nodded, flicked on his flashlight, and made his way into the building. The hairs on his arms and the back of his neck stood on end. The singing voices of demons reached him as he moved deeper into the building. He responded—somehow he'd learned the words while he was in Demonside. The song was about rain and water.

There was a pause, and then the song resumed.

Angus moved more quickly. The air tasted of death and blood. It was heavy and metallic. The college must work their rituals there.

But where were the guards? Or had dispatching them been someone else's job?

He turned the corner and saw the cells of demons. "I'm here to let you out."

"Angus?" A blue demon stepped forward. He knew her.

"Yes." He looked at the cell door. There was no lock to pick. It was magical, and he couldn't use magic because of the dampener. He swore.

The air shimmered, something crackled, and static built on his skin. The dampener was down. He lifted his hands and, without bothering with a circle or any finesse, he ripped the locks off the doors. The demons pushed them open and ran.

The trainees were herding the demons, just like they'd been asked. Angus followed the demons, and they all ran to get out of the building where they'd be trapped and helpless.

A surge of something hit the air, and the dampener came back online. The slap took Angus's breath away, and he stumbled. A demon grabbed his arm and pulled him up. The scent of barbeque hit his nose. The thief was slumped over, dead at the door with the cables in his hand.

Someone would be getting a call that the building had been breached.

Dustin, who'd been on the roof, was now holding the door of the truck open. "Get in the truck!"

The demon at the front stopped short and started to walk in circles.

Angus knew what the demon was trying to do. He was trying to open the void to get home. When Angus got close enough, he tore open the void. Most people would think the demon had been successful, but the demon knew better. He gave a nod and stepped through. The others didn't even pause. They followed.

The trainees watched as the point of the mission went home. No one made any move to stop the demons, and Angus was very tempted to follow them. The void called to his blood. He could feel the heat and smell the air. Then the demons were gone, and the void closed.

"Well, I guess they're away from the college, which was kind of the point," Lizzie said.

Angus pulled himself into the truck. Syg and the van they'd arrived in had vanished. "We'd better get in unless we want to be arrested."

They climbed in and slammed the door closed. The trainees were all alive, but none of them were smiling.

ANGUS WAS delivered to the headquarters at the old school. The corridors were cold, and his footsteps echoed. While there were no dampeners, there wasn't any magic accumulated in any corner either. The other trainees followed him as though he knew where he was going, and he had a vague idea, but he was just following the signs. They'd been told to go to the auditorium.

The underground wasn't impressed that they allowed the demons to escape. But what were they supposed to do? Use magic to recapture them? He expected one of the other trainees to say something about the demon opening the tear… or even that the demon had help, but no one said anything.

It was clear to all of them that the underground wanted the demons for their own use, much like the scarlips. The only person who'd died that morning was the thief, but it could've easily been one of them. If they'd fought with the demons, there would've been injuries.

Risely, the masked warlock in charge, had been waiting for them to discuss their failure, had impressed upon them the importance of keeping demons safe. How was going back to Demonside unsafe, Angus asked? Risely had no answers, but he gave Angus a look of pure hatred.

Odds were that Angus would find himself brushing up against death on the next mission. He was getting used to that feeling. But while he didn't want to die, it didn't terrify him the way it once had. At least if he were dead he'd be free from fighting battles on behalf of people who were only slightly less bad than the college.

He pushed open the door to the auditorium. Many of the seats were missing, and most of it was in darkness, but the stage was lit. A single pale light shone on one person dressed in black—Syg. Another person was almost hidden in the shadows to the side.

"That can't be good," Norah whispered.

Angus knew it wasn't going to be good the moment they were all ordered to go. He'd thought it would be a meeting, but it wasn't.

"Come and get a front-row seat," Syg said, not moving from his circle of illumination.

"Are they going to kill a demon in front of us?" Dustin whispered.

"I don't think this is going to be congratulations for fucking up," Lizzie said.

"We didn't fuck up." Angus took a few steps closer. "The demons escaped when they got the chance."

"Maybe we shouldn't have taken the dampeners off-line," one of the trainees said.

"Then we'd have never gotten the locks open without setting off the alarm." The locks were magical. "We were set up to fail."

"To be arrested by the college." Norah crossed her arms.

The other trainees spoke softly, but worry swirled around them. They formed a tighter cluster.

223

"We could have fled to Demonside with the demons," Angus muttered. But they hadn't, and while they hadn't yet been arrested, things were not looking good. He couldn't leave Terrance behind. The underground had found a most effective way to bind him into near obedience.

"Would you flee to Demonside?" Dustin's voice was curious, not incredulous.

"Yes," Angus answered immediately. "I'd rather take my chances in the desert." He knew how to survive, although he would never again take a swim in a lake—not without a hunter present. His ankle was bare, and his steps too quiet without the bells. He missed the noise of the village. In Humanside he was slinking around in the shadows as though he didn't exist.

They could all be erased, and no one would care.

His mother already thought he was dead—or worse, a rogue warlock. Did the others have family to miss them or had the underground become their family? Like him, they were all around twenty years old.

While they had all volunteered to go to Demonside, they had probably only done so because there was nothing else for them. None of them loved the college, but none of them talked about how good the underground was either. They no longer hoped the underground would somehow make things right. They would have to save themselves.

They all went silent as they reached the last couple of steps. Angus remained standing as the others took front-row seats that had seen far better days. "Why are we here?"

"To remind you what happens when you don't obey." Syg tugged on the rope around the other person's wrists. It wasn't a demon. It had to be a human man from the height and broadness of his bare shoulders.

Angus's stomach flipped over.

No.

He didn't need to see Terrance's face to know it was him.

"Take your seat, Angus," Syg said.

"I will stand." His hands fisted at his sides.

Lizzie hissed at him to sit.

They didn't know that he'd helped the demons across the void, and the underground didn't know, but it didn't matter. Terrance was still going to be punished because he hadn't done exactly as the underground wanted.

If Angus had been killed or arrested on the job, Terrance would've been given the bad news. If Angus had survived and brought the demons, Terrance would have been there as a reward for good behavior.

It was sick.

But Angus had no idea how to break the bonds. Terrance wouldn't break up with him. While he no longer believed in the underground, Angus knew that Terrance believed in what it had once stood for. And the underground had enough on Terrance to turn him over to the college for the smallest infraction. As long as they needed him to keep Angus in line, Terrance was almost safer in the underground's hands than he would have been if he were free.

With a flick of his fingers, the man sent the rope upward, where it tied itself to a rafter. Terrance's toes barely touched the ground.

Angus's nails pressed into his palms, and the scar on his chest burned.

Finally the man removed Terrance's hood. He blinked a few times. When he saw Angus, he gave a very small shake of his head.

What did that mean?

Terrance didn't look away in disgust. He kept his gaze steady and on Angus.

Something snapped. Terrance's face contorted, and Angus realized what the punishment was. Syg had a whip, and he wielded it with the finesse of someone who had done it many times.

Angus took half a step forward, but Terrance shook his head again.

The third stroke drew a grunt of pain.

Angus's nails broke the skin. He couldn't just stand there and do nothing. But Terrance continued to stare at him.

Someone to his right gasped and let out a cry as though they were receiving the lashes. But the underground still needed them. There were plenty of dangerous jobs the trainees could do. Terrance was fully expendable.

He'd be written off as one more troublemaking rogue, even though he no longer had a demon. People went missing every day. He'd be one more, and no one would investigate too deeply, in case they were next.

Angus flinched with every stroke. Tears blurred his vision. He shouldn't regret helping the demons escape. But he did.

Terrance gritted his teeth, but a grunt escaped with each lash. When it became too much, he cried out. The anger broke free and magic flowed from Angus's fingers. He didn't care what happened to him. He tore the whip from Syg's hand, looped around his throat, and dragged Syg to the edge of the stage.

Syg recovered fast and lashed out with magic. Angus was thrown back and landed awkwardly four steps up. He gasped for breath, but he was sure that nothing was broken, just bruised. He raised his hand, but Lizzie held him down. The other trainees restrained Syg.

Angus struggled until he realized that he didn't need to use his hands to direct magic—he'd never seen Saka wave his hands like a warlock. He reached out with his mind and freed Terrance from the rope that bound him. Terrance stumbled but didn't fall.

"I'll take his place. It's me you want to punish, so do it." Angus pushed Lizzie aside and got up.

Syg threw off the trainees and unraveled the whip from around his neck. He glared at Angus as though he judged him unworthy. "We were done anyway."

Syg grasped Terrance's wrist and pulled him offstage and into the shadows. There would be no reunion and no chance to talk face-to-face. If he'd kept himself in check, there might've been. He could've healed Terrance. Apologized. Begged for forgiveness.

Terrance's cries of pain echoed in his ears. And fury burned in his blood. If they thought he'd cave and obey, they were wrong.

226

They had shown their true face, and it wasn't one he could work with. Terrance knew that this day was coming. He expected it, but Angus hadn't thought it would actually happen.

He'd been a fool.

CHAPTER 27

WITH WEK at his side, Saka prepared to reach across the sands. He knew the direction, so he could aim his call. Words were still hard to form, but it was getting easier. Although he'd damaged his mind, it was healing. He would be more careful with his next attempt, but he also wanted a result, some good news to share with Angus when he returned in two days.

Wek's lips were pressed together. She wasn't happy that he trying again so soon.

Eighteen demons had flooded into the camp earlier today with stories of being captured and then rescued.

An emergency meeting was taking place between the leaders. Tapo was assisting Miniti while Saka would talk to the other head mages. Those meetings would bring no good results. Saka didn't think the level approach would hold sway for much longer. The demons who wanted blood would get their hands wet.

If only to give them a little more time, not even the full year, Saka needed to make contact with the distant tribe. And he didn't have long to try before he needed to talk with the mages of Lifeblood.

He pushed his mind into the telestone and out. Magic flowed from the other mages and pushed him further and faster. When he ran out of telestones, he sent his mind and called across the bare sand.

He found only the emptiness of the desert, so he pushed a little further. His mind was hair thin and just as delicate. He could feel the pull of home, as Wek and the other mages sent him their strength.

How long could he wait for a reply? Time had no meaning out there, but his body would tire. If one of the mages weakened, Saka's mind could break.

Fear almost made him drop back, but then he felt the brush of another mind.

This is Mage Saka of the Lifeblood Mountain tribes, seeking contact with mages from across the sand.

Would the other respond or just flit about the edges?

The magic trembled. He couldn't maintain it for much longer.

This is Mage Iktan. The mage's image formed in Saka's mind. He had no feathers, but unlike any demon Saka had ever seen, he had a long muzzle and elegant horns.

For a moment they assessed each other.

You have reached far, Iktan said.

And I cannot remain for long. I have been searching for others. Does the drying affect you?

Iktan tilted his head and nodded. *Our jungle is dying.*

Jungle?

Saka's mind was filled with visions of taller trees than he'd ever seen, lush green hills, and mountains that made Lifeblood look tiny. He responded with what Lifeblood looked like during the rains. *There isn't enough rebalancing.*

Our humans rebalance, but others do not. Who do you work with?

Saka hesitated. Vinland wasn't well liked in the human world— and with good reason. *I fear the people aligned with my tribe are causing the problem. We are trying to stop them.*

Iktan didn't respond for a moment, and Saka's mind started to fray. He had to break the connection soon.

Vinland will be stopped. Then Iktan was gone.

Saka retreated back across the sands. It would be easier next time because he had a name and a face to connect with. He opened his eyes. His lip was wet with blood, but he was upright and awake.

Wek was watching him. "And?"

Saka just nodded. He didn't know what to make of the conversation with Iktan. Was his tribe a potential ally? Which of Angus's countries did Iktan's humans come from?

"I must prepare to talk with the other mages."

He washed his face, drank, and then resettled himself.

Wek hadn't moved. "I am not leaving. If you die, we are all in great trouble."

"Tapo will make a fine head mage." But he had no plans to die. A simple call to the other head mages wouldn't kill him.

"We both know he would not be head mage for long."

That was also true. While Wek might be a very young mage, she was smart when it came to the politics of the tribe… maybe even all of Demonside and Humanside.

Miniti swept into Saka's tent as he reached for the telestone. Saka paused before his fingers brushed the surface.

Miniti stopped a couple of paces to the side. "My meeting is over. Leave us, Wek."

Wek got up and left without a backward glance.

Saka looked up at Miniti. She didn't come in very often. Usually he was summoned to her tent. She looked at the bloodied rag, but she didn't ask what he'd been doing. She probably assumed it was some ritual or further training for Wek. Wek had passed the trials on Lifeblood, but she still had a lot to learn.

"I have spoken to the others, and while your idea of turning humans against each other had merit and was worth trying, we cannot continue with it, given these new developments." She paused. "I know you have an affection for Angus, which is why I am telling you in private. Enough mages will concur with our decision. All humans are to be killed. There will be no more working with them."

Saka couldn't form words, but it had nothing to do with the brain injury.

Angus would open the void in two days, and the tear would open near Saka. If Saka was with the tribe, the other demons would kill Angus. And Saka had no way to warn him. He didn't want to think of a world without Angus.

"Angus has done no wrong. He is on our side." He didn't know what else to say. Angus wasn't just his apprentice. He was his friend—his lover. He couldn't sit by and let him die for the crimes of others. "He rebalances. That is worth more than his death."

"I'm sorry. There can be no exceptions, no matter how demon he is on the inside." Miniti turned but then glanced back. "I know you will do what is best for the tribe."

CHAPTER 28

ANGUS THREW another stick on the fire. It wasn't a big bonfire. The underground hadn't given them much wood, nor had they let them go out to gather more. There was no traditional roast cooking in the flames, no singing or dancing. They had the radio on, but at every break in the music, there was a piece of propaganda—something about how great Vinland was, or that Spring would come when the demons and the underground were defeated.

He wanted to turn it off, but he had to look like he cared. On the other side of the fire, Norah and Lizzie watched the embers fly into the sky. After the incident in the auditorium, they weren't sure they'd be allowed to celebrate the shortest day of the year. But here they were, celebrating nothing.

Without the other trainees or Terrance, Angus couldn't walk away and put his faith in Demonside and his ability to hold on to the magic. They'd have to wait until they were all together, and waiting had never been so hard.

He tossed another branch on the fire and listened to the crackle of the hungry flames. With a little twist of the magic, he brought the sparks together to make a sun and let it explode out. Guards sat nearby, ready to act if anything happened.

What did they expect? Open revolt?

Angus hoped they didn't expect them to flee to Demonside.

The nervous tension that had been swelling in his stomach all day hadn't dissipated. It would be better if they fled that night. Then it would be done. He understood why Terrance had hated the waiting.

Angus demanded answers after the demonstration in the auditorium. But he was tackled to the ground and thrown in a makeshift cell for the rest of the night until he calmed down. His skin still felt bruised, even though there wasn't a mark on him. He didn't sleep in the cell—the dampeners were so strong that they hurt. So he was awake when a note was pushed under the cell door.

One word was written on it.

Run.

He did the only thing he could—he ate the evidence in case he was searched. It was the only food he'd been given, and he'd had hours to realize that it would be convenient if they just forgot about him.

But someone had risked their life to send him that warning. They thought worse was to come, and they were probably right. He fisted his hand and sent sparks high into the air. He needed to do something. If he threw sparks in the faces of the guards, would that give enough time to open the void and fall through? Probably.

Long enough to steal the car and get away? Maybe. But he wouldn't get far.

He lifted his head. Someone was approaching the house. They were being kept in an isolated house surrounded by forest. Even the fence was protected with some kind of magic that hurt to even brush against.

The noise of a car engine filled the night, and Lizzie and Norah looked up. Neither of them smiled. They'd barely spoken since the auditorium, but they all agreed it was too dangerous to rely on the goodwill of the underground.

The guard with the pipe got up. "Looks like the rest of the party is here."

The knots in Angus's stomach almost crippled him. Would that be the rest of the trainees? And if it were, could they really do it?

Angus could open the void fast, but they still needed to get through. They needed to make it clear to the others what was at stake, but they didn't know which of the others they could trust. And Angus couldn't leave without Terrance.

He swallowed and tried to be calm, but his heart raced like a rabbit about to be slaughtered. The rations he'd eaten for dinner didn't want to stay down.

233

Voices drifted out of the house. He heard the clink of bottles, and six people came out of the house—what was left of the trainees and Terrance.

Angus stood and his knees gave a little wobble. He hadn't spoken to Terrance via the telestones since the auditorium. He'd tried once, but Terrance didn't respond. He walked over stiffly, as though he still hurt. Had the underground not healed him?

Terrance held out a bottle of the traditional Solstice mead—sunshine in a bottle, the taste of summer that warmed from the inside out. "As host you get to open it."

Angus took it from him and unwrapped the foil from around the top. Then he undid the cap. He paused for a moment to make sure the mead wasn't poisoned or laced with magic, but there was nothing there. He needed to say something.

"The longest night of the year. This one is colder and darker than most, but summer isn't far away." *It's just across the void.* He raised the bottle and took a drink. Then he passed it back to Terrance, who took a drink and handed it on.

Angus reached for his hand, and for an awful moment, he thought Terrance was going to pull away, but he didn't.

One by one the others drank, murmuring "to summer" even though it was clear none of them believed summer would come back to Vinland.

Terrance moved closer and murmured in Angus's ear, "The stone went flat, I think. I could feel you, but not reply. I wanted to tell you I was all right."

"Are you?" Angus searched Terrance's face for a clue. There was always tension between them after a forced separation, but Angus was sick of it.

"Well enough. Though I can't play."

"They didn't heal you, did they?" The anger simmered closer to the surface. Angus had never thought about killing with magic, but if Syg walked into the garden, Angus wouldn't have hesitated.

Terrance gave a small shake of his head. "They said it's because you interfered."

"I'm sorry. For everything."

"Don't be sorry. Do something. I can't live like this."

Angus nodded. He *was* planning something, but it could get them all killed. Could he live with that? "Let's drink and celebrate first."

Terrance's dark eyebrows drew together. "And then?"

"And then...." Then they either did nothing or they ran across the void and hoped they weren't committing suicide. Although, if they stayed, death was equally assured. It was just a question of when. Maybe he'd become too comfortable with the idea of his death.

Someone handed Angus a fresh bottle. He opened it and got Terrance to sit in front of him, between his legs. To anyone looking, they were just being close. Angus had his hand under Terrance's shirt as they shared a drink and watched the little bonfire.

Angus's fingers brushed the edge of the bandages. He sensed the mess that was Terrance's back. "Do you want the scars or not?"

Demons left the scars until the person was ready to move on.

"No. Neither of us need the reminder." There was a mettle in Terrance's voice that Angus had seldom heard before.

"Sometimes it's easier to wear the physical scar than to bury the mental one." Angus would never forget. Nor did he want to forgive. If the underground thought that hurting Terrance would keep him loyal, they didn't know him. Or maybe they thought he was the same person who'd started college five months ago and was barely able to pass theory—the idiot who was taken by a demon the first time he opened the void.

Terrance turned his head. "And sometimes it's better to move on. We both knew it was coming. Now it's done. Now we push on before the fire dies."

Angus let his magic spread into the wounds to encourage the skin to grow faster and knit together.

Terrance flinched. "That kind of tickles."

"You must have a higher pain tolerance than me, because it always hurts."

"They aren't deep. It stung at the time, but it was more for show. They wanted to know when you'd break. It's why I kept telling you no."

"I tried." He rested his forehead against Terrance's shoulder. "I know you wanted me to just stand there." He'd seen Terrance shake his head to warn. But watching someone he cared about being hurt on his behalf was more than he could bear.

Terrance's posture eased. He'd lied about it not hurting that much. Beneath Angus's hand, the scars faded too. In the morning there'd be no sign of them. Angus took the bottle of mead, and it burned all the way down until heat burst in his stomach and flooded his veins. But it didn't unravel the knots.

"Are you sure about it?"

"Yeah." Terrance rubbed his hand against Angus's thigh. "My parents were jailed for being wizards. I was raised by my grandparents. I took the scholarship because they didn't have the money for any kind of college, and I wanted to play rugby. After one term I knew I had to do something. I didn't want to be one of them. So yeah, I've been ready since I was ten." He lowered his voice. "Since I overheard my grandparents whispering about a cousin who'd defected, and I had to look up what the word meant." He turned a little to whisper in Angus's ear. "If I ever got to represent the country overseas...."

He didn't need to finish the sentence. Angus hadn't known about Terrance's family. He'd never said a word. Maybe it was simply because he didn't want people to know, in case they judged him for his parents' assumed crimes. Angus had grown up listening to how bad wizards were. It was only when he'd met some that he learned the truth. No wonder his father had hated Jim so much.

They drank silently for a few minutes while the other trainees chatted. Angus hoped the mead didn't make them too talkative. Would there be any mead next winter? Would there be any bees? Would anyone be left to care?

His hand was still under Terrance's shirt. His skin was warm as Angus glided his fingers over the ridges of muscle on his stomach. Terrance had always been built, but he felt harder. "Been training lots?"

"I figured my life depended on being good."

He kissed Terrance's neck. Was it wrong to steal a few moments? How long did they have before the guards put out the fire and told them the party was over?

Were the guards—there were two extra—all waiting for him to do something? "I think we should go in. Give those watching something to talk about."

Terrance turned his head and kissed him. "I don't care what they say. We should make the most of our time together."

He hadn't been serious. Terrance had walked in wounded. But he couldn't deny that the mead and the bonfire and the way Terrance leaned against him had put the thought there. "You're well enough?"

"I'll show you the new trick I learned." He turned and pushed Angus to the ground, and the snow crunched beneath him. Terrance shoved the bottle of mead into the snow to keep it upright and turned his full attention to Angus.

He'd almost forgotten how bright the lust could burn in Terrance's eyes.

"And what trick is that?" But Angus was pretty sure he knew. Terrance could turn off his bracelet. It was only then that he realized he couldn't feel the dampener at all. He'd healed Terrance without resistance. His eyes widened.

Terrance grinned and kissed him slowly. "Besides, you need to sober up."

"You want to take advantage of me?" Angus wanted to be taken advantage of right then. Lust tumbled through him and hardened his dick. But he did need to stop drinking so he could open the void in a hurry when the time came—so he could fight if he had to.

"I was hoping the feeling would be shared." Terrance pressed a little closer, but there were too many winter clothes between them.

"It is." Angus threaded his fingers through Terrance's hair and pulled him in for a kiss. Terrance's lips were sweet from mead, and his mouth was hot and hungry. It was impossible to think of anything but getting his clothes off. "Shall we go in?"

For a reply, Terrance stood and offered Angus his hand, and Angus reached up and took it. As they went hand in hand into the house, Lizzie caught his gaze. He gave her a slight nod and hoped that she'd realize that he hadn't thrown their plan out the window.

Inside he shrugged out of his coat and hung it by the door. Terrance did the same, but when he went to speak, Angus put a finger on his lips. It wasn't safe.

"Not in here," he whispered against Terrance's lips.

Angus led Terrance down the corridor and into his room, where he had a very small bag of things to take across. He was ready, even though he wasn't ready in his heart.

But he had to be. Everyone was counting on him. Terrance expected him to have all the answers, and he had none—only a best guess.

Part of him wanted to wait.

Angus kicked off his shoes. "Is there any rush?" He wasn't talking about sex.

Terrance lifted an eyebrow. "We might not get another chance." That was true for sex *and* for escaping. "We either do it or we forget about it and live with the regret." Terrance tugged Angus closer by the hem of his shirt. "You don't seem like the kind of person who likes living with regrets."

His tension and fear were temporarily replaced with mead and lust, and it felt good. He was tired of playing stupid games and only seeing Terrance when the underground decided he deserved it.

Why had they let Terrance come tonight?

Terrance swiftly undid buttons as he stole desperate kisses. He acted as though there were no time to waste and all he wanted was Angus. Angus wanted to sink into the moment, but he was too amped-up, too alert. The last time they were together, it was pure lust. Neither of them had expected more from that encounter, yet they were bound together by hope for a better place and a better use of magic.

Clothes came off and puddled on the floor.

Terrance smoothed his hand over Angus's chest and shoulder and gave it a gentle squeeze. "Magic must be hard work."

"It is. Demonside is a hard place to live." The trainees knew what they were getting into. They had lived there, if only part-time.

Terrance nodded and stepped forward. The back of Angus's knees hit the bed and he fell back. Terrance fell with him. "Tell me."

"About the desert? The lack of water?"

"I want to know everything," he said between kisses as he moved lower.

"It's hot all the time, even when it rains." His stomach tightened as Terrance's lips brushed his hard dick. "The rivers, when they're there, aren't safe to swim in." He closed his eyes when Terrance took him in his mouth and sucked.

Angus took several deep breaths, not because he needed to hold back for ritual, but because it felt so good that he didn't want it to be over too soon. He hadn't had sex with a human for months, not since he'd last been with Terrance. He didn't have the finesse that Saka had, the polished performance, honed through years of ritual. This was raw and hungry and uncontrolled.

Terrance looked up. "Keep going." He slowly stroked Angus's cock.

"I don't know… it's sandy"—Terrance was totally distracting him and making it hard to think—"and red, and life is brief because the rains and rivers don't last long. But magic is everywhere, and it's beautiful." He wanted to share that with Terrance. Because Terrance had lost his demon when the college killed it. He might not want another, but that didn't mean he couldn't expand his talents as a wizard.

Would Terrance and Saka get on?

His worlds were about to collide, and he stilled as that realization struck hard. That was why he was stalling. He had two lives and two lovers, and while they'd met and knew about each other, it would be something else when he opened the void.

Terrance gave him a slow lick. "And your demon?"

"He's...." Another slow lick that circled the head of his now very hard cock. "He's a very good teacher." Angus smiled. "Turn around and let me show you."

If it hadn't been for the dampeners in the house, Angus could've collected the magic they were drawing to them. He could feel it, even though he couldn't touch it.

Terrance moved, and Angus slid down the bed to get into a better position.

"And now you can't talk because you'll have your mouth full."

"That's not a bad thing." Angus tasted Terrance's skin, gave a lick and a kiss on his inner thigh, and moved closer to his cock, a little at a time.

Terrance's skin was soft, unlike a demon's. Dark hair dusted his balls. The musky scent of sex filled Angus's lungs with every breath. He'd intended to show off some of his skills, but that wasn't what he wanted to do right then. He liked the simple lust he had with Terrance. It was worth more than any magic he could gather.

He took his human lover in his mouth, more gently than he would've done with Saka. Terrance did the same to him. The wet heat and the suction made a shiver of pure heat roll down his spine, and he couldn't blame that on the mead. Even though he'd been taught to hold back until he couldn't resist any longer, he gave in as the need crested the first time. He moved his hips, the bells around his ankle chimed in rhythm, and Terrance took him deeper as Angus came.

Angus's groan was muffled by Terrance's dick in his mouth. He shuddered as the sensation rolled through him. It was far better than bottled sunshine or even the promise of summer around the corner.

With the lust out of his blood, he focused on Terrance and the way he moved with each touch or suck or taste. A flick of Angus's tongue over the slit brought the first taste of Terrance's pleasure.

It didn't take long before Terrance rocked his hips in rhythm. Angus took him a little deeper each time and then slowly drew back to just tease the head. That was all it took. Terrance thrust his hips forward as his back arched and a moan formed on his lips. Angus swallowed. The taste wasn't what he'd become accustomed to. It was more salty than sweet. Had it really been that long?

They lay spent on the bed, limbs tangled as they caught their breath.

Angus wanted longer. He wanted more, but that wasn't possible, and he didn't know how to say it. Finally they sat up, and Terrance ran his fingers along Angus's jaw and brought him closer for a kiss. The sweetness of the mead was gone, replaced with a musky tang. "I'm ready for summer."

Angus stood on the back porch, looking at the dwindling bonfire and the very merry trainees. None of them were ready for Demonside. He had his small bag under his coat, and Terrance had put some extra things in another bag under his. Both of them had added some rations. If people were watching the cameras, hopefully they would think it was for the party.

Terrance put a hand on Angus's lower back. "It won't be long until the guards are telling us it's time to leave."

"I know." Angus didn't move.

Lizzie got up and walked over. She climbed the three steps and stood in front of them. "This is it?"

Angus nodded and glanced at Terrance. "No more waiting."

"Okay. I'll get my things. Norah has hers with her already."

"Really?" Norah was organized, but that was very efficient, even for her.

"She's worried."

"So am I. She doesn't have to come." None of them did, but there wouldn't be time for a quiet chat and cool decisions. When they talked about defecting to Demonside, it had all been theory—maybes and what-ifs. But after the auditorium, the plan had become urgent.

"She wants to. I haven't spoken to anyone else."

Terrance picked up a bottle, faked a drink, and handed it to Lizzie. It was still a party—a party with armed guards watching and listening to their every move and word.

Lizzie handed it to Angus. "Maybe we should take one with us."

"Maybe." He took a sip. "I'm going to open the void. Tell everyone that we won't be coming back."

"They'll start shooting at us," Terrance said.

"Yeah. But if I speak to people beforehand, they may speak to the guards before we can leave." There was at least one trainee who seemed to buy the shit the underground was selling.

"It was always going to be a mess. Give me five, and then I'll be back." Lizzie nudged his shoulder as she went past.

"I'll go say something to Norah." He needed to reassure her, but how could he say it would all be fine when he knew it wouldn't be?

Terrance put his hand on Angus's arm. "How many will come?"

Angus studied each of the little clusters. "I don't know."

He hadn't got to know the others well enough. No doubt that was part of the underground's plan—keep them isolated so they couldn't get close.

Terrance picked up another bottle, but didn't take the lid off.

"You really want to take one?"

"Nah, it's a weapon." Terrance grinned. His teeth were white in the moonlight.

Angus approached Norah, who was so tense she was clearly ready to snap. He squatted next to her and nodded at the tipsy man on her other side.

"I didn't think you'd be coming out of your bedroom," she said.

Angus glanced at the ground. "Making the most of it." He had to remember what he was fighting for. He lifted his head to look her in the eye. "How about you?"

"I'm tired of snow."

"That sentiment seems to be going around. Lizzie said the same." They'd all be sick of heat and sand soon enough.

Although Angus had only spoken to him a few times, Dustin sat down and joined the conversation. "There'll be no Spring. It's just going to get colder until we all die, until the world dies, and one college warlock is left standing, laughing that he has all the magic."

"The rest of the world won't let that happen." Angus would do everything he could to stop the college. He glanced at the man on the other side of Norah.

Dustin took a peek at who it was and nodded. "You got something going on?"

Norah glanced between the two of them, but said nothing. Then her gaze shifted. Angus's heart stuttered. Was a guard right behind him? He looked over his shoulder to see Lizzie and Terrance wandering over.

It was time.

Norah scrambled up like a startled rabbit.

Dustin stood and stumbled. "Shouldn't have drunk that bottle on my own."

Angus drew whatever magic was in the yard to him. The guards had stopped talking and were watching the five of them. So were the other trainees. They all knew something was about to happen.

Did he need a distraction?

There was no time to plan one or create one. He took a few quick breaths, but he was unable to find calm. He couldn't look at the guards, but he couldn't wait any longer.

Angus tore open the void, and the heat of Demonside washed over him. "If you follow me, you'll never be able to call Vinland home again."

Terrance and Lizzie went through without hesitation. Norah followed.

Dustin swore. "You're defecting? To where?"

Angus didn't answer. He watched the others. They all got up. Two stepped away and shook their heads, as though to make it clear they wanted no part in what was going on. The other two started toward Angus and the tear. The man was shot before he could take two steps, but the woman ran. She used magic to throw embers at the guards, blinding them for a moment.

She went through.

Dustin looked at Angus and shrugged. "Dead here or dead there."

243

"At least there we'll be free." Angus stepped through and gasped. Something had gone wrong.

There were no friendly tents, no village waiting for them—just endless starlit plains of sand.

CHAPTER 29

SAKA STOOD at the edge of the village. He hadn't been so tense since he'd stood on Lifeblood to be tested as an apprentice. It was hard to breathe, but he had to do this. If he didn't, he was complicit in starting a war with the humans of Vinland... and killing Angus. His feet remained rooted. Somewhere in the distance were other demons. From where he stood, all he could see was sand and stars.

There was a good chance he could die out there. One demon walking the sand was a tempting meal for a riverwyrm, and he'd never lived alone. He'd always had the tribe around him.

He glanced back and saw someone moving in the shadows. Her white skin glimmered, and for an awful moment, Saka thought it was Miniti, coming to stop him. But it was Wek. She stopped a few paces away and took in the sled he'd packed with what he could carry. He hadn't dragged one of those since he was Guda's trainee.

"You are leaving," she said.

"I am doing what is best for the tribe." The greater tribe and all of Demonside, not their small group.

"Some would say you are blinded by love for a human warlock."

Saka closed his eyes for a moment. "Not blinded." But he couldn't deny that he cared for Angus more deeply than he should. "Are you here to stop me? To warn Miniti?"

Miniti would have him staked out in the desert before sunrise. He'd be dead by dusk, with luck.

Surviving out there alone until Angus returned would not be easy.

"No. I do not want to see us destroyed by greedy humans. I used to think all humans, and warlocks especially, were power hungry monsters, but that is the same kind of lie they tell about us."

245

Saka looked at Wek. When had she become a mage? Was it two or three years ago on Lifeblood Mountain? "So what will you do?"

She pulled something out of the shadows—a sled, as though she were ready to travel. "I knew when Miniti announced that humans were to die that you would not stay."

"Everyone else thinks I will." If Miniti thought he'd leave, she'd have posted a guard.

Usi would become head mage with the shift in politics. She'd achieve her goal. The experiment in teaching humans was over, and while she'd agreed it was something that should be tested, it wasn't something she had supported. How many other mages felt the same? Did they agree reluctantly but believe they were just postponing the inevitable?

Angus didn't want to believe that war was the only option, but he thought war would come to Vinland. For a heartbeat his resolve faltered. Was he abandoning his tribe to protect the man he loved, or was he looking for another solution, for an alliance that would help Angus's people fight back against the college and its lust for power and magic?

"They have not watched you and Angus closely. I have. I wanted to know how you worked and why you trusted him with so much." She dragged her sled closer. "I am coming with you."

"I cannot ask that." He didn't want to draw another mage into what could be a death walk. He had no idea how far they would have to travel.

"You did not. I am a mage, and I can make my own decisions. I would rather seek peace."

"We will not get it. The demons we find will hopefully be allied with a country fighting Vinland."

"Then we help them crush the college. That was always the aim of working with the humans, so nothing has changed."

"Nothing has changed." Everything had changed. Saka was without a tribe. He exhaled and started to walk. They'd have to put some distance between the village and themselves before dawn.

Wek muffled the bells on her sled while they snuck into the night. When they were farther away, Saka would unbind his bells. Then they would sing and make noise and hope that nothing thought them worth eating.

TWO HUNTERS had circled overhead, but they had not stopped to ask what Saka and Wek were doing. That was yesterday morning. Since then Saka hadn't seen another demon. In a few more days, he'd leave a telestone. He had six of them ready. It would make it easier for those who wished to contact him.

If anyone did.

He wasn't ready to tell Becha and Lox what he'd done, though no doubt they would know he was no longer in Miniti's tribe. They'd had faith in his plan, and it had been destroyed by those who felt there was no time to waste. The unwritten rules had washed away, and many would bleed on the sand.

As dusk settled and the heat went out of the day, he and Wek made camp. She'd brought her small tent, but they hadn't been bothering to set it up. Saka had left his tent behind. It wasn't really his—it was just the one given to the head mage. He was entitled to keep it, but it would take too long to set up on his own.

It was easy enough to find water, as it had been his job for long to guide the tribe along the rivers. But their food supplies were running low, and they would have to hunt soon. They wouldn't be able to plant if they were to press on and find the other demons.

He lit a fire and allowed himself to remember the planting and the night in the field. It would forever be one of his happiest memories. He started to smile, but a chill rippled over his skin, and he felt a tug at his soul. The void was about to open.

"Arm yourself. The college may have Angus and be forcing him to open the void." Saka moved away from their camp and drew his machete to greet the humans.

The trainees stumbled across. Shouts and the crack of weapons filled what had been a peaceful evening.

Where was Angus?

Six humans came through, but they shrank back when they saw Saka.

Angus appeared through the dark tear, and one more followed him, and the void slammed closed. Angus slowly turned and took in the desert. "Where is everyone?"

"The Lifeblood Mountain tribes have declared that all humans are to be killed on sight." Saka sheathed his machete to make it clear that he wasn't about to do that. Angus had brought six other humans with him, including Norah, Lizzie, and Terrance. "So now I have no tribe."

Angus put his arms around him. "What happened?"

"The demons you freed and sent back? They spoke about what had happened, and the leaders halted the experiment, calling it a failure." He held Angus tightly. "You did the right thing freeing them."

"Did I? If I hadn't—"

"Then they would have died, and the leaders would have found another reason to spill blood." Saka drew back a little. "I have spoken to another tribe, one that lives a good many days away. You were right. There are other demons."

"So they are out there."

Saka nodded. "But I do not know which country they work with. Why are there so many with you?"

"Because the underground was using us. They punished Terrance when I freed the demons. The only way for us to escape Vinland was via Demonside. None of us are going back. No one would open the void for us."

The humans were stuck in Demonside until they reached another tribe of demons.

"Then you had best all learn how to stop the flow of magic so you do not rebalance what was taken across the void."

"What have we done?" Norah scanned the horizon, and fear widened her eyes. "I thought there would be a tribe to live with."

"We are a tribe. You have two mages," Wek said as she came to stand near Saka.

Angus turned to face the trainees. "If Saka hadn't left the tribe, the void would've opened and we'd have been rounded up and killed. If you returned to your tribes tomorrow, as per the usual arrangement, then you would've been killed."

"And if we'd stayed in Vinland it was only a matter of time before the underground handed us over to the college," Terrance finished. "Now we have a chance."

"Says the nonmagic user," said one of the humans.

Saka didn't know that human, and clearly the human didn't know Terrance.

"Terrance is a warlock, though he is currently without a demon." Saka inclined his head in question, not sure if that was still true, and Terrance nodded. "He was as much at risk as all of you. All of us."

How were they ever going to make it to the jungle and hills of another tribe?

He didn't want to dwell on what would happen when he reached there.

They could still be killed.

The humans, with their more delicate skin, traveled better at night. So they slept during the day in the one small tent and walked all night. It rained one evening as they were packing up.

The clouds weren't thick, and the rain didn't last long, but there was no celebration. Angus's lips pressed into a thin line as he folded and packed the sled and did the job of an apprentice without being asked.

No one really talked. They sang and made noise to keep the riverwyrms away, and Saka and Wek made sure that there was food and water. She was a good hunter, able to call prey to her. The humans were busy trying not to rebalance and die, which was a job that required a lot of attention. Not all were succeeding.

Saka brushed his hand over Angus's shoulder. "Survive."

Angus glanced up at him. "They kill humans. Humans kill demons." He looked away. "I should've stayed and fought."

249

"How? What could you have done?" Was he asking Angus or himself? He'd had the same thoughts. Maybe if he'd stayed with his tribe... but Miniti had made it clear there would be no exceptions, and without Angus, Saka wasn't sure he could've kept fighting.

"I don't know." Angus tied the last rope. "We should go. We need to move faster."

"They can't go faster." Not all the humans were used to the desert like Angus was. As much as Saka would've liked to move faster, they couldn't. He didn't want them to collapse from exhaustion.

"Their eyes are getting paler. We don't have a choice."

"I have noticed." Terrance's eyes had lightened, as had Norah's and Dustin's. The others were doing a better job of keeping their magic in. At one time, Saka would have been all about rebalancing. That had been the first thing he'd done with Angus. Now he taught humans how to avoid rebalancing, and he was sure other mages would judge him harshly for that.

Angus turned away. "I brought them here. If they die, it's because of me."

"They chose to come."

When they stopped for a meal later that night, Saka reminded the trainees of how to protect themselves. Angus sat with Terrance and tried to help him. Saka could see the connection between them in those few simple touches. Jealousy prickled beneath his skin, even though Angus looked at Saka the same way.

During the day, when they slept, all in the one tent—out of the sun except for the two who kept watch, Angus slept between Saka and Terrance.

Saka didn't dare touch Angus, even though he wanted to. But Terrance didn't either. They saved their energy to walk and hunt. And tempers were fraying.

Rain fell again as they set up to sleep.

Saka sat outside and placed his hand over the scar he'd made for Guda and let it heal. He was glad she wasn't there to see what was happening. He didn't sleep in the tent that day. He barely slept at all. Tension gnawed at him. Was he walking them to their deaths?

He doubted himself as he never had before, but he didn't dare voice it, even though he knew Angus carried a similar guilt. The humans had followed Angus, and he felt responsible.

After ten days some of the humans were weakening. They stumbled and argued among themselves, and their eyes became paler. Angus's remained blue. His barrier to everything and everyone was solid. It was a tangible thing that few would broach.

He was protecting more than just the magic in his blood. He was protecting his heart—and he expected someone to die.

No matter how many times Saka tried to contact Iktan on the telestone, the other demon never replied. Saka was not sure of the welcome they'd receive. To have walked all that way and strained all bonds of friendship only to have wasted their last days seemed grossly unfair. But he wasn't thinking rationally. He knew the world wasn't fair and that balance must be worked at. All he and Wek could do was keep everyone fed and watered and motivated, though that was harder each evening.

But they were getting closer to the other mage. The magic beneath Saka's feet had changed.

Angus came to sit outside the tent in the damp sand. The sky had started to darken. Soon they would eat and pack and walk. Again. "I don't think Dustin is going to survive the night. His eyes are too pale, and he is too thirsty. We should rest."

"We need to keep going. Rest will not save him." Saka put a hand on Angus's knee. "It is not him you worry about."

Terrance's eyes had turned the color of gold. The big man didn't complain, and he took his turn pulling the sled. But he was losing the battle to hold on to the magic in his body. Saka had grown used to Terrance being near Angus. It didn't bother him the way it had, and he'd come to like the way someone else could break the darkness around Angus. Terrance had a quiet strength that Saka could appreciate. And while they had barely spoken, Terrance seemed to hold no ill feelings toward him. If Terrance were to succumb, Angus would be broken. Magic couldn't heal all wounds.

251

Angus went to speak, but his voice cracked. His shoulders hunched, and he bit his lip as his body shook. Saka put his arm around him, but he couldn't lie and say that it would all be fine.

Nothing would be fine again.

Even Saka had started to feel as though they were going to die out here. The pack of scarlips that had been stalking them for the last two days clearly felt the same. Two mages and their trainees couldn't outrun death.

CHAPTER 30

TEN STEPS. One hundred steps. One thousand steps. Reset. One step. Keep count. Anything to pass the time. The stars were fading on another night. They would stop soon, and in the daylight, Angus would be forced to look at Terrance's pale golden eyes and know he was slowly killing his lover.

He was killing them all.

Angus stopped. He turned around in time to see Norah collapse. The shadows that had been following them all night solidified into a pack of five scarlips. He knew they were there—could feel them—but since Saka had said nothing, he said nothing. The trainees were scared enough already.

Better to be scared than dead?

Wek raced to Norah's side and brandished light in her palm, but it didn't scare the scarlips away. They crouched low and moved as though to circle their prey. The little tribe of humans and demons couldn't afford to lose anyone.

Angus drew up some magic and took a step toward Norah and Wek. He would not let them be mauled by an overgrown kitten with a scorpion tail.

"Scarlips," Terrance whispered. "They're so beautiful in the wild."

Terrance was right. Their blue skin gleamed in the predawn pink. The white of their teeth was bright and their graceful movements drew the eye. Terrance's demon had been a scarlips. He'd tamed Aqua, or at least reached an agreement where he'd give the animal some of his blood, and Aqua wouldn't kill him.

"She's dead," Wek said. She didn't need to raise her voice to be heard over the low rumble that set Angus's teeth on edge. Was it a purr or a growl? Norah was Wek's human trainee, and Wek knelt by her side. "We can't leave her."

"We have to." Saka took a step forward.

Angus grabbed his arm. "We can't leave her to be eaten."

"It's just her body. She is gone." That was true, but it didn't feel right. "We'll leave her out like a mage. We can't bury her. We have no time. They would kill more of us before we were halfway done. We need to keep moving." Saka lowered his voice. "Do you want more to die?"

"I don't want anyone to die." They were here because of Angus. He released Saka, but Saka grabbed him and spun him around.

"They followed you. You did not force them." His words were low and carefully controlled so as not to spread through the night.

"It wasn't meant to be like this."

"It would have been the same with the tribe. How long can a human last here? Now we are finding out."

Angus pulled away and ran toward a scarlips. "Leave us alone."

The animal took a step back and crouched.

"Duck," yelled Terrance.

Angus crouched and gathered magic to him as a scarlips leaped over his head.

"Don't use it, Angus." Saka had his hand raised. The magic he held was red and ugly.

Angus sucked in the sticky night air. He was sure it had lost its usual dryness, but the sky was free of clouds that would bring welcome rain. He glanced around, but he was surrounded. The scarlips had separated him from the group. If he ran, they would hunt him. He fucking hated those things.

"I'll draw them away." Dustin stepped out from the knot of people.

"No." Angus needed to do it. He'd keep them safe.

"We all know I'm next." He pointed to his white eyes. The skin on his fingers had wrinkled as though he'd spent too long in a bath. He constantly drank water, but he was unable to eat. Norah had been the same. "I might as well do something useful with what little life I have left."

"They'll tear you apart." Angus looked at Saka, but he said nothing. Did he agree with Dustin's plan?

The scarlips that was stalking him lunged forward, and Angus threw up a shield that he hoped would stop the creature. The scarlips didn't even get close. It was just testing him. Saka was right. He couldn't keep using magic, even if he was careful to gather from around him. Eventually some of his own would slip through. The longer he was there, the harder it would be.

"This was better than dying forgotten in a college prison. I got to see more of Demonside." Dustin licked his cracked lips.

"We're almost there," Angus said, his attention on the raised tail of the scarlips in front of him. The poison wouldn't kill immediately, but it would hurt and immobilize him so he was ready for eating. He didn't want to die the same way Jim had. No one should die. They were supposed to be on their way to freedom.

"Are we?" Dustin turned to Saka. "Are we?" he shouted, and his voice carried over the endless plains of sand.

"I don't know how much farther it is, but we are closer." Saka's words were carefully chosen and spoken.

"Give me a knife and let me go before I fall over and die." Dustin held out his hand. He'd climbed a building to shut off power and taken other risks on other missions. "They like blood, right?"

"Yes," Terrance said.

Wek was still guarding Norah's body, which pissed off the scarlips that were waiting for an easy meal. That's all they were—meals for the waiting predators. A tiny tribe that was slowly dying as Demonside took everything from them. Wek pulled a knife from her arm sheath. "Norah was my trainee. I failed her."

"You're still needed." Dustin shook his head. "I won't last another day. We all know that. Now before Angus gets eaten, give me a knife."

"Take my blade." Wek held out the knife.

Angus flicked his gaze between the scarlips around him and Dustin and Saka.

Dustin shrugged off the supplies he'd been carrying. "Better to die free?"

"You don't have to do this." No one else needed to die. But Angus had seen Dustin stumble along. He had helped him up and helped Norah up. There was a shake in the young man's hands, and shortness in his breath. But there had to be another way.

"Dead today, dead tomorrow. What's the difference? This way I'm giving you guys a chance. If you don't get there, I'm going to haunt you until you die." Dustin rolled up his sleeves.

"You shouldn't have too much haunting to do, then," Lizzie said without a trace of humor.

A scarlips's tail arced toward Angus. He threw up the shield again and the scarlips retreated and circled to his right, but it stayed between Angus and the group. Another two of the creatures kept Norah and Wek apart. They wouldn't give up.

Suddenly the scarlips all lifted their heads, and every creature looked at Dustin. Dark liquid ran down his arms. Blood. And it was pumping out fast. He'd made a fatal cut.

"Thank you for the adventure… for the chance to be more." He gave Angus a grim smile. Then he ran back the way they'd come. Two scarlips remained watching Norah's body, but the other three loped off after Dustin.

Angus's heart broke. Norah was dead, and Dustin was soon to follow. Angus had failed and failed badly. *He* should be the one giving his soul. A lump formed in his throat and swelled until he couldn't breathe, and a sob tore free. That wasn't how it was supposed to be.

He stood slowly and strained his ears as he waited for Dustin's cries.

Aside from the low grating rumble from the remaining scarlips, there was nothing.

"They'll wait until he falls. The blood loss will make him unconscious soon. The last of his magic is draining freely away, and when it does, his heart will stop. He will be dead before they taste him." Saka picked up the things Dustin had been carrying and added them to the sled he was pulling. Taking on the burden without asking for help. "We must put some distance between us and the death. Don't let his offering be wasted."

Saka started to walk, but Angus stood where he was. He glanced at the scarlips that were waiting for Wek to move. Then he looked at the other humans, and his gaze landed on Terrance. Terrance looked away and then followed Saka. One by one the rest fell into line. Angus had to move. Wek was waiting for him so she could fall in at the end of the line. If they were too spread out, they would look like prey again.

He took a few steps, but his legs were stiff and unwilling. They were going leave Norah there, cold on the sand, with only the scarlips for company. Was Dustin still running or had his blood and magic run out?

How many more days did the rest of them have before, one by one, they collapsed in the sand, drained of magic and life. He wished he'd never mentioned the feathered demon. Knowing Miniti had ordered his death, all of the trainees deaths, didn't make this any easier. The nights spent walking had been a reprieve, but death still stalked them. Angus wanted to be able to sleep without fear. He wanted to be safe and believe that he could have a life that wasn't dependent on someone else's goodwill.

The horizon and the people ahead of him blurred, and his eyes stung, but he didn't fight the tears. He didn't want to fight the flow of magic either. It was exhausting, but he did. He had to keep it together.

Terrance fell back to walk beside him. After a while he reached out and took Angus's hand, but Angus couldn't bear to look at him as the sun lightened the sky.

ANGUS HADN'T slept well. He hadn't slept well in… in too many days. He'd lost track of time. How long had they been out there, relying on Saka for water and Wek for food? He slipped out of the tent and sat in its shade. His skin was sticky, and he was thirsty—but not in the way that meant magic was leaching from him too quickly—and his eyes were gritty. That was from crying. His heart was bruised.

Angus wrapped his arms around his knees and rested his head on them. He must have dozed off. When he lifted his head, his neck was sore, and Terrance was sitting next to him. Terrance reached out with his toes and flicked the bells on Angus's ankle. How could he smile?

"I used to hate these because it was a reminder of what you were doing over here. You'd leave them on even at home." He frowned. "In Vinland. But I like them now. I can hear you moving around. I liked the sound they made when we were together."

"This had better not be some kind of goodbye talk." Angus squinted out at the horizon. The sun would set soon. They'd have to eat and pack and get moving. He was so sick and tired of walking, and he wanted to bathe. His hair, which was overdue for a cut, had started to itch from the sand and sweat, and he was thinking of hacking it off with a knife. He wanted to shave, but there was no mirror and no real point. His clothes were sweaty… but everyone was in the same situation. They were all sandy and sweaty and dirty.

But Terrance managed to make scruffy look good. Angus felt like an unwashed, overgrown armpit. Yet there was still something about Terrance that made his heart beat that little bit faster. It wasn't lust—he didn't have the energy for that.

"You've been avoiding me." Terrance nudged the bells again.

Angus nodded. "Because I don't know what to say. I've damned us all to a slow death."

"It's faster than what the college would've given us."

"Is it? We've been walking for how long? Fifteen? Twenty days?" Everyone's eyes were getting paler. The mages were grim and offered no comfort, only words to make them walk. They had to move faster. The sooner they found the other tribe, the safer they'd be. Hopefully they would return to Humanside, to whatever country that part of Demonside linked to. But he wasn't sure where they were headed.

"Twenty-three."

Angus glanced at Terrance.

"Made you look at me." Terrance smiled. His dark hair had lighter streaks and stood up at all angles. His eyes, which had once been brown, had faded to something that was barely even gold.

Angus looked away. The fear he'd been suppressing surged upward and threatened to choke him. "You have to stop the magic draining out."

"I'm trying. Do you know how hard it is? I haven't spent months here. Norah had spent months, and she still didn't make it. As soon as I get distracted, it slips past like so many greased up worms on a buttered baking tray. How do you catch them?"

Angus's lips twisted into something close to a smile. There was nothing funny about it, but all he could picture was slippery worms sliding down a baking tray. The magic was sneaky, always looking for a way out, a way to rebalance as nature intended.

"I imagine a wall, and the magic—or the worms—pile up against it." When he finally gave in, it would flow out of him like water from a broken dam. And it would feel good.

"I'm not quitting, but it's not getting any easier." He put his hand on Angus's arm. "Don't blame yourself."

"But I do." His words were barely more than a whisper. "We should've made better plans or crossed the border in our world." That would've been safer.

"Do you know how well-fortified the borders are? People get killed trying to cross. It wasn't on the news, but I saw footage. It's not other countries keeping us out. It's Vinland keeping us in."

Angus nodded. Norah, Lizzie, and he had agreed that Demonside was their best chance, but it was supposed to happen later and be better planned.

"This was the only way. Even if Saka had been with his tribe, this"—Terrance pointed to his eyes—"would've still happened. That he left the tribe was a blessing. That he found other demons and was able to connect with them using the telestones was a miracle. We struggled over short distances."

"They weren't meant to be used in our world."

Angus sighed and leaned his head on Terrance's shoulder. "You don't hate me?"

Terrance put his arm around him. "No. No one hates you."

"I don't know what to do."

Terrance didn't respond. They sat together as the sky darkened and the stars came out—so many of them, and it was so beautiful. He'd wanted to share Demonside with Terrance, but not like this.

"I wanted to show you how pretty magic was. How beautiful it could be when it rained."

"You still can." Terrance kissed his cheek.

Angus wanted to believe that.

People began to wake up and move in the tent. Angus didn't want to move.

Saka came around the tent. "You need to eat before we head off."

Angus glanced up at him. They also needed to help pack up. "I think we should rest a night." Resting wouldn't have helped Dustin or Norah, but maybe they would've died in their sleep instead of on the sand. The tightness in his chest reformed.

Saka pressed his lips together. "First one night, then two, then the will to go on leaves. I have seen this before. This is not my first long trek." He held out both his hands. One to each human.

Angus lifted his hand even though it felt like lead. He knew Saka was right. "I know I vowed never to swim in Demonside again, but I take it back. I don't care if there are actual riverwyrms swimming in there with me."

"I think you just want to feast on their flesh," Saka said.

He closed his eyes for a moment to remember the singing and the dancing and the feast after he'd been bait. When he opened his eyes, he saw the sadness on Saka's face, the worry in his eyes. Saka clasped his fingers around Angus's hand. If he missed his tribe and his home, he hadn't said anything.

Terrance reached out, and Saka pulled them both up.

His hands were warm, and his skin was rough. It was familiar and calming... or Saka was doing a little magic to make him feel that way. Was that a faint shimmer or just the starlight on his skin?

Right then Angus didn't care. He glanced at Saka and Terrance's hands. They had spoken on the journey, but it was the first time Angus had seen them touch. It gave him hope. He'd been worried that the two people he cared about most would hate each other, but there seemed to be some kind of agreement between them. Angus reached out for Terrance's hand to complete the circle.

He was sure he felt a ripple of magic run through him.

Saka nodded, and the corner of his lips turned up in a half smile. "One day, when this is a memory that has lost the pain, I would like to know how much magic can be raised with two humans."

Terrance snorted. "Purely for research purposes." But he smiled as he appraised the demon.

They had been sleeping close. Most nights he was between Terrance and Saka, and while the idea had crossed his mind as he'd closed his eyes, they couldn't chance sex when they were trying to hold on to magic. His body didn't actually want it, but Angus hadn't realized that Terrance had thought about it.

"Of course," said Saka. "You will be taught to cut properly and heal too." He referred to the mess of scars that were visible on Terrance's ribs, even in the soft light. There were scars on his legs too, from where he'd fed Aqua his blood. The scars from the whipping were gone from his back, though the memory still dragged Angus out of what little sleep he got.

It all started when they saved those demons from the underground. But he couldn't go back, and Saka had warned him not to run himself ragged with "what might have beens." He'd done the right thing at the time. But many of his right things seemed to add up to a massive mistake with fatal consequences.

Terrance's smile slipped. "And if I don't want to learn any more magic?"

Saka tilted his head. "I think you do, but everything you know about magic, so far, has hurt."

Terrance breathed out. "Right now I'll settle for living. Then you can do your experiment." He glanced at Angus.

Angus nodded, and he knew exactly what he'd agreed to. He'd told Terrance bits and pieces, but he couldn't explain the way it could hurt and feel so good. For a heartbeat, desire flickered, and he let himself imagine being with both of his lovers at the same time. The heat flowed through him, and Terrance's grip on his hand tightened for just a moment.

"Good. Now you have a reason to go on." Saka released their hands.

Angus blinked as he realized his demon had just used lust and the promise of something he'd never thought possible to get him thinking of the future and not the past. But it had worked, and it had worked on Terrance too. The first time Terrance saw Saka, Angus thought he was impressed that Angus had such a powerful demon. Had it been more?

"How close are we?" Terrance asked.

"We *are* almost there. When I reach out, the distance is very little," Saka said.

"How many days?"

"And what do they say?" Angus pressed.

"I do not know how many days. A handful at most." Saka hesitated. "Iktan says nothing. He will not respond. I do not know why, but it worries me."

Angus pressed his lips together. "If we are that close, let me try raising someone."

Saka had not let him do any magic, in case he lost control. Angus was frustrated, but Saka had been right to enforce the ban on humans doing magic. And it looked like he was going to say no again.

Angus lifted his chin. "I'll do it even if you say no."

"You don't have a stone."

"Don't I?" He had the one he made for Terrance and the one he'd taken to Vinland. Both needed to be recharged, but he could do that too.

"Don't drain yourself." Terrance squeezed his hand. "We'll just keep walking. We'll get there."

Angus stared at Saka, and Saka's expression hardened.

"I have seen you and Wek work. You sit out here in the middle of the day while we sleep. She's helping you somehow. Do the same for me." He wanted to know the country the demons were aligned with. If the demons planned to kill them, it might be better to die out here. He hadn't mentioned that fear. If he gave it voice, he worried it might come true.

Saka gave a stiff nod. "Before you eat."

Terrance helped him paw through his things for the stones they'd packed before they left Vinland. "Saka won't forget. He'll expect you to keep your promise."

"Good." Terrance picked up the blue stone. "Or do you not want that?"

"That's not it." He liked sleeping between the two of them. He'd seen Terrance and Saka talk sometimes while they walked. "I didn't realize you felt that way."

"Neither did I. But I made the effort to get to know him because he means so much to you." Terrance handed him the stone. "I want this to work. Saka will always be your demon, but I want to be your human."

Angus opened his mouth, but all of his words had dried up. He'd never thought about it that way. "You are already my human. And I'm yours." He put his arms around Terrance.

Terrance buried his face against Angus's neck. His beard was rough, but for a few heartbeats, he felt more alive than he could remember.

"I'm sure Saka did something when he held my hand, because I don't feel so dead," Terrance murmured.

"Yeah." Angus had a sneaking suspicion Saka had given them a little of the calming magic the demons gave to the sacrifices on Lifeblood. "When it wears off, no doubt we'll feel worse."

As people ate and pulled down the tent, Angus sat with Saka, who held his hand over Angus's as he put more magic into the stone. *Draw from the world, not yourself.* His imaginary wall kept his magic locked inside, but the urge to release it was strong. It was a craving that itched within his veins when he was awake, and he was sure the dreams had only started because his body wanted to release the building pressure of unspent magic.

Even though the night was cooler than the day, sweat still beaded on his forehead as he worked. When he felt the stone was ready, he lifted his hand. "They'll be the closest demons?"

263

"Yes. Reach out without a name in mind, and hopefully someone will respond."

Angus nodded. No matter who responded, he was going to ask for asylum. He hoped the demons weren't aligned with a country that forbade demon magic. He didn't want to rot in a foreign jail.

Saka made the circle, but Angus hesitated. "Are you really curious about rebalancing with two humans?"

Saka's black horns gleamed as he tilted his head. "I am. I do not see how keeping your lives separate makes you happy. There is always a time when you first arrive or go to leave where you are happy and sad, and I can never work out how I should feel. I don't want to be jealous, and for a time I was."

Angus bit his lip and studied his toes.

"Spending time with Terrance has been a good thing. I think you need him. You need a human."

"And what do you need?" Angus lifted his gaze.

Saka drew in a breath and then exhaled. The stars reflected in his eyes. "I need to get the trainees to somewhere they can get across the void." He nudged the stone toward Angus. "Then I can think about what I want."

"And the rebalancing?" The thought was lodged in Angus's head.

The demon smiled. "I want that. That was not said in jest or without meaning. But there is a lot to do first." He touched Angus's cheek. "And I still want you, alone, to myself."

Angus leaned into the touch. "Thank you for the calming."

"It is merely masking the tiredness. Do not be fooled."

"I'm not, but I'm still grateful." Angus closed his eyes and pushed his mind out via the stone. At first he drifted. Then Saka added to the search and pushed him further. He was ten times stronger, and his mind flew over the sands.

The touch of another mind against his brought him to a sudden stop. Then he was in a room with no windows. It looked solid, as though made of stone. A man in a red pinstripe suit stood behind a desk. Under his hand was a skull that appeared to be made of jade.

It was the most elaborate image he'd ever seen using the telestone.

The man spoke in a language he didn't know, and Angus shook his head. The man tried again. *Who are you?*

I'm Angus Donohue, formerly of Vinland. I'm... we are seeking asylum. Did the man even have the power to grant that? *I need to speak to immigration?*

The man considered him for a moment and then laughed. *I'm Priest Cadmael Och of the Mayan Empire Intelligence Temple. I am the person you need to talk to. We have been monitoring your approach across the desert.*

Angus had to steady himself so he didn't drown in the tide of anger. The man had watched two of them die. But that was the Mayan Empire. They weren't known for being friendly to outsiders. *Then you know it hasn't been easy.*

Why are you defecting? You have magic, a demon even, given that you are in Demonside.

I am wanted by the college for.... There were so many reasons. *For joining the underground, for realizing that they are the ones hoarding magic and causing the spread of ice and the drying on Demonside.*

The priest was silent. Angus was sure he was going to say no. After all of their struggles, there would be nothing but death.

Why not stay and fight? What kind of warlock flees?

One who has realized the underground seeks to take power from the college, and does not want to right things. Was he giving too much away? He didn't care. *There are five humans and two demons.*

Yes, a Mage Saka. I have been told about him.

Without a country, the humans will die. They had days, not weeks.

They will rebalance, Cadmael said, as though discussing the heat in Demonside.

More than five deaths are needed to rebalance what has been locked up by the college. If Cadmael didn't grant asylum, could they keep going and find another tribe? Unlikely. They had come as far as they could. They were at the end of their walk.

Angus's strength wavered. He would have to dip into himself to hold the connection. How much power did Cadmael have to form an entire room? Or was Angus actually in the room? But even if he wanted to let the connection go, something or someone had anchored him and stopped him from leaving. Was magic pouring out of him while he was trapped in that windowless room? While Cadmael took his time thinking, Angus used his mind to search for exits or for ways to break the connection, but there were none.

A faint smile formed on Cadmael's lips. *You may proceed to the demon tribe. Mage Iktan will be expecting you. From there the humans will be brought across the void to the Empire for debriefing. You will be a guest until such time as you are deemed safe to the community.*

By guest, Angus was sure he meant prisoner. *And the demons.*

The tribe will determine how to deal with them.

That didn't sound promising. How could he accept asylum if it meant that Saka would die? *Saka and I... he is mine.*

Cadmael's eyes narrowed. *Or are you his?*

Both.

Cadmael nodded. Angus had time to see Cadmael's fingers lift off the skull. Then he was thrown back, vertigo swallowed him whole, and he fell over onto the sand. It was hot against his cheek as he drew in a couple of breaths.

There was no taste of blood in his mouth, so he hadn't ruptured anything.

Saka helped him sit up. He cupped Angus's face, stared into his eyes, and winced.

"I had to." And he didn't want to know how bad the loss of color was. Maybe it was only a little. He hadn't been there for long. But the camp was all packed up and everyone was waiting and looking at him. He licked his lips and said, loudly enough for everyone to hear, "The Mayan Empire has granted us asylum."

Everyone cheered and hugged.

Angus smiled and he let himself be hauled up. Terrance kissed him.

All they had to do was survive for a little longer.

CHAPTER 31

"Is THAT rain on the horizon?" Angus stared at the smudge in front of them that hid the stars that should be visible. He'd noticed it a while ago but hadn't been sure. It was clearly something.

"It's not clouds." Saka stopped walking, and Angus caught up to him.

Everyone else followed suit, and they all stared at the blot.

"It's hills," Terrance said eventually. "I think it's hills."

"I think you're right," Lizzie said, and hope lifted her voice.

No one said anything for a little while as they all took in the realization that they were almost there.

Hope prickled along his skin. "That's where the other tribe lives."

Saka nodded. "Yes."

Lizzie took several steps forward. "Well, let's not dawdle. My eyes are white, and I'm thirsty. I figure I've got two days at most."

Angus glanced at Terrance. His eyes were also almost white, but the thirst hadn't started yet... unless Terrance was keeping that to himself.

It had only been two nights since he'd spoken to Cadmael, and he'd been close to giving up. If Dustin and Norah had been able to hold out for just a few more days....

The lump in his throat swelled, and his heart seemed to grow another fracture, but he held himself steady.

They continued to walk as dawn lightened the sky and even when the sun rose and they would usually stop. The smudge of hills became clear, and they weren't made of sand. They were blue with vegetation.

As they got closer, plants started to poke their way through the red sand. Then the sand vanished beneath a carpet of plants with small, pointed leaves. By midday they were surrounded by shrubs, and they finally reached the shade of the trees. The sunlight lost its cruelty as it danced with the leaves.

No one mentioned rest until they reached a small shaded stream that bubbled up from the ground. It was barely a pace wide, but it was the best thing Angus had seen in a long time. He lay on the ground and stuck his face in the cool water. Then he rolled onto his back.

Something circled overhead and flew back toward the hills. Angus sat up and pushed his dripping hair off his face so he could track it across the sky. Someone had been watching them and was reporting their location.

Water dripped onto Angus's shoulder. He was sunburned despite his shirt, but he didn't care. They had made it. He wanted to lie down and appreciate being alive, but he had no doubt that he'd have to face Cadmael all too soon.

"I vote we stop here and wash and rest for the rest of the day." Lizzie undid her shirt and then glanced at Saka.

Everyone glanced at Saka as though they expected him to say something like "We must keep going."

Saka dropped the ropes of the sled he'd been pulling. "They know we are here. We have earned a rest until they come."

Wek sighed and dropped the ropes to her sled. The trainees smiled and sat. Like Angus, they were sunburned and tired. But they'd made it. They had survived the walk across the desert. They would find out how safe their sanctuary was in due time. At the moment the shade and the water and the plants were something out of a dream. Angus lay on the bank with his feet in the water, and his wet clothes clung to him.

Terrance lay down next to him. "I would kill for a toothbrush, a wheel of cheese, beer, and a shower. In any order."

Angus ran his tongue over his teeth and then his hand over his face. "And a razor."

"It's not that bad." Terrance propped himself up on his elbow. "Just needs a trim."

Angus pulled a face. The scruff would come off the first chance he got. "Do you still have that bottle of mead?"

It was the moment to celebrate. Angus didn't know what was going to happen when they met the tribe or when they crossed the void to the Mayan Empire. He didn't care right then.

Terrance sat up. "Yeah. I think it's on the sled."

He got up and came back a few minutes later. Everyone gathered around in their wet clothing. They were all streaked with grime, but they smiled for the first time in too many days.

Terrance handed Saka the bottle. "Do you want to do the honors?"

Saka shook his head. "Let Angus."

Angus took the bottle of blood-warm mead from Terrance and undid the foil around the top. He hoped it hadn't spoiled in the heat, but when the cap came off, it smelled sweet, with a whiff of alcohol. He took a sip, decided that it was still good, and had a bigger drink before passing the bottle to Terrance.

Lizzie drank, shivered, and grimaced as she handed the bottle on to the two other trainees who'd survived the walk. Wek and Saka pulled faces, but neither of them turned down the bottle when it made a second round.

They drank for those who hadn't made it—for Dustin and Norah, for the trainee who'd been shot trying to cross the void, for Jim and the others who'd been killed on missions for the underground. Their small group was all that was left of the grand experiment—an experiment that had clearly failed, at least in Vinland.

No one knew what to expect from the Mayan Empire, but they had a chance. That was reason enough to celebrate. The bottle went around a third time. The taste was thick and cloying in his throat, and the alcohol hit his stomach and bloodstream hard. The sharp edge of the world smudged, and he leaned against Terrance, who wrapped an arm around his waist.

Saka's grin was wide and unrestrained. Angus didn't have to force a smile. Saka leaned forward and kissed him with a quick brush of lips and nothing more. Saka drew back and looked at Terrance. Terrance shrugged and then hugged Saka and pressed Angus between them. Angus didn't even care that, for a moment, he couldn't breathe.

Lizzie and Wek joined in the group hug, and so did the others.

It was only then that Angus realized how desperate everyone had felt and how well they'd locked it up to avoid making the others feel worse.

Someone laughed, and Lizzie started to cry. The bottle made a final round.

A few mouthfuls of Solstice mead, and Angus was already light-headed. That's what the Solstice celebration should feel like—joyous with the promise of Spring and new life.

They had a chance to start over and fight back, to return the stolen magic and bring Spring to Vinland.

TJ NICHOLS is the author of the *Studies in Demonology* series as well as several novellas. Having grown up reading thrillers and fantasy novels, it's no surprise that mixing danger and magic comes so easily. Writing urban fantasy allows TJ to make sure that evil gets vanquished and the hero gets his man.

With two cats acting as supervisors, TJ has gone from designing roads to building worlds and wouldn't have it any other way. After traveling all over the world and Australia, TJ now lives in Perth, Western Australia.

Website: tjnichols-author.blogspot.com
Twitter: @TobyJNichols
Facebook: www.facebook.com/TJNichols.author

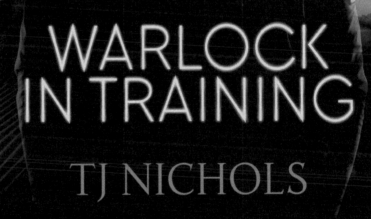

WARLOCK
IN TRAINING

TJ NICHOLS

Studies in Demonology: Book One

Angus Donohue doesn't want to be a warlock. He believes draining demons for magic is evil, but it's a dangerous opinion to have—his father is a powerful and well-connected warlock, and Angus is expected to follow the family tradition.

His only way out is to fail the demon summoning class. Failure means expulsion from the Warlock College. Despite Angus's best efforts to fumble the summoning, it works. Although not the way anyone expects.

Angus's demon, Saka, is a powerful mage with his own need for a warlock.

Saka wants to use Angus in a ritual to rebalance the magic that is being stripped from Demonside by warlocks. If Angus survives his demon's desires and the perils of Demonside, he'll have to face the Warlock College and their demands.

Angus must choose: obey the College and forget about Demonside or trust Saka and try to fix the damage before it's too late. Whatever he does, he is in the middle of a war he isn't qualified to fight.

www.dsppublications.com